A WALKING SHADOW

By

Gary Bolick

Editor: Rebekah Stogner
Cover Designer: Kathryn Geary

Printed in the United States of America.

Attention schools and businesses: for discounted copies on
large orders, please contact the publisher directly.

ISBN: 978-1-947021-49-5

To paint, not the thing, but the effect that it produces.
Stéphane Mallarmé

GARY BOLICK

ROLL CAMERA:

WHEN THE BATTLE'S LOST AND WON

Doctor Malcom Lowenstein stepped out of his aging Volvo and immediately shielded his eyes, the early afternoon sun seemed particularly harsh today. Turning to read the marquis at The Rio, he chuckled then spat out his last mouthful of coffee.

'Set your watch, no your calendar, ' he thought, Monday, Tuesday, Wednesday, the whole damned week, backwards and forward: Penn and Teller. Oh, wait something new, a guest appearance by David Copperfield. Slamming his door, the handle remained in his right hand, "Perfect."

From the moment he woke up, he had begun to dread this particular session. 'But why this one?' he asked himself. Procrastinating most of the day, he suddenly realized that he would be hard pressed to call his old professor, Doctor Matthew Whitlock, for a consult. As he walked quickly across the parking lot and hurriedly unlocked his office door, he dropped his briefcase sending his notes swirling in the wind. After quickly gathering up his notes, Lowenstein checked his watch, realizing that it was too late to make the call. His next patient would be there in less than fifteen minutes.

'Well, I'll do it anyway, the hypnosis, nothing else has seemed to work. Still, it would have been nice to bounce it off of Doctor Whitlock. I'm stumped, but oddly intrigued, even a little excited by this one.'

Jonas Bellingham Ayre, Jonas, J.B. he still was not sure which name the patient preferred. A mix of PTSD and a mild or perhaps severe case of dissociative identity disorder; or not. Yes, that is what made him anxious and edgy and he had to admit, interested. It, he, was actually breaking up the monotony. Looking back up at the The Rio marquis, "Yep, still Penn and Teller."

He was in uncharted waters with Jonas. It was the most excited he had been since his graduate work at Johns Hopkins. Still, he was objective enough to realize that this one had him over a barrel.

As he settled in and began to scan his notes, the doorbell chimed, Jonas had arrived.

Since Dr. Lowenstein only saw Jonas during the six months he was in in from the desert, the first session back was always a little awkward. Their last session had been contentious, devolving into more of a philosophical argument than actual therapy. Dr. Lowenstein had blamed himself. He realized that it was up to him as the psychologist to keep it above board, objective, but there was something about this particular patient that unnerved him. He had welcomed the six-month respite, but now found himself anxious again.

'Damn it, I really wanted to talk to Doctor Whitlock. Get his input on why this guy is getting under my skin. Or is he?' Lowenstein mused. 'Why do I feel so challenged by him? Why am *I questioning* myself? No, don't go there, not now, not enough time. Deal with your own issues, later. OK, OK. Showtime, Lowenstein. Showtime.'

"Jonas, so good to see you. Nice tan. I trust desert life is treating you well. Fine, fine. OK. Since it's been six months, and you know as well as I do, the last session created more questions than it answered, I thought we'd start fresh. I've had great success in breaking down barriers and unlocking doors with hypnosis. If you're up for it, we can try it."

Jonas shrugged and said, "I guess at this point, what could it hurt. Seems nothing else has worked. Fine."

Dr. Lowenstein turned the lights off, then switched on a small table lamp, then turned on a CD player. A nonstop loop of the tide, ocean waves crashing, began to fill the air.

"OK, Jonas, make yourself comfortable. Remember the breathing exercises I taught you. Let's start with those now. Good. Now, close your eyes. Listen to the water, count down from a hundred while you continue to breathe, good. Long, easy breaths. Good. Keep counting and walk back to a place where you really felt safe for the first time. Breathe. Good. Breathe . . .

"Jonas? Jonas! You OK out there? No, don't open the door. The movie's about to start. Grownups, dear. Only for grown-ups and well, we've had this conversation before. Your brother and sister are older. *They can watch.* Now be a dear and play with the dominoes. After a while, we'll all . . . never mind, sorry, the movie's starting."

Jonas Bellingham Ayre, eleven years old, turned away from glass paneled door and gazed out through the windows of the glassed-in back porch. For a moment, he felt relieved as he stared up and into the fire, the red, orange, and yellow fire that seemed to have overtaken the maple, oak and hickory trees surrounding the house. Looking out made it, yes, suddenly, it was much easier to breathe; his mind wonderfully clear. He was soaring, as he watched the brisk October breeze bend and twist, turning the treetops into a living paint store of colors.

Calm and centered, happy, but alone, Jonas now marveled at how in one quick turn away from the door he was freed. Freed and soaring, his eyes hovering easily among the branches, leaping from one to the other. But most of all this warm, calm feeling seemed to whisper to him that he was no longer alone, isolated. Was this an answer?

'Yes,' he thought, 'looking out *there,* the rules don't seem to be so . . . lonely and hateful, it's possible to feel carried, as though bound up in someone's arms, someone who just doesn't ever want to let go. Being here, then, I'm not worrying about being in *there*. I-'

From the adjoining room, the den, *the family room*, laughter exploded. Jonas, J.B. to everyone except his mother, turned quickly away from the windows and the flaming tufts of leaves and stared hard at the glass-paned door of *their room*. Low and piercing the descending sun burned brightly, showering the glass with a reflected mixture of yellow, hot-gold and J.B.'s face, fluttering. Three separate screens displaying three different views of what he felt cloistered up inside on the porch and out there; there where the trees burned, the wind swirled, and birds hung drifting on any and every updraft they chose.

Jonas listened as the laughter continued, and then began to move his eyes from one pane to another. From the top right to the bottom left, up and then diagonally down, the reflecting panes burned, wrestled and combined with the incoming light creating an awkward, long and searing face. Yes, his own riddled with a new angst, a hard, chilling discovery that fear and laughter are twins. Or rather, one person with a Janus-like face: loneliness and elation, both now whispering, fracturing what once was never to be thought of as strange.

'Nothing fits, now,' he thought, 'in between, but not able to touch either.'

More laughter, the reflecting panes still ablaze. The sun was descending as the volume on the television grew louder. Looking out through the glass, the wind was dead, the birds had all disappeared, the fire extinguished and the voice that so often offered comfort and solace was mute. Gone.

From deep within his own protective pocket, the vault where he could always retreat and find some manner of connection, J.B. now *felt and heard* a new, whispering taunt that was trying desperately to find a foothold, issue a reassuring word. Disappeared, exited out with the lights leaving nothing but the memory, or rather a shadow of what once felt natural.

A WALKING SHADOW

Here, adrift, then? Where, now?

This house, his home? When just ten feet away, hovering behind the glass this world's inhabitants, *family?*

"No, no dear, don't touch. No, especially, not me. Run along now. First hand me that bottle and the pack of Winstons there on the table. OK, go."

Suddenly more desert than two-story Victorian, turning the glass-lined walls of the protruding porch into an unbounded Mojave, a treeless, waterless plain that now, strangely, began to seem natural and inviting. What had always seemed a suggestion:

"Don't be silly, Jonas. It's not a real person or voice. It's just something we, I mean, all people do. Children have imaginary friends. Grownups reason with themselves. It's not actually a person or voice. Well, you remember PINOCCHIO? The cricket? Jiminy Cricket. Yes, dear, sort of like that. Go on, now, leave mother alone."

Something *like that* became J.B's newly discovered voice of reason, age eleven, watching the fires burn outside while the laughter through door, burned even hotter inside. A whisper to reassure him that with the separation he was finally free, unfettered, unconnected and yes, a twin of his former self, cast out.

"See? See it, J.B., Jonas, you choose. It always seems to fall down running back and forth between fear and laughter. So, mount up. I had to. Ride, son. See? Three glass panes, all with something and nothing similar to teach you. By the seat of your pants, it all falls apart, then each day asks you to put it all back, right again, up there, pick one or take all three. But don't worry J.B. relax and breathe. It's hard at first, but soon you'll want to stay here. Yes, right here, with me, with us. There? Through that, or any other door? No matter where, now. It'll never change 'cause you'll always carry it with you. Here, there, anywhere. See it? I know, it's hard, now, son, hard. No looking back, still, you choose."

J.B. turned away from the door and stared back out through the glass, tried to pick up the last remnants of the fire. 'Funny, only when I look inside, into the den, away from the trees do I hear him or it or whatever that is. It's gone, now.'

Turning back to the door,

"Simple, now. Simple, but lonely, but don't worry, now son. We'll make it"

J.B. closed his eyes and searched. 'Yes! Him!' he thought, 'a mixture of mine and Leander's voice. It sounded like me, but older, calmer like an echo up and out of a well. And, yes, that was Uncle Lee.'

"Leander? Not in my house, ever again!" Mrs. Ayre screamed at her husband. "Never!"

Uncle Lee, always angering the others with his version of, *"The unvarnished truth. Embarrassing, ain't it? J.B.? Shoot, only one of you I give a damn about. Come on, son, let's go fishing."*

'Yes, of course it *had to be his voice,*' J.B. thought, smiling.

"Jonas! You're so quiet."

J.B. turned, and looked at the door, hesitated, almost laughed, and then ran to the door. Turning the doorknob, he stopped.

"Now who said anything about coming in *here now?* Are you OK?"

"Yes."

"Excuse me!"

"Yes, *ma'am.*"

Looking up and out of the glassed-in porch, the sun had descended below the trees. No fire now, only silhouettes, shadows of what they once were—fading. J.B. turned on the overhead light and noticed that, again, the three-paned door now displayed a mixture of reflections both from the porch, the den and now his own face and the large, jet-black trees looming up behind him.

Looking around the porch, into the den, out into the woods, J.B. now felt as though he was standing back, viewing each and every object at a distance. No longer did he see or have the focus or centered eyes from just a moment ago. It all seemed to be seen from the backseat of the Ford, the Fairlane station wagon. It's all like watching a drive-in movie. Shaking his head, he thought he heard the whispering again, but realized that it was his brother Stephen and his sister Dee talking to his mom and dad.

So, yes, J.B. what'll it be? I've got your back. Always have, always will. No, don't worry, it's confusing. A very confusing place. Just like when you sneaked in to watch your sister shower. I remember. All hell broke loose. Chip off your Uncle Lee's block. Your daddy and momma seemed real concerned. Me? I laughed, took another long drink. Toasted your manhood, and mine.

Funny and lonely all at the same time, isn't it? But you've always had an inkling and notion of all this. It's your place, son. Been expectin' it, been watchin' you. So, here I am. I know, it hits you when least expect it. Me, well someday I'll get to that, tell you when and how I found it. The place, where you are now. The place where the world disappears and all you can do is move on, bluster through and then the next step is to put the pieces back in some order. After they're in place, you smile and call it a life. Right now, let's just say it's like that line of dominoes and all the hours spent standing them up. Winding and curving, trying to square the circle, but always back to Spiral Jetty, your favorite, mine, too.

That's good, son. Real good. Out there alone on the floor of the sunroom, it, your water, finally broke. Alone, son, alone . . . and all the king's horses and all the king's men . . . well, you get the picture, chief.

"Jonas . . . Jonas, start back now . . . easy does it. Jonas, start talking now, come out of it, come back." Dr. Lowenstein said.

Murmuring at first, then speaking stronger and more clearly, Jonas said,

"Dominoes and train stations, a small line shack out in the desert, a tractor-trailer gnashing me to the pavement and that burlap sack, yes, thrown out from a passing train at three in the morning, and inside it? Out comes poor, sweet, but indomitable, my savior: Eva. Then later, her little girl, Tela. All of them, yes, dominoes, too. All arranged, now, and then set in motion. Isn't that how it all works, dear? The canvas painted in arrears. Isn't it . . . isn't it . . . isn't it? I mean, please, again, say something, please."

"Jonas!" Doctor Lowenstein said forcefully, "Wake up!"

'Asleep? Was that my own voice . . . am I, the back porch, eleven? I hope, not, no

I . . . shit! Uncle Lee . . . Leander, mother, Eva and I-?'

"Jonas, wake up, easy now, relax," Doctor Lowenstein's clipped, baritone voice broke in. pulling Jonas up and out of his trance. Reaching out and over, J.B.'s psychologist rubbed his hand and then offered him a bottled water.

"Here drink this. Take a couple of minutes. We'll talk some more, or we can call it a day. You choose."

J.B. emptied the contents of the bottle quickly. After several cleansing breaths he looked down at the armrest, then scanned the walls of Doctor Lowenstein's office, and smiled, saying to the psychologist, "It all seems to fit so neatly—now—doesn't it? No . . . not quite, it really didn't follow any sort of pattern until I met the . . . matriarch, Rosa, Eva's grandmother, Tela's great-grandmother. Biblical, barely five feet tall and maybe one hundred pounds soaking wet, eighty-five years old, Rosa was . . . is, shit! Would not dare cross that woman, ever! No, don't get me wrong. For the most part all I saw was this balled-up fist of . . . sweetness . . . and so very kind. But anyone or thing that put the family at risk? Jekyll to Hyde! Terminator on steroids.

"I met her shortly after I took Eva to the shore. Once she had been reunited with her daughter, Tela, the three of us went inland to Rosa's home. That house. So warm and spacious, huge! Then I realized it was an old mill home. It was actually very small. Tiny. Funny isn't it? I *felt* as though I was inside a much larger home.

"But that was Rosa. She was like a conduit for . . . purpose . . . energy . . . the universe. And the décor? A mixture of Norman

Rockwell and Ornette Coleman. Furniture, posters, pictures, throw rugs from all over the world. Rosa told me that she would go to the lost and found sale at the Carnival Cruise office in Los Cabos. Every spring they had a parking lot sale; put all the unclaimed items, all the souvenirs from the port cites left in the cabins out in the parking lot and took the first, best offer.

"Gene Autry up on the wall as big as life, grinning, waving his hat from atop of his horse. A signed poster, below his picture the caption read: Greetings from the Anaheim Angels and a big Howdy Do from your favorite singing cowboy! Drop your eyes, and there in the middle of the floor was a small, handwoven Turkish rug. Look up and into the opposing corners? Two plastic pink flamingos, ready to charge one another, just waiting for their trainer to blow the whistle. What? How'd I know that? Another poster. One from Flamingo Park St. Augustine Florida.

"Still, by far the most prized among the pictures and posters was a portrait of her mother, Maria. Above the mantel was a wonderful old black and white photo that had been colorized, you know, like those old post cards. That's when I started thinking about dominoes, again. How as a child I was always on the outside looking in at my older siblings, in everything. Every time I tried to become part of the larger picture . . . the family, it was awkward and isolating. So, I gave up and started to rebel.

"Wasn't long before I realized that we, all of *us* do *everything* . . . in arrears. Blindly react to whatever comes our way, stumble over it, then stop and look each way only to switch back and forth looking to find what we believed actually happened. Stopped, we start up, again, and try to come to grips with what had occurred. Paralyzed, unable to punch out or through our own elastic cylinder, we settle on a third alternative, maybe the most elusive and distant dream of all: being real. It sits on your brain like an insidious, persistent nightmare; the image, the person you so desperately want to project out, the one we want everyone outside of ourselves to recognize as being valid, important, yes, real . . . me.

"We take all those random events, set them up and watch them play out like a line of dominoes . . . or a movie. That's what made Rosa so . . . so, unnerving. Yeah, she really was. Standing there under that Norma Desmond photo of her mother, Maria, she reminded me of something I read in physics, about how all the matter in the universe collapsed into a ball not much larger than a baseball right before the big bang: Rosa. Like I said like a knotted fist that was either all love or action, just depended on what the situation called for.

"And there hovering over all of us was Maria, "Are you ready for my close-up, Mr. DeMille? Rosa's ancient mother, all done up in pink and green and yellow. All of it fit, dove-tailed so perfectly into that one, particular place and moment. And yet, none of us really had anything in common, save for the youngest, Tela. She was the ringer, the catalyst in the wonderful alchemical mixture of . . . us. We all, seemingly, had gathered . . . there, of course, it had to be *there* for the expressed purpose of allowing that picture of Maria to bear witness, to cast her shadow down and around us. There we, all of us were held in perfect stasis; another child born, another notion of love and trust brought to life *through her*. Like I said biblical, shame I don't believe. That's heart of it, right, doc?

"The common denominator, Tela, had forced all of us to work in congress. Maria first, then Rosa, Eva and then . . . yes, me! I had a hand in it too. We were all there to try and undo the damage of Eva's mother . . . she was the domino who stopped it all until . . . we made it back to the water, and the gaze of Maria, and then the proud, sweet, dominating stare of Rosa and then . . .well, where to now? That's one of the reasons I'm here . . . now.

"Standing in that warm nest of a house, the family lineage running out in every direction, all connected, reconnected and firing on all cylinders, yes, it hit me hard. Real hard, that is the idea, the absolute understanding of how these . . . all women have the capacity to be stronger, more resilient and thrive in ways completely alien to me, us, men. They had endured and survived the ultimate treachery and . . . Eva's mother? I'm sorry, never heard her name spoken. No name. Rosa refused to tell me, Eva of course could not speak and Tela only knew her as the stranger who had appeared twice in her life, both times with near tragic results.

"Rosa simply shook her head and said, 'Dead.' Her daughter was now dead to her. When she betrayed, Eva, her own daughter, she had given up all claims on life and love. 'Purpose,' she said, over and over again. Purpose. There existed no life or death outside of the purpose of a mother to her child. Period. Then she spat and raised her fisted hand and stopped, then smiled, and said that it was up to her to straightened-out and then restore the line of the family's peace and love, there, right there in the house, under the shadow of Maria. 'By my hand, and through me, and this house and this wellspring looking down on us . . . we will all move on, together, now.' Rosa. A balled-up of fist of purpose. She did it. I saw it.

"What? The betrayal? Oh, I'm sorry, Doctor, Rosa's daughter she sold Eva to a cartel. Whatever they chose to do with her. Laborer, maid, prostitution . . . seems in her case, it was just the opportunity for anyone with enough money to extract as much pleasure as they could from her pain. Just the hot-wired monkey—man—being true to himself. Shit!"

Jonas stopped and closed his eyes. Doctor Lowenstein watched as Jonas mouthed what appeared to be a soliloquy, or a simple laundry list of chores to attend to, or now? He was not sure what. After a few more seconds, Jonas opened his eyes and spoke.

"Sorry. Where was I. Eva! Eighth century, and the alchemist walks me out into the heart of the desert to show me how to stop time and insert myself in the flux of the universe, return to the four basic elements so that I might re-integrate, return myself to perfect stasis. Women can do it here, can overcome the indifference of this world, create life, men? Jabir, the man in the ice-cream suit, first in Paris and then in the desert showed me and my shadow how we can, at least, make a stab at it, approach it, there. So, yesterday or tomorrow and tomorrow plus two more, for you and I doc, what has really changed? Same bird that's hovering over the desert, now, sees, what was there before we ever crawled out of the mud, right? And once we got out, what did we do? Eva dragged me out, but, shit! Sorry. Dominoes. Right. Got it!

"For a moment Eva's mother, Rosa's nameless daughter, stopped that line of dominoes, interrupted the wonderful, flowing line that was trying to make a beautiful, spiraling design. She stopped it cold. But looking up at that faded picture of Tela's great-great grandmother, then looking down at that fist of a woman her great-grand mother Rosa, and then looking over at her recently restored, mother, Eva . . . in Tela, yes, Tela, I saw the great experiment, the alchemist's dream of the philosophers'' stone—breathe—there in Tela."

A long silence. Doctor Lowenstein stopped writing. He reached down, picked up his water bottle and took a long drink, then rubbed the bridge of his nose and smiled at Jonas, then began to write, feverishly, on his legal pad. The afternoon shadows lengthened. Jonas picked at the thread on the armrest. The silence extended into a five-minute respite. The only sound was the doctor's pen trying to keep up with his racing thoughts. Then Jonas spoke.

"Sorry! No way, you can be following me on this. Are you? Let's just say it was pure dumb luck that I was there to offer a hand. Still, when I think about it, I'm not so sure, she . . . Eva wouldn't have walked out from the desert on her own. Walked to the coast into the water, on through the Pacific, no matter how long it took, with or without me or anyone. Eva!

"Maria to Rosa to Rosa's nameless daughter, see how Perfect they can make it. Ice-cold, center of hell stuff that's where Rosa exiled her daughter. Son-of-a-bitch! So, the nameless one feeds it down to Eva and then Tela. Me? Still not sure. I mean, doc, is there a *why* in all of this, honestly?"

"Jonas, the nameless woman, Rosa's daughter. You seem to pause, become a little agitated whenever you mention her. Seems strange that you never pressed Rosa for a name. Is there more than just a little of you there than you'd care to admit?"

"I . . . no! Absolutely not. No. I really don't identify with her, the nameless one. It was just all the shadows hovering there under Maria's picture. We seemed to be like vultures, cave paintings, particles racing and splitting, reforming. Summed up all those months out in the desert, in Vegas, and just watching her, yes, watching her . . . rise up. Shit! I, the word, a word, shit where is . . . the word for it?"

"OK, Jonas slow down."

"Phoenix or specter? Apparition that still haunts me, scares me a little when I think of what she showed me out there, and all that I still don't quite understand, even now. I'm still trying to wrap my head around her, Eva's journey, the pull it had on me, on the whole universe. What kind of force and bond and love did *she,* yes it was Eva that made it.

"Like some collapsing star, or perfect combination of the four elements or I'm not sure, really what, what could have sustained her for all those years, and then with the last best efforts of man to kill it—her—whatever *it is* began to flower—there—out in the desert. Seems all I did was play centerfielder. Catch anything and everything I could run down. Never expected to be Mays running down Wertz blast in the Polo Grounds, '51' series. Sorry."

"No, no. Keep going. I understand about the Eva, grandmother Rosa, it's like the family you never had, right? Or am I way off? No? OK. And the alchemy and the anger, the complete distrust of any other person to actually love or care for you."

"Sure, Bingo. Impossible. I mean you know that, right doctor."

"My feelings, views aren't important, we're here to help you. I-"

"No, I don't mind. Tell me. I mean, I *know* it's impossible."

"What?"

Jonas extended his hand, pointed his finger and laughed, "That's it! All she wrote. Past that it may as well be light years away. Eight billion of us bumping into one another and not once do any of us have one God damned idea what the other is *actually feeling!* See? The wreck took what I thought was mine away. On the porch, standing at the front door listening to the laughter, I was able to leap over it, find *my own place.*

"Son-of-a-bitch, walking away from that smoking pile of car, gone. Earth, sky, trees all laughing, pointing, screaming out, 'Fool!'

Doctor Lowenstein felt his stomach seize up, 'OK, easy. Remember, he's the patient. Be objective, move on, re-direct. But . . . why does that bother me? He's not attacking me personally . . . but is there, can there be any validity in what he's saying. Enough!'

"OK, Jonas point taken. But you have mentioned several times, or I should say alluded to alchemy and this nihilistic obsession and-"

"Paris and Uncle Lee . . . Leander. Both were gut punches. In Paris, well you know about Therese, but there was the bookstore, the old Iranian bookseller in the ice-cream suit. He had the book I ended up with, am still translating in the desert. Leander? Only blood that cared. Gave me the best advice anyone other has up until I landed in the desert. It was his, Leander's voice, I heard, used, hoped to hear, you choose, before I met the shaman, the alchemist in the desert. Uncle Lee died, Jabir the alchemist took his place. Now I'm here still fighting to understand how in the hell I can sit down and play chess with my own shadow. Does that clear it up, doc?"

Dr. Lowenstein smiled, thinking, 'Well, I had to ask. Shit! Focus, come on now, focus!'

"OK, OK, let's go ahead and finish, the hour's about up."

"Funny thing, though, is I eventually chased down and caught my own shadow out there—once. So, tell me, doc, when all the shouting is over, is that all a man is good for? Playing centerfield to any and every woman, dust-up or, OK, OK. Time's up? Save it for next time. Sure. Why not? Just one more domino to put in place, right?"

"Whatever you say, Jonas, that's fine. Next week, same time? Fine."

TAKE TWO:

A POOR PLAYER

Hello, Doctor Whitlock? Malcom. Malcom Lowenstein, thanks for taking my call. You were my advisor for my senior thesis, I-"

"Malcom! How are you? Of course, I remember. Wonderful to hear from you. I mean how could I forget *you*. I thought you were going to take Dennis' head off. Dennis Marx. You two were like two colossi throwing boulders at each other. He the staunch disciple of behavioral, B.F. Skinner and you the champion of analysis, Freud and Jung. Great days. So, how can I help?"

"So, ah Dr. Whitlock, I-"

"For God's sake, call me Matt. We're contemporaries, now."

Lowenstein took the phone from his ear, looked at it, smiled and then continued.

"So, ah, Matt, I tried to call you right before my last session with a truly interesting patient, name's Jonas. I haven't seen him in six months. He spends six months out in the desert, then when the summer months hit, he comes into Las Vegas. Lives in an old line-shack about two, two and a half hours from here, you know those outposts the railroads use to mend track, fill the boilers with water, well when they did that sort of thing and-"

"Whoa! Malcom. You're pulling my leg, right? Wait, no, it's not April first. If any of what you've told me is true, why hasn't he been committed by now?"

Malcom pulled the cellphone from his ear, again, and stared at the wall for a second, thinking, 'Good point. Why haven't I just moved him into a good outpatient facility.'

"Malcom, you there?"

"Sorry, Doctor, Matt. Well . . . I know it sounds like he *should* be under full time care, but I really wasn't sure, before and that's why I tried to call you. Now, I 'm glad I didn't have the time. Big break through last week. Never seen anyone respond to hypnosis like this one. Up to this point I thought it was rooted in his PTSD. He suffered a horrible trauma, but walked away, physically, unharmed. So, of course I have been approaching his treatment with the idea that I could help him move pass the trauma and get on with his life. Just like with a soldier traumatized in combat. You don't ignore the pain, but help them find a better place to deal with it, and then hopefully, they can essentially function alongside of it rather than suffer from psychological paralysis. Anyway. Seems this one, ah Jonas, comes by this naturally. In the accident he mentioned a split, a feeling that the earth and the universe became completely indifferent not to just him, but all of mankind.

"Headed out to the desert to try and see if he couldn't shake it, figure it out. The split only worsened, and now I find out that it started when he was around eleven. I-"

"Malcom, again, I'm objective. What you're describing is something we here at Johns Hopkins treat only in the most guarded of environments. He could be harboring multiple personalities, I'm sure a ton of latent hostility and more, I-"

"Wait, Matt. Thanks, and ninety-nine out of a hundred times I would agree. This is as much about me as him. You see, I'm not sure that I don't believe and agree with him. I won't keep you much longer, it's just I know I'm on shaky ground. He's a little like, this may sound crazy, a mixture of Elvis and John Wayne. No, that's not quite it, throw in a dash Don Quixote, yeah, that's closer. There's just this aura of invincibility and inevitability to his stories, his personality, but most of all what he's seemingly stumbled upon; this hole that bores through the conscious and unconscious. Kind of like a living-breathing black hole. Sorry. The real reason I called is to ask if I can call you back, discuss this case some more and, no, that's not it either. I'm a little thrown.

"Some of the methods I'm thinking about using are unconventional, but I've got to try. I mean, if he is suffering from multiple personalities I could be pushing him over the cliff, but if he is in fact a man who has collapsed the conscious and the unconscious into a working, functioning foil to himself and the universe as a whole, I want to be there."

A long pause ensued. Lowenstein stared at his phone, his heart thumping, his palms becoming clammy. He could hear his old professor's breathing, papers being shuffled, his voice clearing. Finally, words.

"OK Malcom. If it was anyone but you, I might call the psych ward at Clark County General there in Vegas and have this guy put under involuntary observation for seventy-two hours. I trust you. It's more in how you're telling me about him than what you're saying. I can hear it in your voice. You're spooked, but in a good, professional way. Anything else? I mean, sure, call me any time."

"Well actually, there is, Matt. It's why I'm a little more than spooked, I should have told you this right off. This guy, I mean my patient, Jonas, while he's been out in the desert, conversing with his own shadow has been translating Jabir. I almost wet myself when he told me. Yeah, Jung adored that guy, spent the last thirty years of his career quasi-obsessed with the alchemists and how they bridged the gap between religion and science. I-"

A short burst of laughter stopped Lowenstein. Trying to compose himself, his old professor began to laugh even more. After close to a minute, the professor composed himself and said, "I can still see Marx ducking when you threw a copy of **Psychology and Alchemy** at him. Malcom, as much I want to say great, and OK, I still have reservations. Be careful, for both of you. For your patient and *you*. You might not like what you discover. It's more than the patient, now. You're on the chopping block now, too. So, when do you see him next?"

"In about ten minutes."

"Like I said, call anytime and . . . watch your six."

Confused, Lowenstein, pulled the phone from his ear stared at it, then said, "Six? Matt, I'm not sure I follow you."

"It's an old fighter pilot mantra, warning. Six o'clock, bottom of the clock, underneath, impossible to see. That's what you have to be careful of. Take care, Malcom."

"Good to see you again, Jonas, J.B.? Which do you prefer?"

J.B. smiled and shook his head, "At this point I don't think it really matters. A year ago, you could have called me Sparky and that would have been just fine. Jonas? J.B? Actually, both died a long time ago. Not really sure what to call myself now. So, whatever comes to mind, if I do find something that fits, you'll be the first to know. OK?"

Lowenstein nodded, thinking, 'Again, I had to ask. Watch your six, shit! Why stop at six?'

"Sit down . . .J.B., please."

J.B. was looking directly over Dr. Lowenstein's head as he spoke. It was as though there was someone else, someone more important that either one of them, that he was addressing,

"She was, barely, nineteen; her young daughter, almost, three. The cylinder enclosing them held firm . . . was still, perfectly, intact.

"Mother and dependent child . . .the vacuum in nature. Einstein touched on that idea in searching for the comprehensive theory . . . the grail, the philosophers' stone of physics."

J.B. stopped, smiled at Dr. Lowenstein, shook his head, then started picking at the same loose thread on the arm of the chair.

"Cat chasing his tail, right? I always go back to some idea, notion of alienation . . . isolation . . . when all I wanted to say was, 'It was the happiest day of my life!' Watching her as she peeked out from behind the Life Guard stand. She was afraid to approach her . . . her daughter, after so many years, so she hid and watched her daughter laugh and play in the surf . . . just off Los Cabos.

"Happiest . . . but incredibly sad, too. S'why I'm sitting here with you, again. Thought I'd beaten it . . . no, I had, then she arrived."

Arrived . . . but only after being taken, kidnapped. Her . . . yes, *her name* was Eva, her ticket said, Los Cabos. No, not the resort. Just a small clapboard house built in the early fifties, a mile from the coast, barely four hundred square feet. Eva's grandparents had share-cropped, saved, worked nights and saved Green Stamps to put a down payment on a run-down, abandoned mill house. It was unremarkable and blended in perfectly with all of the other worn out, trembling and wheezing houses in the neighborhood. Unremarkable, except for its address: 1923.

Yes, 1923 Angeles Avenue would be a memorial; a punch square into that banker's face. A shrine that Eva had yet to see. Her daughter Tela? It was home, the only home she had ever known, the place where she ended up after the strange lady, barked and screamed at the sweet conductor on a night that was, now, more reverie than memory; a recurring flashback of a time that still felt like an unfinished dream.

Into the arms of Eva's grandmother: Rosa, little Tela and her Raggedy-Ann Doll arrived almost ten years, now. Pointing up, just above the mantle, the picture, Rosa explained to the flowering young woman, "This is a little complicated, but you'll see. It was your great-great-grandmother Maria, *my mother,* see her in the picture? She was delivered in the back of an abandoned school bus in the oil fields of Los Angeles in 1923. Everything she earned as a field worker, maid and mill worker she put into Savings Bonds. Bonds the bank would not honor when she tried to cash them. The starched white bank manager laughed as he put the stack of bonds in the top drawer of his desk, motioned for the guard, laughing still harder as the elderly woman pushed the guard's hands away.

"The last thing she heard as she was escorted out was, 'Alien . . . trash, Henry, here take these over and cash them. Christmas has come a little earlier for all of us.'

"1923 Angeles will be the place they stole from mama," Tela's great-grandmother said, "you'll see."

Each board, shingle, pipe and vinyl floor tile appeared slowly over the years. Some new, some faded, scratched or dinted; still the house braced itself up, rose from its Phoenix-like past and became a shining quilted collection of all the region had to offer. It was now the prize of the neighborhood, a colorful queen bee resting comfortably among her overworked drones.

No more fecal-infested work camps, abandoned buses, or tents. Hanging over the mantel was a picture of Tela's great-great grandmother holding up a Unocal sign, standing next to the rusted-out bus where she had been born. With the addition of tinting colors, it became more hologram than photograph, supernatural, warm and reassuring.

Sometimes Tela would stand and stare at it for several minutes hoping it would speak, tell her where her own mother, Eva, was. Explain to her why she had to hug and kiss the awkward and strange woman from her unfinished dream. Yes, it had only been once, but as soon as that woman spoke, it all returned.

Her great-grams Rosa, immediately knew, now, the story and struck the awkward and angry woman hard across the face, ordering her to leave, to, "Never set foot, again, in 1923 Angeles Avenue until she found and rescued Eva. You! Who are you? *You?* No not my daughter, never again!"

Gone.

"She?" her great-grandma Rosa answered Tela, "yes, sweetness, she's mine, she was my daughter, your grandmother . . . hard to understand. A lost and angry creature, more specter, ghost than woman, now. Don't fret, my little angel, don't fret. She won't bother us or you, ever again."

Add now to the unfinished dream, a new wound for Tela. It was from the other room, just before the awkward and angry woman and great-grams shouted. Tela heard it first, then ran into the room to see the results. It was the only time she had ever seen her great-grandmother raise her hand, not once, but three times. Tela heard the first slap before peering around the corner and seeing the second and the third. Then put a face to the nameless and awkward and angry woman. Grandmother? The shrieking woman ran out of the house holding her face and then stopped. Tela watched through the window as that same woman, still defiant, spat to one side, looked long at the house, start to walk away, stopped again, turned, started to walk, then fell to her knees and wept.

Still watching from the window, Tela discovered her great-grams, shaking her head, whispering, as she walked up the stairs and back into the house. Running to meet Rosa, Tela was halted by the stone-like face on a woman who always smiled. Desperate she lunged for Rosa's embrace and reassurance. Grabbing the back of a chair, she whispered to Tela, "Not to worry, my little angel," as she caught herself and quickly sat down, saying, "Please, child. No worries. I'll be fine in a minute, sweetness, really, just fine."

Sitting down, Rosa looked back up at the photo of her mother, and whispered, "You're right, gone, yes I had to do it. You would have, too, right? It was five, yes, no add eleven to that, yes, sixteen years now, since I got the card saying she had a little girl, Eva. I've never even seen my granddaughter, only *her precious little one* Tela. The one who loves to look up at you, Maria, and says you are alive in there, that you somehow know where her momma is."

Rosa looked back at Tela and then up to the picture above the mantel and continued, "Momma, why do we lose each other? I know I'll never see *my baby*, my daughter, now that I know what she has done, ever again. Worse than dead to me. Still, if I could just find Eva, my granddaughter, bring her here, back to her own flesh, her little angel, then at least there would be some peace with the spirit that haunts this old body that always seems to ask and I can never answer, perhaps you can.

"Is there some elixir, some special mixture that exists somewhere to make this . . . hurting, stop?"

Her head was clear now, so Rosa stood up and then pulled Tela into her arms.

"Come with great-grams. I need to find something. It'll be a treasure hunt, OK?"

Searching the dresser, Rosa found the faded, dog-eared card, checked the address and penned a quick letter to the general delivery address for the migrant camp. It was this letter, tucked in the little girl's Raggedy-Ann doll that assured the safe passage of the crying child, the great-grandchild, left alone in the train station five hundred miles from Los Cabos.

Tela's mother, Eva, barely nineteen, the woman J.B. would only know as *she or her*, later naming her Madonna, *she* never saw the handkerchief. The chloroform they used that gave her a headache that never, from that moment forward, ever seemed to go away. Never saw that same angry, awkward woman who swept her up and with fifty dollars ordered the conductor, "Take this one to the end of the line! Here's the address, and another twenty for your trouble. OK? OK!" And left.

It would be another ten years before *she,* his Madonna, would see her little girl with the Raggedy Ann doll—her daughter—a budding woman, laughing in the surf. There!

The frightened, mute, elated mother thinking as she peered around the corner of the Life Guard stand,

'No, it was not. It cannot be *her*, no impossible, just another mirage in the desert, another illusion, yes one after waking up in the small cabin. Dead, I'm sure, my last vision, I'm dying, and God chooses this before sending me back to continue my penance.

'Or worse. Another one with the smell and the anger and a knife will walk in and it will start, again as they take me and use me over and over again. What was it they really wanted that was so hard and frightening and painful? I never understood it. Could never cry for help, not even as they threw me out into the desert to die.

'Yes, please, on my head, break my neck, please! Landing, the hard fall, the shooting, searing pain, soon I will, blessedly be—dead.'

Black and silent. Nothing. Gone.

Waking, the room was sparse and she was inexplicably clean. Again, she was sure that she was dead; and the cool desert morning a pause, a way station before passing on or into whatever heaven or afterlife awaited her.

He, the nice man, laughed and held her, made sure she knew that she was safe. Spoke of strange ideas and atomic particles and purpose. Called her a racing element in this strange organic collider and somehow it all ends up here in the desert: a new configuration that even the universe itself could not have planned or envisioned or hoped for. Atoms smashing into more atoms and an isolated and lonely man, a wounded woman complete one another, well, for a while.

Each day and night moved on and held up the perfect mirror of how completely imperfect they were as a couple, there out in the desert. But for a moment, a short stretch of time stolen, the elements succeeded in becoming the gold of indifferent love turned eternal and perfect and sang clear sweet ballads in the desert sun.

'He, the nice man, laughed as I never heard anyone, save for the asylum, when I worked there as an aid to the nurses, holding them as they thrashed and spit and screamed, then miraculously they would smile and laugh as though they had just discovered the sound of . . . laughter? I wonder if she, my little girl has ever laughed? Can she laugh? Is she alive to even smile?

Neither of them had reason to trust or love or accept the other, and still, they did. Why? The desert.

Yes, the desert *required it*.

And the two of them?

She never, could not speak, and he? He could not stop drinking or shut up.

And the desert; with all of its light and sand and colors?

Working through them, from the inside out each grew stronger and more fragrant, new green shoots from the ashes of the fire, both of them—flowered—in the desert.

Yes, just like the last dream before sunrise, it lingered in the alchemist's eyes, there, there is where I can finally find the philosophers' stone. So clear . . .

Quick write it all down.

Here and now, there.

There.

In the desert.

A WALKING SHADOW

Strutting and Fretting

So, J.B. our third week now. You said you wanted to cram in as many sessions as you could, before . . . you still intend to go back out there, even now? Sorry. That's you're call." Lowenstein said to J.B. as they both settled in for another session.

"I feel like I know a lot of the facts, the nuts and bolts, but you've mentioned outwardly and I heard a little of it during your hypnosis a change in the timbre and tenor of your voice. As you were coming out, waking up you seemed to be gazing at someone or something. You want to go there, again? Is it OK to go there with me?"

J.B. shrugged. Took a long drink of water, and said, "Why not? It's not like I want to deny or hide it. It's like an over-heated piston firing in my head. It's never stopped, runs me into the red, you know like a gauge, constantly. It started way back with the dominoes and only ran hotter and faster as I gathered more proof, evidence that this."

J.B. stopped and waved his hand as though painting a mural, "This shit we call interactions, trust, devotion, love. It's fine if the furnace door hasn't been opened up."

"Furnace door?"

"Uncle Lee, Leander. He schooled me on that one. The rest just dropped down behind in single-file. The wreck and Cindy and all the rest of the women were just more evidence and support of what I knew all along. Eva? Shit, when I think about it, she was the only respite or rather the perfect hand played at the wrong time, set me up for the worse kind of fall."

"And that is . . .?"

"You ever see The Cincinnati Kid? The kid, Steve McQueen's got him, got that tough old bird Edwin G. Robinson, gonna take him for all he's worth. Boom, royal straight flush to his, I think it was a full house. Anyway, smug as hell, he says, "No kid, just the right play at the wrong time. See? You thought you had me earlier. You're good kid, *real* good, but I'm still on top.

"No, not so much me, men. Always the right play at the wrong time. We'll never feel the universe, never know what it's like to have another heart beating just to the south of our own."

"And the voice . . . first you said it sounded like Leander, then Jabir and now?"

"Not really a voice doc, a persistent, insistent revelation that constantly turns over, reminding me that as hard as I try whenever I reach out, the only thing I'm ever gonna touch is the tip of a very short stick, a stick *I'm holding*. Yep, you guessed it. That same stick I'm holding is gonna somehow or some way find itself rammed right back up my own ass."

"So, J.B. how would you describe it. Where does it take you?"

"Here . . . "

Paris . . . St. Germain, the Latin Quarter, the Islamic book store, the book, skimming it quickly, yes this is the one, on the first page,

"When speaking of the animal's design, contained therein, is theory, not practical application."

Outside looking in, each of us is a random collection of ideas in similar looking vessels that never bond with our surroundings. The ancients knew from the start, tried to bridge the illusion of inclusion, tried to find a place to make the theory—work.

So, it was always meant to begin and end in this desert, that was the illusion that drove him to the spot—here—the old Salt Lake Line, slowly piecing together the abandoned line shack, restoring something that was never there to begin with, save for the nagging notion, If not this, then what?

Walking away from the verdant hills saturated with maple, oak, poplar and dogwood, exiting the rolling green fields of western Carolina, trading the autumn colors, the spectral splash, like an over-turned paint truck every fall for the arid, empty space punctuated only by more absence, he found the illusion-less place that allowed the engine racing in his head, and the jackhammer in his chest to idle.

It will always begin and end in this desert because the random, unchecked movement of him would always dream of a place where it could finally become uncluttered; where nothing in the landscape would fool, re-arrange or dupe him into believing that his fractured time would pay off.

"Pay it off fast . . . son!" the old man, his great-uncle Leander, snapped. Born, raised and tattooed by the Depression made him almost plead with the rain and wind and sun to ease up! Bend a little so that this day might weigh lighter, work a little easier for just a short   stretch . . . please.

"Pay it off, or it's surely gone. Long-term, short-term contracts are nothing more than a fixed argument designed for you to lose. Secure? Shit! Banks and snake-oil salesmen, as close as two coats of paint. So, pay it off, son, then hide. Dissolve into the forest, mountains, wherever it suits you. Dissolve, retreat into whatever will silence that demon crouching on the hind side of your brain, the one who's whispering, 'That's right he does it, they all do it cause they can, they will. Check your pockets and hide your wife. They'll do it and laugh 'til they cry.

"They take all of what's most important: the heart and soul of the man staring back at you in the mirror. Steal what you love and care and need most from your own self. Hellish. See it's not enough to win, they have to see you lose, everything.

"If you let them steal that from or break that in you, you'll owe more than you can ever dream of making or finding cause you've become a bottomless pit, an abyss, and no amount of water, dirt or love will ever fill it back up, ever."

Leander stopped. Looking at the ground he scratched a circle in the powdery, red clay dirt, then stamped his boot clean. Spitting, he wetted the inside of the circle, and then smiled. After a long minute, he shook his head, and looked over at J.B., home from college.

"Shit son, I'm spent. Never knew one man who saw the same thing as I did while we were both staring at, shit, say that bucket of water over there! One sees a still life, a perfect painting. The other wants a big, long drink of it to quench his thirst. Third man wants only to wash up, and then eat. Fourth? Why he wants to pour it over that young thing standing over there, so he can watch her blouse mold around those sweet, firm breasts. One bucket of water and four separate universes. So, son, you choose.

"Made love to a lot of women, passionately, completely, lost my whole being up inside each and every one. And yes, even there, up inside, as connected as two people can possibly be, the two of us are still reaching and touching and feeling two separate things. It' over, I . . . I pass. It's yours now. It's yours."

"We're all an elaborate arrangement of complex, beautiful theories. Share one. Gone on, make yours mine. See what I mean, son?"

So where can it be found? Where is a place that possesses the complete and permanent absence of hope? A place to exhaust all hope, and by doing so, disarm the indifference of the universe? The desert. Go out and test yourself, hold your hand over the fire. Then run. No man can ever withstand a universe, or worse, the sense and sound and heart and loss of knowing it was and will never be excepting of you . . . for too long. I knew one man who lived there and it not so much as broke him as it tortured and isolated him to the point that life was impossible. No, son not lonely or hard, impossible.

"Salvatore Ledbetter, just Sal to his friends; and daddy was his closest. Quiet and hard-eyed man, would look right through you 'cause he never saw anything more than what was behind his own eyes. Hollow, always thirsty.

"Daddy was sitting in the saloon across the street from the stable. He said he saw both of them leave the stable about the time Sal came by to

pay his boarding fee. Two strangers, only been in town a week. Thought it was strange how they left as soon as Sal, arrived.

"After paying the stable master and tipping the groom he crossed the street for a beer. Sal asked the barkeep about the two drifters. Shrugged his shoulders, walked away, then turned and asked, 'Is your wife named Minnie? Was she in yesterday, with your boy across the street at the dry goods store?'

"Sal heard the cries and moans a quarter mile away from his farm. One was higher pitched and hysterical, the other, forlorn. Sal, was called "ghost" because he was the best trapper anyone had ever seen. Could surprise a deer in an open field, pick up a sleeping bear cub, scratch its ears and not wake it, or the mother.

"Sal appeared in the bedroom door, his little boy's throat had been cut, dead, slumped over in the corner. His Minnie was tied to the bedposts, one had finished, and was watching as the other began to violate her.

"He was quiet and meticulous, the sheriff told daddy. Gutted and fileted, those two drifters, put 'um up in the smoke house. Sal was going to feed them to his hogs. He buried his wife and son under a large willow overlooking a bend in the Yadkin River.

"As I was saying son, I've only known of one man who was cast out into I guess you could say the indifference of the universe. Sal, told daddy, that each and every moment, became frozen, still as a photograph. He felt like he was walking from one segment of time to the next.

"Those eyes of his were like two holes vacuuming up everything they slammed into, but not letting anything back out. Seems that once a man's gone through something that is way past acceptable he can't ever really completely go back, step completely out of that place. Breaks the elaborate web of dreams we spin to make it through each day. If you're lucky, and nothing rips through that patchwork of illusions, eventually you got something you can call a life."

"So, yeah, doc," J.B. said, "That's about as close as I come to explaining where I've been, where I am, and where I hope to go. The wreck? Collapsed everything into a simultaneous reaction. An entire life, well, it's all happening as though, yeah, nothing is separated. Is it ever really?"

"The collapsed cylinder, is how you described it before, "Lowenstein added, hoping to come out on the other end, right?"

"Yeah, that's right. I know I can't change the expansion, the movement of this path, life, whatever I find myself in the middle of, it's just, just once, I'd like to connect. Eva made me step out of myself, but to where? What's the next step after."

"Let's try, OK, again next week?"

"Sure, why not, the air-conditioning feels nice."

Heard no more

(One morning in the desert)

We will demonstrate that each one of the components that make up this world constitutes a world unto itself.

From the *Book of Divine Nature*
Jabir ibn Hayyân
Circa 800A.D.

Standing over the remnants of a decaying carcass, he could piece together that it had been a mongrel dog and probably lame, judging from the irregular knee joint. It was probably riding along with his master, a transient, he was, undoubtedly slow on his feet, too, a soiled and worn Ace bandage had been used in a feeble attempt to set its broken neck.

'I bet they hopped into an open boxcar in the yard,' he thought, 'just as the engine lurched forward, straining to gear up. Probably at night when it was cool, and the yard watchman was asleep or drunk or both. I can't imagine that his master, I'll call him: Jim, would have asked him to jump. No, the dog must have instinctively followed him out of the car. Dogs, the most flattering reflection a human can possess. No matter what you say or do it's the hope and love in their eyes. We really don't deserve it, they do.

'Jim probably tried to sneak out while the dog was asleep He was going to let him ride all the way to Mexico or Salt Lake City, hoping someone else would take over for him, maybe give him a place, a home, a purpose, I'd like to think so.

'Anything with lungs, moistened membranes, warm-blooded that *chooses* to pause here in the desert will be rejected. S'why I'm here.'

Looking down at the disappearing carcass made him suddenly aware of the buzzards overhead, the heat and the wind, his drying lips, burning eyes and the swirling eddies of sand. He took a long, deep breath and smiled.

Looking in either direction, watching the rails of the Salt Lake Line pinch together before disappearing into the desert, he does not see another train, nor, more importantly, does not hear another rumbling toward him. Nothing, except for an occasional blast of furnace like heat and its accompanying wind making, still more, lazy snake trails in the sand.

Again, glancing down at the evaporating dog, then peering over at the old line shack, and up into the violent blue sky, he takes a second, longer deeper breath, 'I feel absolutely—nothing.'

Calm and absence, space and release. 'Is there a place, here, for the spirit? What of the mind that creates the idea of spirit, that cannot tolerate this nothingness? Reduce it down, 'What is his essence here, yes, here in the desert?

'Yes, the perfect place to envision water—the desert. Ideal spot to open to see what's inside yourself, to feel and explore, and possibly lay to rest all that is useless. Useless?

'Isn't it all useless, save for the man in the mirror? As long as *my universe* is stable

Then, yep, it's fine. Shit!'

A small skeleton in the sand, an old line-shack in the desert, touching the rail, turning his ear to the wind: silence. So even out in the desert he was confident that there would be no distraction. And yet, they, still, arrived, like apparitions on a Scottish moor, even in the desert, or perhaps, more so *because* of the desert everything falls away, save, the voices and faces and spirits that inhabit the long, deep channels that are so impossible to locate, except when isolated or exiled, or fleeing.

Yes, J.B. had, chosen this place so that he could reap the rewards of its stark and perfect isolation, could look inward and see displayed outward the rising sap, the ooze of his particular and singular world as it welled up and out from the center of his head. 'Lancing the abscessed boil,' he mused.

Numberless and immeasurable, but his particular choice. Ruler, subject, and kingdom all here now—of one—a restoration. A restoration of the original wiring, where else, but in the desert. Only here could *he* find peace in the only universe of any substance or importance? Where else but in the center of his own self exposed. No questions or diversions, here, this world unto itself. So, could he unwind, and then re-wire the circuitry of Jonas Bellingham Ayre?

Here, where the world's largest hour glass was—broken. Spent and spread out, all the time that the earth as ever experienced piled up, then spread out; stopped, started, held and released the collective gathering of all observable time—in stasis. And he?

He, yes, no more than just, *he now.* Would he adjust to the heat and the impossibly dry wind? Or would he become just another grain to be tossed and rolled and scattered before coming to rest—here—there—the desert: "Complet . . . cheri, complet, salut," Therese, cooed after the third time they made love."

'She really did just go, didn't she. Left *me* here after using me as, how did she say it? A wonderful diversion, a wild, perfect fuck, before settling down to raise a baby, but his, not *my* child.'

Here, the perfect place to center and return to each and every moment bubbling up from the central well deep inside of him. Funny, always bringing out the thought of water, here. Water and mirrors, the gift of isolation within himself, here.

FADE OUT

FADE IN – RURAL SOUTHERN LANDSCAPE. TALL PINES, OAKS AND MAPLE TREES. CRICKET AND CICADA WINGS SCRATCHING THE AIR. TWO-STORY VICTORIAN

GARY BOLICK

CLABOARD HOUSE WITH A WRAP-AROUND FRONT
PORCH.

FOCUS – YOUNG BOY, ELEVEN, ALONE ON THE
PORCH

On the front porch, eleven, as his elders, all of them:
mother and father, brother and sister held court around the
table. Banished to the outside, too young to participate, too
unschooled to know or hear or contribute. Staring first at the
doorknob, the shining, brass orb, the voices seemingly
emanating out of this metal, then turning to watch the late
afternoon sun die slowly into the crown of oak and pine it
seemed that the voices were hissing, burning the back of his
head. And the isolation? Reflected back into the last light of the
day. And still more voices, laughing and cajoling. The sunset?

A movie! Yes, just make it a movie. Perfect, now. He, Jonas
is standing behind the last row watching, and always there
listening to voices that were of some vague connection, but to
what and whom and where. Keep rolling, work it out. Better
now. A good flourish.

Sitting, scratching a pattern into the railing and the stairs, he
would have remained there, save for, no, he still was not sure what
pushed him up and over and away. Turning the knob, pushing the
elastic wall until it almost snapped, saying to the table warm with
laughter.

"Jonas! Were you called? No sir, no I don't think so, you can
just turn around and-"

*OK, remember, deflection! Slight-of-hand always trumps the heavy
hand, s'right, remember casting out from under that willow tree. Got you
back J.B., you and me, you and Uncle Lee, go on, now!*

"Just going to my room, now."

43

"Fine dear, just fine."

FADE OUT – SILHOUETTE OF THE DESERT BEHIND THE FULLY-GROWN JONAS aka J.B. FOCUS- TIGHT SHOT ON JONAS'EYES

'There on the porch, both front and back, the Janus-face of exile, the house, never a home, just my first desert. Now here, feels like home; natural, now. He could still hear his own words fly out and pause, hover and die from no response. Just like, here, now. Looking over at a rising dune, the billions of spent words and notions were all here, all assigned a place in time, still not moving. See? All here, there! No past, or future. All still, but screaming and burning, like a match, unable to extinguish, here. Now.

FADE OUT

SMASH CUT HALLWAY

JONAS, AGE TEN, LINGERS, LOOKING INTO THE KITCHEN.

Mother is irritated, nervously smoking while grooming the oldest: the daughter. Smiling, she winks at Jonas' older brother, the "gifted son". A martini glass is on the table. The father is reading the paper, angry at the interruption.

Mother (dismissively): "That's fine dear. Supper will be ready in an hour. Don't be late. Run along, dear."

FADE OUT

FADE IN

LONG SHOT OF ELEMENTARY SCHOOL ROOM

THE SOUND OF GLASS BREAKING, THUNDEROUS LAUGHTER, SQUEALING

CUT TO AND FOCUS ON TEACHER

Teacher is female, mid-fifties spinster, intellectually and sexually frustrated.

Teacher (bordering on rage): "My little dears . . . silence! Please, I must insist so, well, you *really,* I mean it! Do you really want to test me, today of all days? Fine!"

Errant and insistent, an eddy swirling endlessly with the prepubescent voices all quieted by the thunderclap of Miss Landover. Frozen in the front of the classroom glaring under the halo of large block letters: cursive verses print, primary numbers forming a spiraling jetty under her feet. Born full grown and in full battle raiment (from the head of, well, no one was ever sure which God could or would have dared to have dreamt her up) she ruled the fifth grade and even caused Principal Burden to seek shelter upon occasion. Forcing the wind and the rain, the sun and the moon to follow her dictum and rage, her postulates, but most of all, "My rules!"

Searching under the desk: the lost world of former students and their forbidden graffiti. Underneath and on top of desks, boys scanned and probed and wished for elusive notes from the lost underground of ancient comrades. Anything and everything hidden to discover and then to share at recess. Yes, curious for the words, and a place one of the older sixth graders had mentioned. Held back a grade, yet again, Kyle was a head taller, and lord of the playground. He laughed, knowingly, when speaking of a place called The Bermuda Triangle.

Yes, a hidden, forbidden space—there—where you, the uninitiated would soon learn is a warm, moist fragrant triangular shape of soft, supple hair, a place where all men, eventually find themselves lost. "No man, once there, ever comes back the same, trust me, I know!" he boasted.

J.B. searching for graffiti found only odd scribbles, and then an ominous warning, clearly written, as though the desk had been turned upside down, and the words stenciled cleanly and clearly on the center of the seat. He stared long and hard, tried to ignore the words, but could not, would not look away.

A WALKING SHADOW

The Triangle? Nowhere to be found. It was or would be something of a *cause-célebre* for Miss Landover and Mr. Burden. For J.B. now? Nothing, only the stenciled warning. But that was more than enough to create suspicion in Miss Landover's eyes. Surveying her troops, she noticed that when called on, Jonas would not answer. His head was nowhere to be found, tucked neatly underneath his desk. Miss Landover assumed the worst.

Striding brusquely across the front of the room, Miss Landover turned quickly to her right, her crepe soled shoes squealing as she arrived at the third desk down where J.B. was still lost, studying the curious message, in block letters: "If they can kill Kennedy, then no one is safe. November 22, 1963."

Miss Landover pulled J.B.'s face up to front her own as he started to read the warning a third time. Her breath was toxic, a mixture of licorice and garlic. He saw her mouth moving, but only later, did her words register.

"Don't lie to me, boy! At your age, my word! I would have expected it out of, never mind. Mindy, honey, don't fret, I'm sure he didn't *see* anything. Off, young man. Off to the principal, now!"

LONG PANNING SHOT OF PARIS

CUT TO SMALL FLAT IN MONTMARTRE

"Now, cheri! Please take me. Remember me in this moment. Love? No, no, it is because I will never have this love, again, the love *I want* but at least I can have this moment as *I* choose. Compris?"

The tower, Delaunay's twisted and protracted destruction and resurrection of the Les Champs du Mars, the war fields in the form of Eiffel's slender, black swan stretching its neck up from under its wing in the late afternoon, the mist and fog covering the winking and blinking of the waking city below it. Her hand threading into his, her eyes drowsy and soft and full of affection. Just a moment, she and what little he had ever tasted of those perfect wings covering, enclosing and reassuring him—gone.

TIME LAPSE OF SUNSET ON THE DESERT

J.B. out walking along the rails.

Yes, come and go, gone. The burlap bundle hoisted off the passing train, late, without the aid of a full moon, he never would have seen the glint of silver capped teeth, the large, brown hands, two sets, swinging the potato sack up and out of the box car; seen the smile, the other hand pulling out the bandana to wipe his brow, close the door. Gone.

Moaning, he heard the sack speak before he saw it move. Thirty? No, younger still, but looking like fifty, her tongue mutilated, her face? A constellation of scars old and new. Used, and used again, for whatever, "The man will pay for." Dropped in the desert to die, here. Away from everything that a man might value as real and good and necessary. That was why he was there, and now she was with him, silent, save the frightened eyes, an occasional moan, and giving him the eerie sense that he was in a movie again; standing on the porch looking out as the voices from inside, like those he heard from the passing train, laughing.

He chose this place, she was left for dead here. Together, today, this morning in the desert, they seemed perfect for one another.

Time has been . . .

(In the desert . . . a moment ago)

A WALKING SHADOW

First light, a gentle updraft is quickly desiccated, again. Its first and last whisper of hydration? Errant vapors, whispers of morning dew clinging only to scatter like exploded dandelion fluff. Holding steady as the dry lift increases, a vulture cranes its head, surveys the desert floor: nothing. No small rodents or larger creatures struggling—dying—no carrion—only wild flowers, cactus and the occasional, wind-induced, rose-shaped, eddy in the sand.

Descending, a pause, another updraft; floating higher, now. Its eyes ease up, relax and broaden to scope the entire horizon: rose to cream and finally azure. A thin patina of sunlight, restless and warming melds with the wind and light all supporting the flux and patter, up and down, out and back, that is the constant stasis under its wings.

A moment later. Actually, *moment,* strains the thought. Less, still, when seeded into the collected time of the universe's womb, yes, barely an instant ago that she, with her hand and song and smile, humming while seated at the spinning jenny pulled raw animal hair into wool. Or him, Beethoven, his impossible 9th composed in the silent quadrants of his voiceless brain. And what of the pixels hatched from a radio beam caught like the sizzling heat from Walter Johnson, The Big Train's hand: the Hubble Telescope giving us the backwash thrown forward, and of course, the ever present, insistent mushroom cloud, yes, born, bred and refined—here. Our brief, insistent spot in time here, no more than, was it ever here? When stepping back, a few million, throw in a billion years. Yes, above floating those wings saw and felt this place as its own. Us?

Each eye amazed, stilled and flummoxed, wondering, How was I ever connected to any and all of this, ever? What was it the catcher said after spitting out his chaw? "Sheeit! That weren't nothin'! Just his little 'ol change-up." Then paring off another chaw, rolling it in his mouth, he replaces his mask, crouches down and flashes another signal. He drops down his index finger, slowly rotates it and says, as you nervously dig in, "Strap in good, Sparky, here comes his jumpin' *angry* heat."

Try as we may it just never seems to include any of *us*. "So of course, bien sûr, cheri, we annihilate it! Compris?"

The curious creature, the bipedal dreamer: man. Such a quick blip, barely a scratch or mark on a timeless plain, so anxious and angry that he was never included, so yes, "That's a wrap! Print it! Strike the set!" Gone. Re-runs? One can always hope, right?

"Wait at second! Who hired this guy?"

He was the weak, observant one. Not at all like the others, no, not like them, at all, *he* was the first of *us*. New wiring, perhaps, or just a mutation that left its indelible mark, on walls, in caves, saw one thing in his head, another outside and decided to marry the two. Tolerated, left alone, not a female, but too frail to hunt. Not a child bearer, nor a hunter, a lone observer always perched up on a ledge, there up on the hill above the river and its valley to watch the fixed tableau that moved like his own chest, imperceptible, but moving, breathing, alive and animated if you had the time and patience, and were given the luxury to simply observe it all unfold. Creatures above and below, colors that moved with the wind and the light, all of it connected and peaceful, all of it seemingly orchestrated until he extended out his own hand. Reaching out, where did *it, his hand, and he?* Where did any of him or the others fit into all of this magic?

So, when the females were out with the small ones. The hunters? Gone. Alone by the fire, the shadows fanning out, licking the walls like the tall grass and water reeds blown by the wind. Closing his eyes, yes, there he was, perched once more above the verdant fields, the river silent, save for the distant wash of whitewater just past the sweep, the bend in the river, like a heron craning its neck, its head, suddenly, plunging into the water, out of view. Blinking, again, the erratic, bob and weave of the fire's shadows jumped. Again, closing his eyes, he smiled.

Being asleep, but not, inside of the cave and the interior of his own head seemed one in the same: grass and ibex, the wind combing the long green, its long, easy strokes threshing out prancing, leaping herds of creatures who appeared to move in and out of the land in the same manner he felt his own chest rise and fall. Restoration of place? Close, but still falling down.

He plunged his hand into the rough-hewn mixing bowl, mashing and matching, grinding and watering the paste gleaned from the soft, staining minerals. Rising up, he walked over and used the shadows as a living stencil to shape the form of the great beasts leaping and prancing. Wall and shadow giving *his* vision body. Pausing, looking up and around, for a moment he felt as though he were standing inside of his own head.

From a waking dream, the most fragile of them—the father of *us*—all—reached up to soothe the heart of each despairing descendant birthed from that moment. Awake and probing, painting and lamenting, this precursor of *us all* attempted to re-attach that which was discovered and lost all in the same instant it was observed. He was so unlike the graceful creatures who seemed but an extension of the water, air, forest and fields, so he attempted to paint them into his own waking dream in hope of restoring himself to the sanctuary that was home to them, yet so hard, cold and unforgiving to him.

Pausing for a moment, he smiled as he saw it appear, there, the connection, made possible from the extension of his own hand. There the awkward, perfect strokes fused the ibex and the antelope, the great bulls, the cows without hesitation onto and into and now leaping out of the walls. Yes, it was his and becoming more, perhaps a part of all of us until adding the simple outline of his hand. He wept. Ah, yes, close, but still not *there*.

Of all that was in and of those walls, flying, snorting, prancing, galloping, and soaring, all that was matched and made lovely from what he had seen and felt from his perch, all these images became the simultaneous expression of the serenity and perfection that was seen outside, also felt within him, and successfully a living part of these walls. Yes, here, as though it were out there, or from the shadows and from his dreams. It was, all of it, there, the cave as a cathedral, a timeless, new dream. The two were one, here, but the only thing, completely out of place was, yes, one thing: his own hand, it alone, did not match.

A seed discovered, cracked and flowering all in the same instant and into petals of anguish, fear and alienation that grew stronger and enveloping as each of us continues to flourish and grieve. Grieve? Yes, because at arm's length there is the ceaseless and mocking realization that we are hostage while others soar and prance above, below and around—*us*.

Thirty thousand years, really not even a moment, earlier, it began, and still the isolation, the indifferent shrug reverberates and reinforces the waking revelation that he alone discovered and attempted to solve. By reaching up to re-install all of us he set down a marker, a moment for each to study and resolve, to ponder and forever exile us in the heart of the dilemma: How to extend an individual dream into and out of a place hostile to his very existence? For in each of us is a simple, completed dream to share. But how and where and with whom? In each there is the rage and the silence that petitions while suffocating the love wrestling in the womb desperate to push out, be touched and made whole, again. Here?

"Back again, back again, back in the warm waters of momma's belly," goes the refrain of the song sung wrung from the cold, steel-clawed winds felt from riding under a boxcar, the parallel lines of the track and it wooden ties only inches away.

In becoming man, the damning dilemma was an unfortunate fix, a needle that never seemed to deliver enough of the drug to last long enough to survive, save for a moment in transition, a dream or perhaps making love. That dream? Yes, the one that has eight billion separate versions. How to share it? How indeed, the hot-wired monkey—man—asks each time the sun appears and he has not a clue, still, where the time stops or goes or waits, and for what?

Still, yes, that most pressing of problems rears its ugly head and allows the prefect diversion. Yes, understood. Whoa that was a close one. So? What to order for breakfast, this morning. Yes, a close, shave that one. Too close.

"Cut! Bring in the extra!"

THIS MORNING

He heard the major chord first; a sustained, full C, but the train was not in sight. Odd for the desert, he thought. Yes, strange, sound before the image, a complete reversal of the accepted, the ordinary, the reality of the desert's flatness. Everything so close, seemingly within arm's reach, when, in fact, the shrub, abandoned depot, or mountain are ten miles away. A desert constant, the unresolved *tompe-d'oeil* that the brain attempts to correct, but never succeeds. Still, he has never *heard* the train before seeing it approach at his particular point in the desert: his winter home, the abandoned line shack on the Salt Lake Line. A relic of another, slower place in space and time.

Again, the long, full blast from the engine's horn, but still no train in sight. He walked back into his cabin, looked at his sleeping palette, 'Yes, I *am* awake.' Returning to the rails, he scanned the parallel lines of steel that ran endlessly in both directions. Again, the visual slight-of-hand, as his eyes followed the rails out, slowly collapsing from two equidistant lines into a single, bold black stroke that disappeared in both directions. A third blast of the engine's horn, arrived, and still . . . no train.

He reached into his pocket and pulled out a small plastic bag filled with pills and pot. Counting the pills, surveying the weed. 'Same as I had yesterday, so no, I am *not* using, I'm sober, now.'

He stepped closer to the rail, dropped to his knees, then stretched out on his stomach, placing his right ear directly on the warming face of the rail.

"A baby sleeping in mama's belly," is how Shep described it to him eighteen months ago. Shep could calculate the distance and time from the whisper and the faint vibrations he heard and felt in the rails. 'This guy's like a bottle-nosed porpoise out of water,' J.B. thought.

"Don't rush, none, you hear?" chuckling as he stood up and brushed himself clean. "Seven miles, shade over eleven minutes 'fore she gets here. Gives me time to tie up tight, have a smoke 'fore I jump up on or scurry up under her. Damn I hope there's an open boxcar. I hate sailin' the blinds underneath, just getting' too old to hang on up under there, have trouble stayin' awake down there, up against her belly."

Shep appeared, one night, a new constellation, discovered and fallen alongside his cabin. Walking out to urinate in the morning he saw the old man curled up asleep inside his Bronco. He fixed him breakfast, supplied a bed and books, liquor and conversation. 'A week and a half of graduate school before that apparition disappeared,' J.B. mused.

'Fifteen miles close, to forty miles an hour, so figure about twenty-three minutes, so why haven't I seen it, yet?'

Standing up, straightening his back, his eyes followed the rails out until they were no longer steel, but simply a part of the distant desert. No sign of an engine. A gentle breeze pushed sand and scrub brush swirling past his feet. Another stronger gust followed, and then another and another after that creating a series of eddies—roses in the dirt—everywhere.

'Can the wind do that? Pick up a sound, like a hurricane and jump it? Sling it forward?' He closed his eyes and took several deep, long breaths. Opening his eyes, he saw a vulture climb up and hang on an updraft. Scrub mesquite held fast against the gusts of wind. A slight hint of water filled his nostrils, and there, again, the full, melodic C.

'Funny, no drugs, no food, not even a cup of coffee. Just awake and I hear the approaching train before I see it. I know it's there, I felt it in the rails. Like knowing a star is there before the light arrives. Wonder if anyone else has ever *felt* or *heard* a star before they saw it?'

THAT AFTERNOON

We whittle down our lovers, you know, systematically pare away everything we don't like or accept as being something that reflects back to us a perfect image of ourselves. No, doctor, not like Pygmalion—worse.

"Objectifying her doesn't quite catch what I'm driving at. Shaping the image or personality to fit your needs is narcissistic, reprehensible, but hell, everyone tries to do it, and no one seems to really object. No, what I think is going on, and at a much deeper level is when we make love. When we are making love, we are trying to transform our lover into a sustained idea or feeling that bridges the outside world to our own particular universe. Bend it—her—to shoehorn that person into your particular place an alchemist at work in his laboratory.

"The dance, the seduction, each scent, the sight of her, her taste, eyes, doesn't matter what color, green, blue, brown or the sweep of her hips or the way her breasts nuzzled up against my chest. Even the soft, wet feel of her vagina, the release, our release, *my* release inside of her it's till just a marker. *My marker.* I admit it."

Lowenstein nodded, showed an animated lift of his eyebrows, thinking, 'Well, the gloves are off. A lot of rage where I least expected it. Of, course it has been percolating since he was eleven. The accident only acted as a catalyst. The curve ball, here, is Eva. The redemption. So now he wants to line up all the women, one by one, load and fire. How to push back, help him move, without re-opening, revisiting . . . well, he seems to think there is no going back it's always there, the disconnect. OK, we'll just see about that.'

"Don't look so surprised. I know most, no, no man really wants to admit to it. Not at all PC. I don't care. For a moment she is everything I want suspended, right there under me, and me? I am suspended between two worlds, she becomes the place where I escape the natural world and add my own particular world on top of, thrust it inside her. I am completely transformed. If she would let me, I'd take her three times a day. Who wouldn't? Each time we make love gives me a window of a couple of hours. We're basically screwing everything, both literally and figuratively to solve the build-up, then find the release. It's the place where science and poetry, painting and music and . . . murder originate. Withhold the love and sex and it's not long before the axe comes out, anyway, enough of that, that's another hundred and fifty dollars, right?"

Lowenstein felt his pulse thumping, a quick sliding drip of sweat race down the center of his back. He knew that the anger and the rage were a mask for fear; a profound longing to attach to something of permeance. Hyper-sexual, J.B. was still the shunned child on the porch, the lonely friend of the raging Leander. One woman after another and the prostitute, yes. His safety-valve. He always made a point of paying for one in particular. 'OK. She's it. Either it opens the door or we go down the rabbit hole,' he thought.

"So, J.B. . . . what's a poor schmuck like me to do?"

J.B. stopped cold. It was as though he was just now realizing that he was talking to another person. After an awkward, sheepish smile, he stood up and walked to the window, where he began to survey the strip mall parking lot. Desert Dry Cleaners-Slots, Seven-Eleven-Video Poker, Subway, Arlen's Spirits-Slots and Jimmy's 24-7 Lube, then over to the marquis at The Rio: Penn and Teller. 'Do these guys ever take a day off? Last time I was here: Penn and Teller!

What was it Shep sang? Back again, back again swaying under momma's belly. Sailing the blinds back and forth from here to there. Six months in Las Vegas and then back to the desert, 'Cockroach scurrying from the heat so that he can enjoy the middle way,' he thought.

He could hear his wristwatch ticking; an old Timex that Leander had given him. The ticking mimicked the clatter and chatter in his head. Often it would calm him, bring him back to moment, help him look out and get past the back of his eyes. Leander. Yes, "No man, I know of, save for Sal, stayed there. Lived in that vacuum and poor 'ol Sal, just plain hollowed and thirsty, looked right through you on to the wall behind you 'cause all he saw was the backside of his own eyes. Wounded bear trapped in his own skin."

Lowenstein watched J.B. and paused, thinking, 'This could screw both of us. He's like a little brother who was just beaten-up by the neighborhood bullies. Look at him, big nervous cat uncomfortable, pacing, trolling the grass, yep. Dare I? Why not.'

"So, J.B. Shari's? The world's most famous brothel, isn't that part of the ritual? Isn't her name. Let me think. What? Yes, Toni? Is she good? Does she even come close to that French piece of ass? Be honest, now . . . close? How could she? Didn't you say you can still smell her, I mean, the frog, la femme fatale. Wakes you up in the desert. So, does Toni do if for you like, what was her name? Therese? Right? Jonas? J.B.? No wait, how about Guy?

Ever try that name? After all that wonderful piece of French ass bore *his child,* not yours. Right?"

FADE OUT – The Doctor's voice grows increasingly faint.

FADE IN – ELEMENTARY SCHOOL – J.B. sees himself seated at the principal's desk.

It was the principal, Mr. Burden's, labored breathing, his tongue popping after shoving, yet another, peppermint into his mouth. Just as then, now, he could not put his finger on why he was being disciplined.

FOCUS – Jonas the ten-year old child.

Voiceover - J.B., the adult, speaks:

Why do I feel like Dr. Lowenstein is disciplining me? Why, even as the owner of my own company, when asked a simple question, even by a floor worker, did I always feel challenged? Always seems to come back to that to why am I always so uncomfortable when all I am trying to do is address my own feelings. Is it possible to have two sets of feelings? One for the person you are trying to deal with and the other, your own. Where is the line? Where is it, the space within yourself, where is it possible to accept another's thoughts and ideas as authentic and meaningful? Is there room for another's emotions without sacrificing your own? Is contentment just another word for isolation? Wall yourself off, even in a crowded room, and smile.

FADE OUT.

CUT TO MISS LANDOVER'S ROOM

The truth? Mindy, the girl sitting behind of him in the fifth grade claimed he was trying to look up her dress. J.B. dropped his pencil. When he reached down to pick it up he saw some writing. It was a long sentence in block letters, even had quotation marks and a date beside it: graffiti from the ancient past: "If they can kill Kennedy, then no one is safe. November 22, 1963". Who actually said it? Why was it there? Who took the time to put it there, and why were they so scared?

All these questions to answer so he stayed to read it a second and a third time. It both scared and interested him. He felt like Indiana Jones. It seemed very important, almost sacred. Then, just as he was about to raise up, Jonas saw Mindy's legs move. Slowly at first, then completely spread out, he saw the space where her legs disappeared and there, yes there he saw a pair of thick, white cotton panties.

He was confused. 'Yes, she, she *wanted me to see* . . . something, but what? What was it that was so special there? No, this cannot be what Kyle spoke of, so what, where can it be?' Confused and still, frightened at what he had just read, it was Miss Landover who made the issue clear—to herself.

Suddenly, the hard, cold hand of Miss Landover was pulling him up. The bank of fluorescent light blurred, a flash of heat then cold ran through his body. Looking behind him Mindy was blushing and nervously shaking her head "no." It was all the circumstantial evidence that Miss Landover needed to convict and hang the accused.

"Listen to me boy! I've got a mind to blister you right here and now! No, better yet, let that, ah, Mr. Burden handle this perversion. Get up. Off to his office, pronto, boy!"

Her breath was, if that were possible, even stronger, and more acrid than before: a mix of rotting eggs and vinegar. Her eyes: two slits and growing narrower. Add this crime to the earlier ones of spilled paint and upset pencil boxes, Miss Landover was well into Poland, massing her troops for an incursion into Russia.

Mindy whimpered as she suppressed tears, Danny, the asthmatic, pressed hard on his inhaler, desperate for a good, deep breath. The air was heavy with history, a humiliation and a memory that was Miss Landover's and hers, alone. Still, all would have to suffer in some fashion as it blew out the top of their teacher's head.

Festering for fifty years. Yes, fifty years it had lain dormant, until now. So, looking up into her face, J.B. saw the fear and pain of a frightened young girl and the rage of an isolated, unloved middle-aged woman running from the classroom, her dress soiled red, and dripping, the children laughing, the dismissive teacher shaking her head, "Deb Landover, really? At your age, you should know better by now than to come to my classroom unprepared for, my word, get out and don't come back until you've cleaned yourself, girl."

The door slamming behind her as she started to run for the restroom. Yes, the door was closed, but not sound proof, so Deb could hear the parting shot of the teacher as she said, "I guess they don't have time to teach hygiene in the hills, do they class? Now, now settle down, God takes pity, loves his hillbillies, too. Now turn to page twenty-seven, don't think we'll see Ellie-Mae back in here anytime soon."

There was just too much carnage and collateral damage to wade through to try and explain, so before Jonas could take a good deep breath, and try to explain what had actually happened, he found himself standing in front of the principal, Mr. Burden, waiting for his sentence to be handed down.

"Got to admire your, ah that excuse you came up with, son. Almost had me going, too. Son, I'll have to call your mom and dad. Nothing wrong with liking girls. Just not appropriate what you did, son. Hold, it! Don't try and deny it. Miss Landover caught you, son. Guess you really don't understand that bringing in the name of Kennedy won't help you much either. It's kind of strange, or did you really see that written up under the desk? Don't lie to me, son. Just make it worse on you. Do you even know who John Kennedy was?"

J.B. was looking out of the window, alone, again, with his thoughts. The principal's voice reminded him of a movie voice over or a commercial that was trying to sell him deodorant or life insurance. Yes, he had heard his parents talk of Kennedy, but he did not know the date or the exact year. His fascination with the graffiti? Why would someone post the warning there? Why was that little boy or girl; had it been a little boy or girl? The lettering was perfect and the quotation marks? Who said it? Why was he or she so scared? And why couldn't it be said aloud? It was a warning, so why hide it? Or was there something else to it? What was the world thinking about, and made them so scared, back then?

He looked at Mr. Burden's face. Rose, almost red, creased with thick jowls hanging from his neck. He noticed that he wore a lot of cologne, but there was still a faint sour-sweat smell that filled the room.

'He smiles, too much,' J.B. thought, 'smacks his lips, and makes too much noise rolling all those peppermints in his mouth. Why is he always adjusting his pants? So, what is he really after me to say?'

He thought of Kyle and the older boys. 'Got it!'

J.B. cleared his throat. The principal looked up and said, "So, son, you ready to come clean? Tell the truth?"

"I just wanted to see, you know, sir, if she had hair down there."

The principal grinned, shook his head, and then reached down to adjust his trousers. He stared at J.B. for a long moment, smiled, popped another peppermint into his mouth, and chuckled.

"God, I wish I was your age, again. All of it so fresh and new and never mind that, son. I'll talk to Miss Landover. No need to call your momma and daddy. Kennedy assassination, got to hand it to you, son. You're good! Go on, now, run back to class before I change my mind. But mind you, son, don't find your way back in here again. Do we understand each other, son?"

J. B. nodded his head and replied, "Yes sir, we do."

Walking back to class, J.B. felt an odd contentment running through him, thinking, 'The truth meant a lot of trouble.

Telling Mr. Burden what he really wanted to hear made it a confirmation of what Miss Landover wanted to believe. So, the truth is simply a measurement of what someone wants in that moment.

'Mindy had on thick, white underwear. She opens and closes her legs all the time. I never got to talk about what really scared me. What I told Mr. Burden, and what Miss Landover believed happened, did not have anything to do with what I was really feeling or explain why that person thirty years ago was so scared.

'Seems like if you're talking to someone and they ask you a question, the answer they really want is, Give me anything, but please, no never! Not the truth. Still, better, yet, tell me something no one is supposed to talk about, something that's never supposed to see the light of day. Something we all carry around. Something we think about, but never talk about that makes us anxious and aroused. Now, take it and make into something that is about, yes, *yes me!* The one thing I'm always desperate to hear and see and touch. There really is no truth except what is most important to what I am trying to own and or throw away: people, places and even love. The only truth that honestly matters is my own, and even that has to be changed, constantly, to fit the particular time or place or moment.'

FADE OUT

FADE IN – PYCHOLOGIST'S OFFICE

J. B. looked at Dr. Lowenstein and saw Principal Burden sitting next to him. A few moments later Burden slowly fades away.

"So, doc, right hand at the right time?" said J.B. as he stared back at Lowenstein.

"May be, it just may be, let's see."

A WALKING SHADOW

APPARITIONS ON THE MOOR

Two Years Earlier

CUT TO DESERT HIGHWAY

Off in the distance J. B is standing, watching his memory unfold again.

J. B. Voiceover: "Shit! At least once a day . . . every day, back here, again!"

CAMERA PANS OUT TO FOCUS ON J.B.'s FACE THEN MOVES UP AND DOWN HIS BODY: CLENCHED HANDS, SWEATING FOREHEAD, OCCASIONALLY TREMORS

Out in the distance J.B. shakes his head, clenches both hands into tightly-balled fists. His heart will not slow down, no matter how hard he tries to relax. A patina of sweat covers his face reflecting the late evening sun. 'Each time,' he thought, 'same, absolute silence in the center of my head. Absolute zero right before the plunger is pushed. It's the God damned waiting, sweating it out, waiting, just waiting for the breath to be sucked out of me and, then, the mushroom cloud appears.'

It was late in the afternoon, January, the sun was low, almost parallel with the horizon. J.B. was leaving the factory, driving south on Highway 93. His wife, Cindy had called, she had just started her period. It was fine, he told her, we'll keep trying. His voice, this time, was not as resolute, and hers was more shadow than whisper, hollowed out and resigned, "Fine hon, sure, I mean, if that's what you want."

J.B. held the cell phone out at arm's length and stared at it, thinking, 'Shit! She was the one so hell bent on starting a family.' Putting the phone back to his ear, he heard his wife rummaging around in the kitchen, distracted, as she finished up the call.

"I probably won't be home when you get here. Bring you something? There's nothing here to fix for dinner. I, whatever. I got to get out of here for a while. See you when I do."

Cindy Laring Ayre was bored. A year ago, she had bumped into an old high school acquaintance, J.B. Ayre at an NPR fund raiser. She had finished all of her classes and was about to start writing her thesis for her master's in behavioral psychology. Once that was done she wanted to council disadvantaged children, "You know all the different shades of brown, Mexican-Americans, illegals, Native Americans and God, don't get me started, *so* cute! And, my word! Would you just look at *you,* now. Course you were always so smart, just never noticed what a hunk you were, sorry are now."

Six weeks later they were married and in San Francisco on their honeymoon. Cindy had always been aloof and distant when they were in English class. Or was she? J.B. thought to himself when looking at her sleep. I was the head case, withdrawn and trying to square the circle, constantly challenging all my teachers, but too shy to ask anyone, let alone someone as pretty as Cindy, out.

For a year they rarely left each other's side. She was fascinated, drawn to a man, "So well-read, speaks French, and owns his own company that actually *rewards* rather makes indentured servants out of its staff. Let's make a baby, the thesis can wait."

After five months and no + sign on any of her pregnancy tests, Cindy was growing tired of the desert climate, but most of all the routine of dutifully having sex when she was ovulating, only to be frustrated every time it ended with her monthly period.

Her Master's thesis still sat languishing on her desk. It was, at least a year, from being completed. She had tried working at the local free clinic, counseling, youth offenders and recovering drug addicts, and hated it. 'Perfect, another misfire!' she thought. Looking up at the calendar she counted out the days until she figured she would be ovulating again. 'Why bother,' she thought, and picked up the phone to tell J.B. the disappointing news.

Since they were not likely to have a baby anytime soon, J.B. suggested, What about Paris? He thought it would be the perfect solution. If they timed it just right Cindy's first month being pregnant would be in Paris, a perfect place to celebrate. If they got another - sign on the pregnancy test, Paris would be the perfect place to try again. He had not counted on the third alternative; a disinterested voice saying, "Whatever, see you when I do."

Click. J.B. Looked at the silent phone, shook his head in disgust and tossed it onto the passenger seat.

Pulling the visor down did little to block out the sun. Even sunglasses only partially dampened the glare. A tractor-trailer pulled up on his left and was content to stay in tandem with him. Cindy? Where was she going and why so distant? Looking to his right the desert was, well, the desert: open and running up to the mountains, scrub trees and cactus, and yes, so completely vacant and relentlessly, soothing.

After a power outage at the factory, three sick calls and two angry calls from distributers, the desert and its expansive expression of uncluttered space was—refreshing. He mashed down on the accelerator, passed the tractor-trailer and eased into the left lane, put on the cruise-control and looked out to the desert on his left, now. Again, the tractor-trailer pulled up, now, on his right. J. B. sped up to lose the roar and crowding of the semi. Flipping off the cruise-control, J. B. pushed his Prius to its limits, steered back into the right lane and was, for the moment, alone, again, to enjoy the trip home, sort out his thoughts. 'Just ease back let everyone pass me on the left and, son-of-a-bitch! What is this asshole's problem?'

Again, back on J.B.'s immediate left a long line of massive rubber and steel, sixteen wheels at eye level, roaring, fish-tailing with each gust from an ever-strengthening cross wind. Pressing down hard on the accelerator his car lurched forward, away from the eye-level line of wheels. Looking side to side there was—finally—only the desert opening up and running into the horizon. The sun was descending behind the mountains, the knot that had become the back of his neck was dissolving, the vise clamped on his temples, loosening, allowing the thoughts of Paris. 'Yes, Paris and Montmartre at sunset.'

He remembered one twilight, there. Nineteen years old, perched up on the granite steps looking down, a thick layer of fog, cream and slate colored, a cat curling up at the base of the Eiffel Tower. *La tour Eiffel,* Delaunay's masterpiece suddenly become a Chinese wall hanging, three rough strokes of ebony against the soft, curling back of rice paper. It was all so connected, an extension of what he felt for her, for Therese, as his hand threaded so easily with hers. And those eyes: two black orbs bobbing under the lazy lids of exhaustion. They had spent the afternoon up on the hill, in her friend's cold water flat. He could still see her lithe torso stretched out as she raised the sheet, whispering, "Ici, près du moi, chéri, plus près du moi: Here, closer to me" and so they made love a second time, and then slept. Thinking, now, do I dare take Cindy there? Do I risk losing that day if I—

J.B.'s Prius was airborne, spinning, then suddenly it was not. Looking up to his left he could read PETERBILT on the front grill of the semi only three feet from his face. His car was angling away from him as the screech of the trailer's pumping brakes infused the air with its buckling vibrations, and the smell of rubber, searing, and the sound of metal and concrete trying their best to grind each other into a fine powder. The driver? J.B.? Is that really me . . . him . . . me? A part? What to do? What to say? Harder, faster, louder, closer the god damned grill is only eighteen inches away. Shouting, heard by no one but himself, a simple, but emphatic, "No!"

CAMERA FOCUSES ON J.B. STANDING ON THE SIDE OF THE ROAD WATCHING

J.B. Voiceover: "Each second was an hour, a lifetime. Moving so fast and everything around me at a complete standstill.

CUT TO PYCHOLOGIST'S OFFICE

J. B. paused, took a breath and continued, "I didn't know what else to do. Right at the moment I knew that the truck was going to flatten me, I felt everything pull away. Sound, color, the desert, all fled. There was no longer any connection between me and the natural world. I, whatever *I am* was there, but without any connection whatsoever to the world around me. I was still there, waiting for the truck to flatten me. It would be over quickly, I knew that. It was the complete, I mean, total, absolute indifference that the moment forced on me. *That, yes, that* was the thing that was really the most unsettling. In that moment I understood that any and all things—human—are inconsequential to the earth, universe, all of . . . this. The world was perfectly serene, indifferent and I had absolutely no part to play. It as if the entire natural world shrugged its shoulders, and said, "So?"

"Looking back at, well no, I think of it constantly, now, but in shouting out *no?* Don't we all do that every day? Don't we all, in some way, demand the same sort of attention, and each day there is no one there to listen. Am I not right, Doc?

"The planet completely withdrew its presence from me. Do you follow me? No, not at all like being alone or feeling isolated. It was a palpable rebuke. Even loss of hope—hopelessness—implies an alternative. Even nothingness postulates a possible out, a place that can or will fill the void. Even the notion of Hell reassures the damned that they were expected and will have company.

"When I screamed out No, even the sound of my voice just stayed there, did not release out into the air. It just hung there right in front of my face. A rebuke saying to me, 'You finally got it, chief! Nothing outside of you has a point of reference to or with you. And, oh yeah, try and explain that to someone, 'cause all you're gonna get back is, Don't affect me, none. Piss off!'

"No, doc, not a near-death experience. It was more like an absence-of-life experience. From that point, I've looked forwards and backwards, dissected the present and all I can come up with is that I'm just some isolated particle bouncing around, clamoring for a place on a planet that in no way is interested, one way or the other whether I survive or thrive or exist in any form."

J.B. walked over to the window and stared out. After a moment, he turned back to Dr. Lowenstein and smiled, "Right. You guessed it. I'm just a barrel of laughs at parties, now. But it's why I pulled out all the books I bought when I was a student in Paris. The ancient alchemist, Jabir. And Jung, Carl Jung. He spent the last part of his life wrestling with the split in science and the spiritual. He thought the alchemists had the answer. He postulated that the alchemists knew that they would never solve the mystery of turning base metals into gold or find elixir for eternal life, the Philosophers' Stone. No, they just hovered over their cauldrons, and became suspended between two worlds, got outside of themselves for a few hours before coming back to be here again—alone. Like I said, a real barrel of laughs!"

J.B. Ayre crawled out of his mangled car and paused. Mozart continued to play into the desert twilight. Out of the crumpled metal, rising up from the long trail of skid marks and scarred concrete, Mozart's "Jupiter" Symphony played on from the untouched CD player. Crouching by the side of the road, he looked out over the desert, silent scrub trees, the occasional cactus, brush, sand and the air was cooling; the sun was a sliver of orange slipping over the broken rocks of the mountains. A few stars were earnestly trying to be noticed, and Mozart.

"God must have been watching over you, son," the raspy voice of the junk dealer barked down at him.

Looking up, he saw the random toothed grin of Wayne Leadbetter. "Weren't but a few hundred feet behind that semi when he clipped you. Shit! Thought I'd be washin' you off the pavement 'bout now. Like I said, God must have been watchin' over you, son."

'God?' J.B. thought, 'Interesting plan, that. Maybe the battery went dead on his I-Pad. Just needed a little diversion while it was recharging.'

J. B. smiled, nodded his head, and then threw up.

Wayne was kind enough to offer, J.B. a ride home.

Looking out of the passenger side window, J.B. fixed his gaze on the passing line of telephone poles. T-shaped, long bowed lines that dipped and ran out of sight, only to continue, running away. His eyes slid along the lines, running and then up onto the cross beam and down running, again. Now a skip. As the pole approached, just before the instant of the leap: thwack! It was Wayne's Durango, "Number three piston, spark plug's foulin', she'll skip right on time for the next, oh, seventy-miles and then it'll just be a racket. You OK?"

J.B. nodded, and looked back out of the window. Run, click, jump and run, he was back in a tunnel, the metro: Pigalle, Anvers, Barbes Rochechouart, Gare du Nord, Garde L'Est, Chateau d'Eau and finally Strasbourg St. Denis *his stop* home. It was over, Therese—gone.

FADE OUT

FADE IN – FOCUS: J.B dressed in the same shirt and tie he was wearing at work and in the accident is now standing on the

Métro platform watching as the passengers, including a younger version of himself, exit the subway car.

'Always standing back, watching ever since I was, what, eleven, maybe younger? I could not have been, nor will ever be as close to a woman as I was with her just a few hours, check that years ago, shit, is there any difference, now?'

It was one a.m. the last run, as the mechanical doors opened and the electric voice barked out over the P.A. for everyone to exit, J.B. looked up at the Au Printemps advertisement and felt his stomach collapse. 'It's where I first saw her, in cosmetics, she was waxing and shining some poor old, blue-haired. When she looked at me, staring, the woman watched us both looking at each other.

It was the night after the afternoon in Montmartre. Just hours ago, they had stood, exhausted from lovemaking, staring down at the Eiffel Tower in the distance. A moment later, on the corner just a block away from the Pigalle metro stop, they had coffee and pastries and it was then that she told, J.B., "Kenya. Guy is taking me with him. I'm pregnant with his child.

Today, this afternoon, I owed you— us—as much."

Guy Le Blanc, thirty-five, his travel magazines were at every kiosk, café and bookstore. It was J.B., ironically enough who was responsible for introducing him to Therese. Knowing her love for all things photographic, J.B. surprised her with opening day passes to "The Waking Dream—Photography's First One Hundred Years" an exposition at Le Petite Palais. Possessive and naïve, Therese was *his* discovery, *his* to spirit back to the states. He never counted on the rest of the world seeing her as he did, and more.

"You, such a long, exquisite torso, those legs, your eyes are, *mon dieu!* two watering holes out on the Serengeti plains. Sorry, I have a compound in Kenya, I often go to shoot, no not guns, photos on the Serengeti. Sorry, so rude of me. My manners? Guy. Guy LeBlanc and I would love to photograph you my sweet."

And he was not alone. The moment J.B. ushered Therese into the grand salon there was an audible, collective pause, silencing the room. Therese, literally, parted the waves of admirers as she walked into and through the crowd. Each head: both male and female turned to admire this strange, new woman who by simply putting one foot in front of the other, possessed the entire salon.

Not until he was on his honeymoon in San Francisco, watching a fog bank appear and then roll over and consume the Golden Gate Bridge did J.B. have a proper reference point for that moment. Yes, on *his honeymoon with Cindy*, the fog: Therese kidnapping him, again.

"A long, ivory tendril training up and out from the forest floor thick with the new, translucent green of spring," was the first line of a prose poem J.B. wrote at the tiny desk in his one room, cold water flat after just meeting a young woman sipping espresso at Comme   Chez-Soi a small café off of Place Daumenil. He was anxious and excited and desperate for her to text him her number.

Walking up from the Bois de Vincennes, J.B. had paused to look at the fountain in the center of the traffic circle. Every morning and evening the water was turned on so the circle of stone lions growled out rooster-tails of white water. After a few minutes of watching the lions, the excited children pointing and tossing coins up and into the hydrant-like rush of water, he turned and headed for the metro station, and home.

But as he turned it was—there—the long, slender leg stretching out of the slit in the side of her ankle length, mint green skirt, the outline of her breasts pushing, gently, up against her   rose-colored top, the broad-brimmed straw hat hiding her face only served to heightened his interest.

Moving closer, J.B. watched as she curled her auburn black hair around her pinky; the sun was low in the sky, just above the trees, so when she turned to pick up her phone, she was framed—

sky, sun, bottomless brown eyes, the faint brush stroke of a smile—
Therese.

It was six weeks from the end of his year in Paris. J.B.'s French was more than passable, he could kid, cajole and his bone-dry wit was beginning to sift through the haze of English to French to even include some *argo*: slang. But the clock was ticking, she seemed to be gathering up her belongings, 'It was now or wait this had to be . . . perfect, but- No! Just do it fool,' he thought, 'do it.'

Pulling out his cell phone, J.B. quickly scrolled through his favorites, there, perfect. Elvis! As he moved up closer to her from behind, he turned the volume up to ten and allowed "The King" to take over. Therese dropped her cigarette when, from two feet behind her, the lyrics of "It's Now or Never" blared out. Turning, she discovered J.B. lip-syncing Elvis Presley as her friends rolled their eyes laughed, pointed, and finally applauded.

'A complete fool,' he thought, 'but at least she notices me.'

Therese smiled, studied him.

A full head of brownish-blond collar length hair, parted in the middle, swept back and partially covering his ears, soft full lips, hazel green eyes and, 'charmingly, wonderfully nervous even though, yes he's looking me over like I'm the shiniest toy on the shelf, the one toy he *has to have,* so cute.'

Two drinks later, Therese gathered up her phone, purse and cigarettes, reached over and squeezed J.B.'s cheek, "Such a cute puppy! Call me. What's your number? Good. When I get home, I'll text mine to you puppy. OK? Good."

She leaned over and curled J.B's hair around his ear and then touched his lips gently with her index finger, saying, "Don't pout, I just *adore* puppies. Ciao!"

Therese modeled to fund her own struggling studio. She was a disciple of the "Old Guard": Atget, Man Ray, Cartier-Bresson, Adams, Evans, any and every renowned photographer who worked in the black and white.

"I adore the digital world, I'm not a dinosaur," she explained as she dunked her croissant into her coffee. It was Saturday morning three days after their first encounter. Still in bed they were listening to Mozart's "Jupiter" Symphony sharing fresh croissants and coffee, talking, still caressing and barely able to resist the urge to make love, still another time.

Nuzzling her neck, running his hand gently across the inside of her thigh, J.B. put her coffee cup down and kissed her deeply. She kissed him back, even more intensely than he had hoped, then whispered, "Doucement, cheri, easy, puppy dog, no one is taking me away from you, at least not yet."

Then she smiled. And J.B. in a panic, thought, 'No! Please no. Not *that* smile, again.' It was as though he were trapped in a movie, watching himself being deconstructed, used for some plot line that he had no idea where or how or when it would take place. A sharp twinge of angst seized J.B. stomach. As he was about to speak, Therese, put her finger to his lips, saying, "Shush. Don't. Please not so sensitive. Only kidding, right? Not yet? Can be a long time, no?" Again, the twinge and the indecipherable smile he was learning to accept as a red flag. Stop—cowboy. Now!

"So, puppy-dog, where was I? Atget! Extraordinary! People thought he was some derelict traipsing around dragging that cumbersome camera. Genius. I've even thought about using one of those old contraptions, glass plates, the images are so vivid and don't even get me started on Daguerreotypes. I, sorry. Be a good, sweet pup, pour me another coffee?"

Showering, J.B. moved from movie to vivid dream, there, in his arms, head thrown back the water cascading over her closed eyes, enveloping her long mane of auburn black hair, breasts, thighs, Therese was morphing in and out of the stream of caressing, hot water. Touching her and the streaming water were one in the same. The rose scented soap, their bodies, juxtaposed, twisting, now, a new helix creating a third alternative: real and imagined—merging.

J.B. felt as if he were standing in the back of his skull peering out through two portals that slowly came into stereoscopic view. 'Again, always standing back, watching. I could not be any closer to this woman, and still, there I am back in there some *where* . . . but where, God damn it, where? Watching. But she, damn it, look at her. She's fine; lost in all of this.'

Opening her eyes, Therese looked at J.B., smiled and whispered, "Please, now."

As he pulled her gently up and onto him, J.B. felt her warm, moist enveloping loins seize him. Inside of her and she pulling him still closer, locked, the water cascading down around and into them. Outside, the traffic was spooling up. Horns blared, brakes screeched. In a playground below their window, children squealed. On the corner a saxophone and a drummer played for spare change. They heard and felt and saw nothing of any other world, save for the one where they found themselves, here, in the shower, suspended together.

As Therese eased off his cradling thighs, unloosed her hands from his waist, they stood, slightly apart, staring into one another as the splattering of the water from the shower seemed to grow louder. 'Yes,' J.B. thought, 'What? Why is that coming to me now? Jabir, OK. Yeah, "When the colors are revealed that signal the attainment of the stone, the Philosophers' stone. You must first distill the water before it can be channeled into the process, the proper progression. The perfected water, then the fire and oil and finally earth."'

"Dry me off, puppy dog, then run for a baguette, sausage, lots of red wine. Quick."

After a long lunch and a walk through Bois de Vincennes, Therese, curled his hair, kissed J.B. deeply and said, "So puppy, go home for a while. We play some more tomorrow. Ciao."

Under the thin, anemic light of his desk lamp, J.B. wrote of the day, recorded each and every moment with her, channeling, bridging it to wondrous book he had found in St. Germain at the

Islamic book store. The ancient merchant appeared to have stepped out of THE ABRABIAN NIGHTS. His white linen suit seemed to turn into a long flowing robe every time his voice rose in awe and admiration, "Only one, sir. Just one. This book, by Jabir himself. You speak French, very good, he has only been, just now translated into French. Coffee, a pastry? My pleasure, a little nicety for any and every one who purchases a book from me."

Writing, J.B. compared their—his and Therese's—long shower to one of the first passages he had read and subsequently translated. *We in our separate, walled-off worlds were dismantled for a few minutes. The philosophers' stone, the dream of the eternal circulating light was trapped and held like a baby bird cradled in a pair of gently enclosing hands, between us. Almost one, almost out of exile, new colors together we were wrought out from the basic elements of the other—there.*

From a single point forged in this particular space and time, the colors spread out, through and pierce both sets of eyes, seemingly opened for the first time. A new horizon, sunrise and sunset—shared—and expanding.

A child dropping cat's-eyed marbles into a glass cylinder, counting off the numbers as the iridescent mix of orange, blue, green and yellow become vertical, now, horizontal as the light streams in to make circular as the new, unschooled hand rotates it. The room? A kaleidoscope at his command.

The trick? How to recreate the child in the man, the little girl in the woman as each opens up to the other. Circling the square. The simple act and still, "Why is it so rare . . . have we ever . . . honestly touched?

SAMASH CUT – PYCHOLOGIST'S OFFICE

J.B. picked at the same loose thread in the arm of his chair. He looked at Doctor Lowenstein, started to speak, stopped, the said, "That's how close I thought we were. So, when she left with Guy and then that sack, the burlap sack, Eva, Madonna landing at my feet, it split. As real as anything, more real, just like that fucking PETERBILT insignia, my own fucking shadow, there, right there. Even flipping me the finger. Asshole.

"Wait, follow me on this one. No, not what you might be thinking, Doc. I wasn't chasing my own shadow. It was a clean, clear outline, separate from me, a walking shadow. In front, behind, sometimes it was a hundred feet away from me. Like the voice in my head, or me seeing myself standing behind the last row of seats in the movie theatre. Except this time, it was the outline, the shadow that was watching *me*. The wreck only made it clearer, cleaner, more, well-defined.

"I knew something was up with Therese. I went looking for that moment the instant it stopped. That shower was her one big push through to a place of her own design and construction. She just dragged me along with her. I was there inside of her, call it a cylinder, her particular world. Amazing.

"It ruined me for any other relationship. Crossover into a woman's private and particular untouchable place . . . . shit! That's right doc, right hand, but at the wrong time. You end up in a space that is totally unguarded and open, where else is there to go from there? The wreck just brought it into high definition, Cinemascope, IMAX, whatever! You get the idea.

"So, when that sack was thrown out and I just happened to be standing there, the indifference of it all was—cheated. The randomness of me being there, it all made sense, at last, to me. The desert, the translation of the alchemist, Jabir, the heat, the isolation, two broken people: one a man, the other a woman, but with not one thought of sex. It was the foil, the compliment to the shower with Therese.

"Bigfoot, the walking shadow, stopped. No more strutting and fretting. Yeah, yeah, I know, MACBETH, I played him in college. Still remember a lot of the lines: Tomorrow and tomorrow, life is but a walking shadow, a poor player that struts and frets his hour upon the stage.

"Anyway, no, wait, let me clear this up. I only called her the Madonna for my sake. Out there, in the desert, there is no place for gods or men or anything that the desert does not like or choose.

"You see, it was a truce. The most hostile, indifferent place on earth was curious about us, actually wanted to see how it would all play out between us. I actually saw the desert smile.

SAMASH CUT – PARIS – COLD WATER FLAT
(OK, Everyone, find their marks. This a print. Roll!)
Yes, hold it, there, gently. Remember for her that this is where the moment for her was created, made it necessary for her to fly up and out, seek the shelter that only someone older and wiser could insure. The moment that the perfect love was sacrificed for security. Hold and possess her, Therese? No, never. It was something cut in stone, imprinted long ago, by and through something once painted on the walls of caves thirty thousand years ago. Yes, us—the elder of the tribe—always culls out the youngest, sweetest most pleasing for his own, right?

Barely seventeen when she left Rennes for Paris, fled home for uncertainty. She orphaned herself by design to escape her abusive father's late-night visits. Chose the unknown to silence the frigid denials and evasive eyes of her mother, "How you twist . . . everything! Just pray you don't ever have a daughter or grow old so that his touch, never mind! You'll see, then, won't you?"

Therese's mother stopped, turned her head away and motioned for her daughter to leave. Taking a step towards the door, Therese paused, looked into the mirror, saw her mother's back hunched over, shaking. Turning, she reached over and held firm—stilled—her mother's vibrating shoulder. It relaxed, instantly, as the remainder of her body soften. A long, heavy sigh followed by an almost imperceptible whimper.

And then her mother's face appeared. As though exiting, no impossible, this nightmare was ongoing; a momentary pause.

There, just there, a pause. Poised in front of Therese was an apparition rising up from the moor: her mother's face bleached to a bloodless white, her eyes, colorless. But it was the sound, *her voice,* the frail whisper of a trapped woman slowly winding down, that made Therese pause to step outside of her own boundaries, to see the fear and humiliation of, 'She is just a woman,' she thought. 'I've never seen anything but *mother* until we shared *his* awful rage.' And suddenly they were there *together* sharing the same isolating cylinder: 'No, it's not shame, it's *his* self-loathing that is here, holding the two of us—hostage—now.'

Therese gasped, then, suddenly, remembered to breathe.

"It was in that particular moment, no, cheri, it was the one immediately following, yes then. Yes, that was the moment," she later told J.B. was, "The moment I decided to choose poverty, isolation, whatever it would take just as long as I could leave. But there was Mama. What would *I* be leaving her to fight? And then it, she, the woman buried deep inside of her, spoke."

Like a worn-out, barely audible vinyl phonograph record her mother whispered and warned, "Better me, than you or . . ."

The needle lifted for a moment. Dust hung in a ray of sunlight, the clock above the sink counted out each and every second. The table, each chair, the canisters of sugar, flour and salt pressed cold and hard against the stagnant kitchen air. The needle dropped.

". . . than the Osmond girl, next door . . . or Sylvie . . . the young flower girl who passes by on Wednesdays or . . . understand . . . understand me, child?"

Again, the needle lifted. Mother and child stared long and hard at one another. The older attempted to cry, but found that all her tears were too deeply hidden, impossible to call up, now. The daughter? Separated from the same breath and skin that made her. Therese looked back into her mother's unchanging world that for the first time seeing it as a place frozen. A hard, pernicious standstill, where nothing or no one dared move out from the tyrant's grasp. Therese, now, outside, as though she were holding her mother as a book at arms' length. Reading aloud from a time whose actions, thoughts and purpose were all sloughing like so much dead, flaking skin. Each canister, the dust filled light, the ticking clock were all unconnected; each, in its particular way, looking for a place to hide until, there it was, the scratchy whisper of a worn-out record, playing, her mother's long death running down in front of her. *That was the moment; her moment, Therese.*

"You have the right, no, my permission, hear me good, righteous good, child! I'm not looking! Don't see a thing. Will never question it. I will move heaven and earth to protect you, if you will do what I should have done years ago. There in the upper left-hand drawer is my father's fileting knife. I've sharpened every day for a year now. A razor's edge. It will pierce and slide easily through any and every type of flesh, even hard, poisoned and putrid understand? All I ask of you is do it after he has fallen asleep, fast asleep next to me. I can help you and it will appear as if done by my hand."

The color was streaming through her mother's face now; the dewy, slate-gray of her eyes—glistened, again. Walking over to the knife drawer, Therese eased it open and looked at the gleaming blade of the polished knife. Thought of her father, smelling of an entire night's wine and a week without bathing, his fingernails, crusted and cracking, his breath and touch and fists striking and pawing and fondling and laughing. None of it, though, was worse than his cooing and sighs, and the release and the satisfaction of the lightless, black stalking, fully realized.

Reaching down, the handle fit comfortably in her hand. Holding it up, her mother smiled. Still, it, even his crime was not enough to force her hand. Not yet. Not just a month shy of seventeen. Putting it back, Therese eased the drawer shut, walked over and kissed her mother on the forehead and whispered, "I'm, no . . . sorry."

Her mother took her hand and kissed it, looked into her eyes and nodded in affirmation, whispering back, "It was unfair of me to ask you, child. Let me help you pack."

Thirty minutes later, after putting a hundred francs in her daughter's hand, Therese's mother, said to her, "Find a place to protect yourself, and there, let his poison run out of you, make yourself new and whole again. Make a gift of yourself to you, first. Walk out and never look back before he takes any more from you."

"I felt like Emma. I know it's silly to imagine myself as Madame Bovary, but as a young scared girl it helped me gather up the courage. Anyway, as soon as I turned seventeen I got out, fled to Paris. I waitressed and it was there a man left his card. A modelling agency. Then I started wanting to be on the other side of the camera. Control."

(And stop! Print it! Everyone, good work. Take five!)

J.B. looked out at the desert rushing past: black. Glancing up, the sky was a shroud of pin lights. Above, muted starlight, below, the consistent skip in the engine as a flood of cool night air streamed over both of them. Looking over, Wayne's head was thrown back as he took a long drink from a pint of Jim Beam. After a loud exhale, and smack of his lips, Wayne offered J.B. a drink. The sweet burn of the brown liquid was an instant revelation. Looking at the bottle, J.B. smiled and nodded at Wayne, then took another drink. 'That particular shade of brown, the bourbon, more auburn or chestnut, yes, like *her eyes*. And the label, the contrast of the black lettering and clean white background, of course, like everything else, then and now, and that afternoon, after the exposition at Le Petit Palais, a reminder of Therese.

Safe, yes, safe is the word *she,* Therese, used. So, it was and is now, I just walked   away . . . safe. So, why do I feel worse than ever?'

SLOW FADE OUT.

FADE IN. LATE AFTERNOON – STREET CORNER CAFÉ - PARIS

"I am so sorry, cheri. It's just that with Guy, I'm safe. Much, much, maybe too old, yes, but not so old that we cannot still grow in some way, together. He's always wanted a child. I was flattered when he asked. Sorry, I know how that must sound, hurt you. I was surprised, Guy and I had never met before. It was at the exposition. Funny, though, not funny, strange, it was all because of your wonderful surprise for me. Again, I'm so sorry, seems everything I do for my own benefit *hurts you*."

Therese reached over and curled J.B.'s hair up and around his right ear, caressed his face, then stared into his eyes for a few seconds. Her eyes moistened before dropping away.

"But that's why I asked Anne for her flat in Montmartre. I wanted one afternoon to be just as I imagined, dreamed it could be from the moment I left home. I wanted it all, everything under *my* control and safe, at least once in my life."

Therese stopped, closed her eyes, took a long, deep breath and then began running her index finger around the lip of her coffee cup. The waiter approached, asked her if she wanted another and without looking up she shook her head, no.

Still staring at her cup, her finger still tracing the lip, she continued, "Very quickly. It was the instant you looked, no, crawled into me through my eyes. My God, how you focused on the most vulnerable part of me! Immediately, I knew that you and I are too much alike. It would be so very easy to love and get lost inside of each other. I knew that with you I would be allowed to let go completely! And boom, you would be there to catch me. That's scary, no control. Beautiful, but disarming. Compris, cheri? Understand puppy?"

Her hand moved from the coffee cup back to J.B.'s face where Therese began to trace the outline of his nose, lips and chin, saying, "We would have been so incredibly happy and I'm afraid so very poor. Our love would have turned to resentment, or worse."

She turned her hand over and with the back of it began to caress his cheek, then abruptly stopped. Fumbling with her clutch purse, Therese quickly pulled out and lit a cigarette. After taking in and letting out two puffs of smoke, she ground out the remainder of the cigarette, looked down at the sidewalk then back at J.B. and said, "I was already pregnant when we were together that afternoon in Montmartre. Wait! I know. How can a woman, no that's not right, how can I? I, do such a thing? Easy. My future was there inside of me. Safe. For one afternoon I was unhooked from my past and the present? It was what I chose to make of it. What I would have chosen had, well, that really doesn't matter. At least for one afternoon it was all in my control. I was in the arms of the man I would have, maybe should have run away with. You see? I did run away. For a day. That day will sustain me, will grow along with the child inside of me. Jonas, my sweet puppy, you were my coach ride. Silly notion, I know, but just like Emma racing through the streets with her lover in that coach, the flat on the hill, Montmartre was our horse-drawn coach."

J.B. looked confused.

"Emma, Madame Bovary," she explained. "She seized complete control for her own reasons. I've read that passage a thousand times, the horses running wildly, the carriage racing through the city, and so for a short period she was free to love on her own terms. Emma made love to him for *her* reasons, she wasn't there to fulfill another's wishes. In the closed confines of the carriage, racing through the city, all the world just an opened door away, she stopped time and the world, made them her own.

"I'm leaving for Kenya, tomorrow. Guy wants me to see all that Africa has to offer. He has an office and a bungalow there. He wants our child to have a different perspective. I'm not sure, but it sounds good. I had *my moment*. That was your gift to me. I hope someday you'll understand how important you were and will always be to me, puppy. Kiss me."

FADE OUT.

FADE IN – DESERT HIGHWAY - NIGHT TIME

Staring out of the window J.B. realized that there were no more telephone poles and the engine had ceased skipping. Two coyotes were barking, their howls were muffled, at least three miles away. Still, black air surrounded the truck. The truck? Where exactly was the truck? Focusing, he saw the reflection of an unusually bright star in the rear-view mirror. 'No, not a star, a light . . . a streetlight. We're not moving.'

Blinking his eyes, he saw the front of a one-story stone and glass house; flat roof, large double-doors of smoked glass, sandstone, mortar, river rocks and steel. 'Nice mix of the desert and modern, wait, that's *my* house!' Home.

Looking over at Wayne, he saw that the Jim Beam was gone, the neck of the bottle was sticking out from under the driver's seat, and the brim of his CAT Diesel hat covered his eyes. A soft growl of fifty-gauge sandpaper smoothing splintered pine filled the cab. Wayne was out and did not appear ready to come back anytime soon.

J.B. pulled out his wallet, took three twenties and carefully place them in Wayne's shirt pocket. Before easing out of the truck he looked at the front of his house and studied it. Again, he felt as though he were standing behind the last row of seats in a movie house perched in the center of his head. He tried to bring the front door closer, connect it with a feeling of attachment, security, routine, all the sentiments of home, but they all stopped short this time, hovered, stared at him from a distance. Closing his eyes, he tried again to pull himself up closer to the inside of his own eyes, to climb out and touch the screen, just up there, almost can, then . . . there.

"Shit! No!"

The grill and the screeching, the large capital letters: PETERBILT, and all the air escaping, being replaced with the suffocating silence of abject indifference. Stuck and holding, then bending, the grill—THERE—RIGHT—THERE—the truck pushing the car into the interstate, the cement unfazed, unflinching, the car, like the top of a sardine can peeling back onto itself. The road, time, the air, the music playing on. Wait. No. Yes? 'Is that a bird chirping? I can hear each note—suspended—there, at least two hundred feet away, but it's right—there.

    SLOW FADE
    LATE MORNING LIGHT INTESIFYING TO FULL LIGHT
    LONG THICK TUFTS VERDANT GREEN
    PULL BACK TO EXPOSE A LONG COLONADE OF
    WILLOW TREES LINING
    A RIVER BANK

"There, now son, start counting backwards when you wake up it'll all be over" . . . *there? Told you I'd be there for ya. Damn straight I would. Easy, son. Easy. Let Uncle Lee hold you for second, get your wind back. Son of bitch, that was a piece of work you just finished. A piece of work. "*

J.B. was back under the grand willow, the largest of the string that lined the Yadkin river. "Big Boss" willow, marked the preferred fishing spot. It was there, he and Uncle Lee would start fishing at four, the pivot-point, Leander called it. When the night gets underdressed and the day, still too drowsy to get up, pulls her close.

"Quiet and warm, sensuous and well, Jonas, seems everything and everyone . . . fits." Fish and talk and watch the new day roll in. Most often, Lee slept as their fishing poles and lines remained restive, calm; no fish but that is not why they were there, here on the small pier jutting out from under Big Boss to watch black turn to slate-gray, rose and then salmon, salt white, finishing in a hard, cobalt-blue. New day. Nudging his great-uncle, Jonas could not wake him, this time.

Nothing had changed from the other mornings. Same oak, pine, poplar and dogwoods interspersed in the dominating line of willows. Sitting under the same big willow; but the air and the river's face filtered out now to black. 'Breathe, or not?'

"It's your choice J.B. or do I call you Jonas here?" his great-uncle asked as the black twisted and turned enveloping, no, not a dream, it was surgery and he was alone and felt the simple easy pressure of the black pushing down past the point of release, and *there* he was calm and free and knew that another level had been reached. So, that by pushing past the ever-expanding, viscous, corporal black there would be another release.

"S'right, son. That's where we said good-by that morning. Now, you're here on you own. Shit, that was some piece of work you just finished. Make up your mind. I was old, too old, and tired, past the point I could recover enough to make another day, palpable. You? Tough one, just more work heaped on the one you just took on a couple hours ago. You're call, son. I'm with you.

'Shall I go there?'

"Son, Jonas, J.B. Hold out for a little, no, not just yet, Jonas. Sure, it's here, not there or anywhere, son. You're right there is some peace in a place that strikes the perfect balance. Your fancy laboratory people with funny sounding names, yeah, it's here, just like they said. S'why I like to fish so much in this one spot. In each part of one particular day, the single rage and persistent demons of one can be silenced, for me, here. You got a taste of my choice and solution, still, you'll need you own, son. Your own.

"That's a choice to make later, though. It's hard now. A fucking, jagged piece of twisted work, but you'll know, though. You'll separate at first, see your shadow stand up on its hind legs and neigh, buck and run away from you. Time to invade the land of the Lotus eaters, then. Search your own heart and place and purpose for the misinterpretation of your own best self.

"S'what your shadow's tryin' to show you. Just find a place like this, quiet and solitary to flush yourself out of you. Make him own up and teach him what was always your best part, the stuff you keep hidden from yourself; hardest thing a body can do is accept the best of himself. Why? Do that and where else you got to go? That's when the fun really starts. Like being out in the desert without any reason for being there, save for the fact, 'There's no place left to go.'"

FULL LIGHT, BIG BOSS WILLOW AND THE RIVER SLOW FADE OUT
MOMENTARY BLACK
FADE IN STREET LIGHTS SUBURBS

Opening his eyes, J.B. was back in front of his house. Wayne's snoring, now, was in full bore and growing louder. A full two blocks away, it sounded as though the junk man was sleeping right behind J.B. staring at his house.

'Fine as fine can be,' he thought, 'good 'ol Lee, Uncle Leander. Haven't thought of him for a while. God, I miss him, always seem to think of him, or he returns on his own, who knows. So yeah, maybe I should just keep going deeper. So, will I find China in the center of my head? He said deeper, but where? I couldn't break out of my own head with an A-bomb, right now. I, fuck it. Is there such a thing, can it be created or am I just now discovering that I am my own, aerodynamically-perfect, custom-designed, lest one forget, wall-to-wall carpeting, mag wheels—black hole?'

Extending the house key out to unlock the front door, J.B. saw that it was ajar. Pushing it open, he heard music, muffled, coming from the back of the house: the master bedroom. Crossing the living room, he tripped over a small kettle weight. Cindy's yoga mat was spread out where the coffee table usually rested. The kitchen lights were on, an empty bottle of Kenwood chardonnay was on the counter. Walking into the bedroom the bank of vanity lights over the bathroom sink glared. Sweating under the intense light were the uncapped containers of makeup: lipstick, eye shadow and base. The air was heavy with cinnabar, Cindy's favorite perfume. A red laced thong and stockings were draped over the shower door.

J.B. walked over to the clock-radio on the night stand and turned it off. Looking around the room he felt empty of any connection to anything anywhere in this room, or the remainder of the house. Picking up his wife's nightgown he sniffed it, nothing. Though, heavy with her scent and cinnabar all emotion had been syphoned off and suspended, replaced with complete indifference-the spinning car-the sound of the bird-the screeching-then-Mozart-The Jupiter Symphony.

Again, the tunnel, the backpedaling view seen from the rear of his skull. Every object and smell should be comforting, but now felt like he was scanning a blueprint or a diagram of a place that could not possibly be, come on! Is this really *my home?*

Walking back into the kitchen, J.B. looked over at the chalk board where he saw a smiley face and the name Desert Bloom written. Desert Bloom was their favorite bar in nearby Lee Canyon. J.B. stared at his wife's handwriting, the quick, clean sweep of her cursive lettering, the oversized capital letters D and B that dwarfed the letters that followed. He thought of Morse Code, typewritten letters, fonts and shook his head, thinking, 'Shit!'

Deeper and deeper and, yes, now, even deeper into complete black., the letters and their lack of significance loomed up and then smashed flat onto the floor. *What was* and *what is* no longer exist. Neither of them offer an option as to what or will be the possibility of who or how or where *I can exit out and become something more than a shadow of what* . . . 'Well, I really don't what the fuck of . . . *what—now?*

J.B.'s head pulsed like an overworked jack-hammer. A heavy sweat broke out, washing down from his forehead to saturate his body. His hands shook, and his breathing became shallow. And the house? He swore it was collapsing onto his chest.

'The grill of that truck, there! Now-here-in my own fucking bedroom! Is there no alternative, is there anything at all to replace, to fill up this vacuum? Or was it always there? Hiding like a virus. Maybe it's been there all along, and I'm just one of the unfortunate Joes who didn't get vaccinated. Or wait. And that blackness, it never really leaves me. Am I just a jelly stain on the road and this is just the last code closing down? Fuck! Will anybody give a shit? *Can anyone give a shit?* If you're not in this shit-hole, how *can you care?*'

The room continued to press inward. His clothes were now saturated and his mind was without a filter. Sounds, smells, touch, light and the taste of his mouth were flooded and confused by the lack of direction. 'No one, no schematic, no principal, teacher, mother, father, nothing there, not even me. So, what is real if it all floods in at the same time and speed? What is the choice if everything happens occurs in the same instant and−stays?

Stripped, unschooled and adrift, I am in and of and lost in a place without boundaries as all and every possible message is sent down, in and through me, relentlessly. If I could only split some of this away, step out and away, please for a . . . moment, please. J.B. dropped to the floor, curled up into the fetal position, his eyes-wide-open, seeing nothing and listened to the deafening roar of unfiltered sounds that flooded his ears while the inside of his head failed to recognize any of them as−familiar.

Total blank. Rushing water, static, light and dark, smells, and nothing to compare them to, save that they were there, and refused to leave. J.B. stood up, undressed and sat on the edge of his bed. Looking across at the mirror, he saw a strange nude man come to inhabit his new body. Looking back at him it seemed that who or what was there in the mirror was looking past him and into something still deeper and beyond−behind−the reflected image.

Deeper still . . .

A WALKING SHADOW

"Son, you there?"

St. Germain, the Latin Quarter, the Islamic book store, the book, skimming it quickly, yes this is the one, on the first page, "When speaking of the animal's design, contained therein, is theory, not practical application." Read that part again, son. It's how I ended up under Big Boss, the design, we're all a whole lot of theory. Each and every day the practical application is tested. Well, you know, in baseball, if you fail six out of ten times, that is, you bat .400, you end up in the hall of fame. Theory. What I'd give if four out of ten days I connected. Understand? I found this tree, son. Maybe the opposite's true for you. What was green, now needs to be barren.

Outside looking in, a random collection of ideas, all collected in similar looking, but separate vessels that never find a bond or foothold that can or will bridge them to another or worse the very our surroundings that drove them deeper into despair. The ancients knew from the start, tried to bridge the illusion of inclusion, tried to find a place to make the theory—work.

So, it was always meant to begin and end in this desert, that was the illusion that drove him to the spot—here—the old Salt Lake Line, slowly piecing together the abandoned line shack, restoring something that was never there to begin with, save for the nagging notion, If not this, then what?

Walking away from the verdant hills saturated with maple, oak, poplar and dogwood, exiting the rolling green fields of western Carolina, trading the autumn colors, the spectral splash, like an over-turned paint truck every fall for the arid, empty space punctuated only by more absence, he found the illusion-less place that allowed the engine racing in his head, and the jackhammer in his chest to idle.

It will always begin and end in this desert because the random, unchecked movement of him would always dream of a place where it could finally become uncluttered; where nothing in the landscape would fool, re-arrange or dupe him into believing that his fractured time would pay off.

"Pay it off fast . . . son!" the old man snapped. Pay it off . . . or well, it's surely gone."

Still staring into the mirror, several minutes passed as he tried to look past and then through the reflected man. 'If there were some use, something tangible to grab onto each day. . . instead, it's up and down, light and dark, like water through a sieve.'

Opening the medicine cabinet door, J.B. moved the swinging mirror to front the larger fixed one. His face, tiled wall, the door, stretched out like an endless, restless snake of the same reflection. Stopping, he stared long and hard and saw only unblinking, blank eyes returning the same stare as before. Nothing. 'Or is it?' he thought.

He remembered a passage from the book he purchased in the Islamic bookstore, something Jabir wrote in the eighth century, "Everyone is well aware of the accepted rules, public knowledge, that pervades, directs our everyday lives. What is misunderstood, though, is that this accepted knowledge is of little use to anyone in the particular. But anyone who takes the time to carefully read my works will find the root cause and goal of the question that he alone asks of himself."

'Sure, why not? But here? In this house? At the factory? With Cindy? Yes?'

He looked away and then back into his reflection repeating the only word he had shouted out during the accident, "no."

He showered.

Stepping out of from under the rush of near scalding water, he put on his robe, and walked. Exiting through the back door of the house, he opened the fence gate and continued. Walked to no place in particular, just walked. Walked away from the grinding metal, the compressed air of the inside of the car as it fought along with the windows, the frame and the music: Mozart, his Jupiter Symphony and yes, the entire landscape as it tilted down. All so amazingly slow as the screeching and the howling of the semi's brakes bucked and snorted. Walked away from his cylinder, his place and time left there in the confines of his car. Walked away from his sense of being shrink-wrapped: exposed but never feeling or touching. All gone, now; all screaming the same farewell as he had when he shouted above the din: no. He walked. Then, paused.

Staring out into the night, his eyes only registered the slip and slap of his eyelids keeping his eyes moist. Again, at the back of the movie theater, looking from behind the last row of seats up at the screen. Anything outside the limit of his eyes went unnoticed. He started to walk, again.

He was outside of the glow of the street lights, away from the highway, and surrounded by nothing but the desert. Dropping his robe, he felt the rising heat and cooling breeze dry his body. Looking up at the sky, the stars pulsed. Another sweep of wind and he heard only rushing air, smelled the heat of desert cooling itself, felt his heart slow, relax. No more walking. This is home. As the sand and heat swirled and rose, he bent over, scooped up a handful of sand began rubbing it across his chest, over his legs and arms. A gust of wind hit him, making the sand particles restless and dancing, soothing. Yes, home. Home, now.

FADE OUT.

FADE IN - LATE NIGHT – BAR/RESTAURANT –

Lynard Skynard's "Free Bird" is blaring out in the background, but is almost blocked out by the even louder conversation and bar noise.

Just a moment ago, a small tribe of *us,* the original illegal aliens, modern in every way, perfectly lean and destructive, bipedal locusts migrated out of Africa to forever alter *them.* Everywhere *we* tramped, we seized and burned, raped and rendered *this* and *that* and *yours* until, well, it is as though it has always been: *My own!* Yes, just a moment ago is where the idea took root and still flowers, now. So, it was and is and will always be strange, actually odd that a fight did not break out for *her.*

Each alpha dog, (re: human Go ahead, put 'um all in this hat, reach in there, you choose.) had already thrown in a chit, declared that her scent was now—his—alone. It was only a matter of time, a few more shots of Jim Beam, three more songs, hopefully AC/DC or Skynard, before each of the pretenders would start up and not rest, not finish, until he had vanquished by word or fist, or both, "That, there son-of-a bitch who thinks he's gonna take her! No, sir! Mine! Hear me? She'll be under *me* 'fore the night's out. Or what? What the fuck did you say to *me*? So *that's the way* you want it? Fine by me, boy!" (Or something equally as astute, get the picture?)

Yes sir! For as long as it takes to own as much of her as I, wait, that's just it, I want even more of her than *she even knows*. Once we've finished the deed, there's more, I will own her and everything about her, 'cause once I have her, God have mercy on the soul who crosses me. Her stain is mine, and I will always and never, ever be free of her. No, she ain't got a God damned thing to say about it. She's mine! End of story.

Yes, man, ah check that (Mankind). Ain't nothin' changed. What's a couple hundred thousand years? Really, not a moment, but just an instant ago, so it is really the same as then it is now. There will be no other left standing, until I have her, all of *her* for myself. Understand?

"Easy, Dex! Easy. Have another beer, the shot of Beam's on me. Bartender's gonna call the law. Easy."

"Risk, un-shirted Hell if you cross me, son! Understand? That there Grade-A Number 1 piece of pussy is . . . mine!"

"Yours? Excuse me, shit for brains. What would a sweet slice of pie like that want a dumb shit, little piss-ant like you? Go back to the farm, Gomer!

"Whoa, now you two. You, don't make me strip that hell shirt off of you and, you there Slick, run out and play in the street, sonny! Step aside and let a man who knows what makes a real woman scream for more, take over. Got it, Fire Marshal Bill? Got it Timmy?"

Yes, *Cindy* had that kind of effect on a bar full of *us* and *them*: men.

Her right leg extended out from the stool. Long and tanned, a patina of satin-gold that ran like a streak of morning sun up to rest inside of her cream-colored lace skirt. Powder-blue and sheer, her blouse refused to let a man's eyes rest, as her blonde hair moved back and forth, revealing and then covering, then revealing once more: the top of her breasts. Checking her watch, she wondered why J.B. was taking so long. After ordering another vodka and soda she looked over to her right, and smiled at the gentleman, then she turned left and accepted a light for her cigarette from the man, his eyes, now slits, as he extended the lighter out, saying, "Not, a problem, it's what a man's supposed to do for a woman, excuse me, a lady. I may be out of line, but God, you're just so, I mean, *real dad gummed beautiful* is what *you are*! I, yes, ma'am, your welcome."

He is blushing, thinking,

"If the truth be told, I just want to hit you over the head and take you home, chain you up, never let you go. Maim and kill any man who as much as shows up at the door. Don't even have to knock 'cause I know what he wants. You! Yes, truly, that's how really pretty you are. That's' what you stirred and started up in all of us! Not more than a second, just a moment ago. But don't pay no attention to them. It's just me, now. Me! And you and me! You and me. And I'll kill you if you don't agree. Cause I can't even stand the thought of anyone touching you, after me, even though I ain't had the chance to touch you, yet.

"And so, yes! Yes, you are, you are the one for me cause, well, it's all that I see and taste and imagine now, right now! Yes, you! You will be. mine, you hear me? Mine! No, I really can't say any of that, so I'll settle for."

He speaks,

"Willard's the name, ma'am, a pleasure."

Willard and Austin, Fred and Dex, John and Dusty, D.J., Warren, Sam and Eddie, it was the court of Henry the Eighth, Dodge City and the Caves of the Dordogne: Chauvet and Lascaux, and the high plains settled with mail-order brides. That smile, the easy manner of her lithe, air-brushed, full-figure, moving and twisting as she adjusted her thong, clutched and released the tantalizing, plunging V-neck opening of her blouse. Kingdoms and wars, ships and cars have all been won and lost, sailed and crashed attempting to possess a female like—Cindy. Yes, Cindy.

CUT TO THE OUTSKIRTS OF THE DESERT TWO MILES FROM THE SUBURBS
J.B. HAS STILL NOT GONE TO THE BAR

Staring up and into the full moon, J.B. walked himself up from the last row of seats, from the back to the front of his head, reached up and massaged the cameo, burning and pricking the outer membrane of his eyes. Hovering, just above the irises, the light grew larger and brighter as he sat on the floor of the desert looking up into the night sky. Windless, now, warmth seeping out like the air from a leaking tire. Still, black, cooling and white, there was no filter or wall, nothing to impede the free exchange between him and the desert night. It was four a.m. before J.B. put on his robe and walked back home.

CUT TO BAR PARKING LOT – Cindy's car tires squeal as she exits out onto the street.

Cindy mashed down on the accelerator of her Miata, the traffic light turning red just as she cleared the intersection. Looking in the rearview mirror, she was relieved that there was not a policeman in sight. She was pleasantly drunk, able to drive, but sure that she would fail a sobriety test. It was a little after two, traffic was light, she was tired, but frustrated. J.B. had never arrived. She was relieved, but a little hurt, and feeling neglected.

'After all,' she thought, 'No! Screw *him*! He's the one so big on gettin' me knocked up and *he* doesn't show up! Why the way they were checkin' me out I, raise my pinky and . . . whatever.'

She lowered the windows to allow the cool, early morning air in. She was still aroused. Waiting for J.B. at The Desert Bloom, dismissing one potential suitor after another had taken her back to her high school and college days. Looking in the mirror she smiled, saying, as she adjusted her skirt, "Just like little toy soldiers. All standing at attention. A smile, a wiggle, all I'd have to do is wave my little finger and presto! Mine!'

Cindy looked back into the mirror and shook her head, 'Why did I settle on J.B.? Sure, he's cute, and there's the business. Sure, it's all been, well, yes, interesting. At least, for a while. Kinda miss it, though, when all I had to do was wink and nod and, whatever, I-'

She stamped down hard on the brakes as the entrance to Mesquite Ridge, the gated community where they lived, flashed past her. Backing up, she turned into the entrance, waited for the bar to raise and continued driving home. Stopping short, Cindy looked at their home.

'If not J.B. then, who? Do I really want to be pregnant? They say you never really get the tightness back, anywhere. Diapers, poop, night feedings, bloating. First one, then another, my God, three? Shit!'

Pulling her car around to the back of the house, Cindy noticed that the back door was open, and the bedroom lights were on. 'So, he just couldn't make it?' she thought. 'It better be good, whatever the reason . . . and to think.'

She thought of the line of faces, all anxious, almost desperate to sit next to her, court her, possess her. Looking back at the house, the opened door, and thinking of J.B. in bed, asleep, knowing he would want to make love when she crawled in next to him, she paused. Climbing back into the car, Cindy eased the seat back, loosened her bra, and stretched out to sleep. 'Asshole!'

Exiting the desert, J.B. stopped to study the line of street lights bordering the road. Peering out from inside the dark into the expanse of light lined up in from of him, he thought, 'Just another shadow out to haunt the night, hovering. And always behind the last row of seats. Why? Why do I always feel like an observer on everything? Even my own life. It's always been like that. Always felt like I never had any control over any of the action playing out in front of me so there was nothing else to do except retreat back into what was bouncing around inside of my own head. It was there I could put a story together that included me. Still, I always go back to the story . . .

Up there . . . on the screen and here . . . home, the desert, Therese, Cindy, and that fucking truck that just tried to grind me into a fine powder?'

J.B. thought of the projector, the process, the images repeated over and over again to give the illusion of movement, action and sense. Then he thought of the truck and the grill just inches away and how it slowed the inside of—everything—to a halt; and how he felt when he stepped out of the crumbled car.

Stepping out and clear of any connection to the *living* while remaining alive; becoming a series of still photographs, photographs that I was taking and also being handed. Is there a way to step back into any, wait is that, is it really a *natural* flow of time and life? What will be the *new natural?*'

He turned his back to the wash of light swarming in front of him and looked back into the desert night, 'Home? Why not? It seems to be the only spot where the two mirrors, the one inside of my head and the one I found earlier, fit together, become foils for the other. A place that might silence it, calm all the voices, at least give me a semblance of peace when the landscape pulls back, laughing, asking,

"You, butthead, you still here?"

J. B. crossed the deserted street and entered the security code into the entrance gate. Walking toward the house, the idea of moving out to the desert seemed more and more like a reasonable and welcomed alternative to, well, everything, now. Just the thought of going to work at the factory, made his heart race. Then he thought of Cindy and the trip to Paris and trying to have a baby and then back to . . . Cindy! Her car was parked outside. The garage door was closed, but the lights were still on in the house. Looking closer, what he had first thought was the reflection of the floodlight was the back of her head flush up against the driver's side window.

Walking up to her Miata J.B. started to tap on the window, but paused to study her. Her legs, long, tanned and exposed up to her red lace thong, were stretched out across the passenger seat. She had unhooked her bra so that her breasts pushed firmly up against her blouse. 'What was true twelve years ago in high school was still true today. Not a man in the world could pass by her without lingering, hoping, dreaming. She still doesn't know about that day. Why should she? I never told her I saw them.'

J.B. studied her, thought of high school and then the NPR fundraiser where they met just a year ago. 'The attraction? More for the possession than the person, go on admit it! You wanted to bed her as much as the next guy, so you tweaked the reason, took revenge on Therese through fulfilling a fantasy. If there was no Therese, then why not Cindy? There was always going to be a hole that would never be filled. Without Therese, even with enough money and time and children would it have ever been enough? Now that fucking PETERBILT truck. No, all that did was speed it up, cleared out debris, pushed me closer to where I was already going.

'Can't blame Cindy for being everything I thought Cindy would be. She's great. Everything as advertised. Why should I tell her? Would it really have made a difference if it had of been me instead of Don?'

Eleventh grade, spring, and yes, J.B. could hit the curveball, even a hard splitter, and he was fast. In gym class he coasted the last ten yards so as not embarrass the others in the yearly proficiency test, dropping back to join the wave of boys running the length of the football field.

"See you at this afternoon's tryouts, Ayre," the gym teacher and baseball coach barked out, not bothering to look up from his clipboard.

"And they'll be no slacking off when you play for me, son. I saw you pull up, Ayre. Lenny, my best pitcher, told me all about how you hit everything he could throw at you. Said it was like you was playin' softball even when he gave you his best heat. Son, that shit don't sit with me t'all, you hear me? No sir! Got a good mind to wear you out for fakin' it, never did cotton to a slacker. Course you'll find that out soon enough, boy! Four o'clock, on the baseball field. Be there if you know what's good for you!"

Again, J.B. felt the involuntary seizing up, he had known since childhood facing the impossible task of trying to figure out who or what or how to please the adult looming over him demanding that he be the son, child or relief valve for whatever it was that he or she wanted: "Is *this? OK?*" . . . mom, dad and now coach! Shit! He felt the barometric pressure plummet, forcing all the air from his lungs, the loss of oxygen, suddenly replaced with an intense panic. J.B. thought he had learned to control it . . . 'Breathe and get out of here, now,' he thought, 'go. Just nod and go, and it will be fine, shit!'

"You hear me? Son!"

J.B. stopped and turned to face Coach Barnes. The sun was just to the left of the coach's head, his arms akimbo. Spitting, Coach Barnes repeated his challenge.

"You! Ayre! You better be struck deaf. Cause if you don't answer me. Hell is the easiest thing you gonna have to deal with after disrespecting me!"

J.B. was back behind the last row of seats, again, looking out through his own eyes. Time walked away, sat down and had a smoke as it watched—J.B.—now. Still, time, the moment, crossed him, decided to play with Jonas, not J.B. Back on the porch, searching. Time, the moment, began to extend all, just like the porch.

Trying to hold fast, Jonas listened, felt and watched as all his life up to that point and everything imagined to follow stretched out in those year-long-lifetime seconds. Rubbing its cigarette out, whispering from behind the last row of seats, time snickered, "Remember what Einstein said, 'An hour's time. You tell me which passes more quickly? Sixty minutes seated in front of a beautiful woman or putting your hand on the hot burner of a stove. It's all relative, son. Stretch this out, enjoy it! Shoot, I just fired-up another cigarette."

Pulling in a long, satisfying drag off a Camel, then laughing, time waved him on: "Go on, son, Jesus! This one's a real piece of work. Make it last!"

As the pressure inside J.B. grew, time fired-up and savored yet another long drag and waved him on, hissing,

"So it's Coach Barnes, now. Before it was mom standing over you with *the belt*. Don't forget the principal's office when you been accused you of looking up her dress. Wait, you hear them? That's your whole family, laughing and talking, all warm and fuzzy, all of them, minus you, in the other room. What was their favorite line? Too young yet, to join in, such a child. What? They never were, little, young, alone? Finally, you are summoned in or ordered or challenged, but never simply included. So, when cowboy? When you gonna mount up? Grow a pair, when? Jonas? Where's J.B.?

"This Coach, top of the line, Grade-A son-of-a-bitch! Look at him going to town on his nose, even pauses to look at what he's picked out, like it's some long-lost toy. Are you really going to tell this Neanderthal what he wants to hear? You know you could beat them all this time, that's why I've stretched it all out, sped it up for you, slowed it down for him. Your light years ahead of what he's thinking. Been around the field twice while he's still studying his second booger.

"It hasn't been more than three seconds. Not bad, right? Don't mention it, it's what I love to do. Go ahead, beat them all this time!"

"Coach Barnes, sir? No, no not in my or any other lifetime, My answer . . ."

FADE OUT — Time is shaking his head, laughing as he tucks his Camels back into the sleeve of his t-shirt and exits.

FADE IN- Early afternoon. Principal's Office.

Principle Dunlow looks up from his desk, shakes his head and motions for J.B. to sit down.

"Coach Barnes tells me you've been awfully disrespectful. Says he was showing some real interest in your future and that you repaid that with-"

Fred Dunlow turned his head to cough. A full-faced grin spread out across his face. He pulled out his handkerchief to cover his mouth, but still could not completely hide his amusement from the collateral damage of another "Coach Barnes melt down."

Clearing his throat, the principle tried his best, but failed in appearing stern.

"Now, where were we? Yes, Coach tells me when he asked you, in his own particularly sweet and caring fashion, to try out for the baseball team you, ah, let see if I've got this right, you turned your back to him, dropped you gym shorts and how do I put this? In my day we called it shooting the moon, correct?"

J.B. nodded, yes.

For a moment, Fred Dunlow forgot that he was the principal. He took off his glasses, rubbed his eyes and then stared into J.B.'s eyes.

'No profanity,' he thought, 'and Mr. Ayre, J.B., did not actually threaten that blow-hard Barnes, with anything. This kid is easily the most gifted athlete in the school, but all he wants or ever wanted is to be left alone to, hell! It's not mine or any one's business what he does with his time or anything, for that matter, now is it?'

Glancing down from J.B.'s eyes to his back pack, he saw a copy of Kafka's "In the Penal Colony" sticking out from a side pocket.

J.B. noticed that the principal's eyes were softening, a grin had replaced the forced show of authority.

Reaching into his desk, the principal pulled out a pad of blue paper. Across the top of the page on the first sheaf, printed in bold letters was the word: TRANSFER.

"Here, Mr. Ayre, take this to Coach Barnes. Feel free to drop by my office, anytime. We'll talk about Kafka, Faulkner or well, anything you like. Nice job, son. Nice job. Good day."

Exiting the principal's office, J.B. saw Cindy Laring standing under the outstretched arm of Don Butting: all conference quarterback and starting point guard on the basketball team. Last week, in a pick-up game after school, J.B. had scored on him at will, and stolen the ball twice from Don.

Cindy sat next to J.B. in English. Don simply "hung out, now." With just six weeks left of school, and already assured of a full ride at State, attending class was the least of Don's concerns, now.

J.B. watched them. It was as though a vacuum had encapsulated Cindy and Don. Standing in the hall, people moving past, teachers entering and exiting the principal's office, but these two could say or do anything they wished, without any fear being disciplined.

Don reached down and touched Cindy's breast. She did not stop him, just smiled for a brief moment, then gently moved his hand down to his side, squeezed it, and whispered, "Later."

Later, cutting through the teacher's parking lot, then over a small hill and then down through a small thicket of trees, J.B. was able to circumvent the baseball field and eventually arrive at the student parking lot. Easing through the fence that divided the school property from the outside world, he picked his way over a well-worn path used by the students to smoke, drink or take part in any and all activities forbidden on school property. Just as J.B. was about to duck through another hole in the fence, he stopped. He heard it . . . her, before he saw what was transpiring. As though hitching a ride on the wind he heard her slight whimpering, his moaning. Yes, before he saw it, there was sound.

Down in a shallow ravine, behind a small stand of honeysuckle and oak trees he heard an insistent plea and then a moan, awkward and unsure, but unceasing. What he thought was her moan was actually the sound of a male, pleading. *Her voice* was clear and steady and assured.

Easing up to the crest of the ravine, J.B. peered through the trees. There he saw Cindy, her blouse open, her breasts exposed, Don was nervously and awkwardly fondling them. Don's zipper was open, his penis exposed. J.B. heard the word, "Promise" used over and over again. Then he saw Cindy shake her head and emphatically say, "No." A moment later, though, J.B. heard, "If it'll make you happy, I really need to get home."

J.B. watched as Cindy knelt and then eased Don's penis into her mouth.

Yes, he had heard both before he saw them . . . he heard the major chord first; a sustained, full C, but the train was not in sight. Odd for the desert, he thought. Yes, strange, sound before the image, a complete reversal of the accepted, the ordinary, the reality of the desert's flatness. Everything so close, seemingly within arm's reach, when, in fact, the shrub, abandoned depot, or mountain are ten miles away. A desert constant, the unresolved tompe-d'oeil that the brain attempts to correct, but never succeeds. Still, he has never heard the train before seeing it approach at his particular point in the desert: his winter home, the abandoned line shack on the Salt Lake Line. A relic of another, slower place in space and time.

'Yes,' J.B. thought as he looked at Cindy asleep in her Miata, 'I heard her before I saw her—them—there in the ravine, and I stayed, too long, then returned twelve years later, and got burned, or did I? She is my wife now. Hottest girl in the school, right there in the car, Cindy Laring . . . Ayre! Imagine that, I won. But what? Maybe when I stepped back into that ravine, ask her to marry me, all I was doing was giving into to coach Barnes. Shit, admit it! It was to get even with Therese. But even if that were Therese asleep in the car, even *she* couldn't change any of this, even she couldn't move me up from, no, it's worse, worse than being behind the last row of seats. I'm staring back at myself now, shit!'

'Cindy, Cindy, Cindy, I apologize, honestly. I never really took the time to find out who you are, what you love and where you go when the world doesn't make any sense to you. That's unfair. Not even a toy deserves to be treated like that. Still, it went both ways, you never did dig too deeply with me. Shit, some pair, we are.'

Looking at his soon to be ex, J.B. smiled, 'Always looking for the mysterious, certain one. I've often wondered if during all that searching that maybe I've ever missed something dropped right in front of me. While I was looking one place, the perfect person-

answer was there, lying there, right at my feet, but I didn't notice 'cause I was too busy looking for *that* one?'

"J . . . B, buddy! Really? You don't have to do this," Miguel said as he placed his hand on J.B.'s shoulder and squeezed. "Take some time off, I'll cover, you've built something good and honest here. Only place, shit, anywhere like this. Google it! Seriously. Type in: "Boutique clothing design and manufacture Mexican by Mexican designers, workers and staff." I guarantee, you'll get back: "Did you mean: In your dreams, Pedro!" At least not with a U.S. address. You've really done something—" Miguel paused to study the floor under his feet, collect his thoughts, find the appropriate words. In a voice an octave lower and discernably softer he said, "You're treating these, *my people* with a respect that's been long-overdue them. And-"

He held his hand up halting J.B.'s attempt to interrupt him, "And you're on to something very special here. You walk away now, you're just handing me all the glory. I-"

J.B. was shaking his head, smiling, motioning for his foreman, Miguel Sanchez, to stop. But before speaking, J.B. stared at him for a long moment, closed his eyes and then opened them to look for an even longer time into Miguel's eyes, thinking, 'Round, large and gleaming, back on the front porch, yet again, staring into the brass door knob, listening to the warm, sweet laughter inside. Hushed words, the smell of coffee and the four of them around the table. Never once did any of them look at me like Miguel, he really does seem concerned about *me*.'

Turning away from Miguel, J.B. looked out over the production floor. Fifty sewing machines, a beehive droning, the pushcarts of teal, salmon, cream and olive cotton, wool and silk moving up and down the symmetrical lines that formed the perfect grid of tireless workers. Why such drive and determination? It's a part of them. They own a third of all of this. Yes, *them, those people, vested*, so why wouldn't they feel and work and achieve as passionately as anyone else.

When a cart laden, heavy with new fabric would stop next to a sewer, there would be an occasional glance up at J.B. or Miguel followed by a smile, a wave or a wink, then instantly back down into the metallic, machine gun-like purr of their sewing.

"Our numbers are through the roof!" Miguel's words filtering into and halting J.B.'s reverie.

"Last quarter our earnings were up twenty percent. Next quarter? We're on track to bump it another five, maybe six percent. Macy's, The Gap, and now Banana Republic, with our stuff in those stores it'll be only a matter of time before we can market it under our own label: Ayre Apparel, shit, you even thought of the name. We'll have our own chain. You're just gonna hand it all over to me? I-"

J.B. held his hand up a second time, it was the anguish in his friend's expression, a look of earnest protest. Yet, again—Therese. She had the same anguished look on her face as she melted away, her hand dropping slowly down as the metro car disappeared into the tunnel. This time, though, it meant nothing. J.B. paused to consider that. 'Yes, it actually did not feel like anything. Imagine that, even Therese can't budge me off this one.'

"Miguel, it's perfect this way, I want, no, I really need to do it this way. It's how I, it's something, listen it's gonna sound strange, something . . . I heard it first, then I looked for it and finally discovered where the sound was coming from; only it was an idea, a notion, a feeling that this was, correct . . . right! I woke up to it, made the decision after sitting out in the desert the other night. Besides, this way I-"

J.B. stopped talking. He realized that there was no good way to explain how he had arrived here; spell out how he had come to the conclusion that it was best to sell everything and move to the desert. 'Miguel would have me committed,' he thought, 'shit, I'd do the same with him, only he didn't do the tango with a fully loaded tractor-trailer. But, still, I'm not sure that this is what it is really all about. Am I being honest or just giving up?

'Hard to tell, what with the smells and the sound and the slow, awkward silence that continues to pile up, one-on-top-of-the-other. Every second of every minute. Just one photo after another, handed to me, so hours become lifetimes, days become a millennium, so yeah, I better get out from under this.

'And fast. Why? Well, take that fucking phone call, the one from the trucking company. My trucking company? No, his? Who? Dino? Yes, My company. No, sir! We're following up on the claim, the wreck, you!'

'Oh, right. Still, what's with the attitude, I was the one who was almost plastered flat, and you? You are?

'The dispatcher.

'What a piece of shit, so detached, dismissive, like he was reading the Sports Page to me. Just giving me the run down on all of last night's box scores.

'Dino? Let's see, Driver Twenty-seven Coded Red Alpha. Highest rating. Red Alpha means he's licensed to haul any and every type of freight local or cross-country. Twenty-seven stands for how many years he's been balling the jack for us. And sorry, you didn't ask me for all that, now did you?

' Dino Frederick, one of my best drivers, well, at least I used to think so, can't rightly say that *now!* Wait, says right here that his daddy's real sick, terminal. Right here; Orange, dash ninety-six, code for medical cross-reference . . . sorry, there I go again.

'Guess his mind wasn't where it ought to be. Still, it's plumb amazin' he stopped that rig the way he did, yes sir! She was fully loaded, forty thousand pounds of cleaning equipment. Probably would have had use some it to clean you and your car off the pavement if he hadn't stopped her the way he did, yes sir!

'So yeah, see? Which is it now? My delivery man or Dino? How in the fuck will I ever keep anything straight, now? If I don't do this now, then there won't be anything left to sell.'

J.B. felt the weight of Miguel's stare, shook his head, apologized, and spoke.

"Miguel, last night I took a walk. You know, one of those watershed, soul searching ones. My marriage is a bust. And besides, I got into this business kind of sideways. You remember? Anyway, it's you. You're the one who found and hired all these people. Me? I just got lucky on a real estate deal. No, stop! Don't say a word. There's a whole lot more to it, I just don't want to go into any more detail. Bottom line is you deserve it.

"Besides when Cindy and I split, it'll be a whole lot easier to pay her off in cash. Trust me, you don't want her sticking her nose into the business. No, sir, it'll be yours, lock, stock and barrel.

"Come on. Let's go to the bank, have this notarized. Don't be *too* happy just yet. You're on the hook for eight million to Nevada Trust."

The two men hugged. J.B. whispered, "It'll be worth ten times that in two years."

Twelve years prior?

A friend from college while they were in the Keys, celebrating graduation had invited him out to Las Vegas.

"J.B. my man. I know, I know, just hear me out. You think I'm full of shit, but just listen. I know what you think of France and Paris and literature and these translations of yours. Jung and Proust and this witch doctor of yours, honestly? What's you call him, Jay-Bo?"

J.B. choked on his beer, laughing, "Jabir, eighth Islamic philosopher masquerading as an alchemist. I stumbled onto his master work. Small shop in the Latin Quarter. Thought I'd see Rod Serling step about, you know, 'Submitted for your approval,' old guy in there was amazing. We talked for most of the afternoon. The first ten chapters of "The Book of Six-Nine Treatises" had just been translated from the Arabic to French and I landed there in this bookstore

and-"

His friend Jack had dropped his head straight back, feigning sleep, snoring loudly.

J.B. smiled, "Touché, asshole!

"J.B. my man! Five letters: V-E-G-A-S! Come spend a long weekend with me out there. Mom and Dad are going north to Portland, I've got an uncle in Oregon. Sure, I know all about castles, cathedrals, art and history, that Old World shit. Three days in Las Vegas and you'll trade in the Old for the New, and never look back. No, don't answer now. You said you'd be back in September. I'll show you all the nooks and crannies, wait, scratch that. All the nookie there is to had and more in Vegas. And the desert. Don't shake your head, no. If you've never been out in the desert, get ready. Strange and mystical, really. Come on, dude! Don't take too long, I'm outta here tomorrow. Toss me another beer."

J.B.'s long weekend, continued, twelve years and counting. He had, as his friend Jack had counseled, dropped the Old World for the New. He went to work for Jack's father, Don, who owned a commercial real estate business in Las Vegas.

Since his best friend Jack was the son of the owner of Don Jessup Holdings, J.B. knew that his options were limited to being a good salesmen, and little more. All the executive positions were reserved for any and every one with the last name: Jessup.

Fair enough, J.B. thought. It still did not prevent him from learning the business and perhaps opening up his own business one day. That is if he really enjoyed the work. Las Vegas and its night life were fun. Still, he imagined that it might all start to wear thin after a while.

After his first "hit" J.B. was hooked. Jack's father, Don, was so impressed he came by J.B.'s cubicle and praised his initiative, "You remind me of myself thirty years ago. Outstanding. I'd offer you something higher here, but you and I both know it'd only hold you down. Wish Jack had your drive. Keep it up, son. Stick 'um, then turn the knife three times, is what I'd always say. Once for me, once for the company and one to make my dick real good, and hard, cause with the commission I just made, Watch out, sweetie, Papa's coming to Shari's tonight. You don't know Shari's Ranch, about an hour from here. Why, with your talent and intuitive, they'll name a wing after you, just like me, boo-ya! See you later, J.B. Keep it up, son, keep it up and use it wisely, that is . . . stick it to 'um, son. Stick it to 'um! Damn, nothing like being twenty-three and just startin' out. OK. Fun's out of the way, let's get serious.

"Let me get to the nuts and bolts and used rubbers of the deal here at Jessup Holdings. I know you're anxious to break out and run with the big dogs! Like I said, you'll probably own your own place, but first you've got to understand that this kind of work is a real bitch, and not the kind that'll give you a blow job every single day, even after a good day's work. Good, start, J.B. good start.

"If you want to be like me, own your own place, you're gonna have to do all the real shit work, for me. Yes sir, for a while, it just simply sucks and not in the fun way! Get it son?

"Anyway, a couple more sweetheart deals like the one you just pulled off and lots more hard work, in say, maybe seven years with the equity you build up from working for me, you'll be on your way. Keep it up, stick 'um, son!"

It was four years before collateralized debt obligations were about to usher in the Grand Recession. Land, real estate and flipping property made crystal meth seem tame. J.B. stayed and worked, first cleaning and remodeling rental homes, warehouses, strip malls, anything Don could leverage short term and unload fast. All the while he learned the basics of finance and most importantly of all, reading eyes. Watching Don, and his stable of high octane brokers, J.B. absorbed and calculated, how this all might become a part of his own twisting and jumping DNA. His way out and into his own business. The answer? Foreclosures in the desert.

Why? It reminded him of a line from Jabir, his alchemist from the desert country that was not even called Persia when he wrote his magnificent rumination on man.

'Foreclosures in the desert,' he thought, 'what a fitting and perfect description of something, almost pallandromic.' It was a small cluster of manufacturing plants Don had acquired when Homeland security raided and closed the "sweat shops" just north of the Arizona border.

J.B. took out a loan and bought all seven of the buildings. Don was elated, but confused when J.B. offered to take them off his hands. Miguel Sanchez, the senior Hispanic broker at Jessup Holdings, though, was curious, then defiant and aggressively challenged the new "Anglo's" motives in buying up the property.

Looking one way and then the other to make sure no one was in listening range, Miguel ducked into J.B.'s cubicle, pulled up a chair and shoved his face into J.B.'s, challenging him with, "Thought you were different, thought you southern boys had a little more heart than that. I see what you're doing. Wait a few weeks, go in clean them up, hire some more illegals, slap a new name on it. Turn a quick profit, and leave. Why if I-"

"You want a job?" J.B. interrupted.

Miguel stared at him, his face reddening as his hands tightened into fists.

"Sure, I loved to make a profit and then some. That's why I want *you*, Miguel, to do all the hiring. Find me people, no, professionals and artists. People you know, personally. People that you would trust with your life. I'm going to strip all the equipment out of six of the buildings, renovate the largest one, retrofit it, sell those other six and put everything into that one building.

"So, find me the most talented seamstresses, the hardest working machinists, and the savviest salesmen you know. Go where you are most comfortable, tell them all it will be for real wages and benefits. It will be our New Albion in the Nevada desert. It-"

Miguel was shaking his head, holding up his hands, "Maybe you should try breaking the pill in half tomorrow, Gringo. What in the fuck are you talking about, man?"

J.B. burst out laughing, "You're right. Sorry. I promise, though, it wasn't the Mescal or any other drug talking. It's about rubbing their noses in it, making them nod their heads, open their wallets, making them admit, 'I had no idea.' So, find them. Tell them I want them to design and create clothes that they have always wanted to wear, but could not afford to buy. Better, yet, clothes that they have never seen offered to *them*, anywhere. Most of all clothes that scream of their own roots. Tell them to close their eyes and dream. Pull it up from that special place we all keep hidden, deep down and-"

"Deal," said Miguel, stopping J.B. cold. A moment later they shook hands, laughed and smiled like two school children meeting, and realizing that they would soon become best friends.

Within a year, the experiment was working. J.B. had paid off his note, and was the owner of a small clothing manufacturer, run and staffed with Miguel's hand-picked, Mexican and Central American workers. All legal, documented, well-paid and vested in the business.

"Yes, it'll be perfect. If it weren't for you it never would have happened," J.B. said to Miguel as he signed the papers.

Miguel smiled sheepishly, shook his head and signed the papers. Looking up, he started to ask J.B. what he was going to do now, but was stopped before he could speak.

"Me?" J.B. said, "I could see it in your eyes. You were going to ask me why and how and where will I go?"

J.B. grabbed Miguel's shoulder and squeezed hard. A moment later as his eyes moistened, he confided to his best friend, "It was pretty good until it wasn't. Now? No wife, no future and no place that feels like it's my own. What? Where will I go? The desert. And Vegas. Split my life into two equal parts. Six months, the winter, when the desert is tolerable. When it's too hot, Vegas.

"One's a perfect mirror of the vacuum inside of my head. The other? You understand . . . man's got, well, needs, never claimed I wanted to be a monk."

"Are you sure about that Padrè?" Miguel asked. "Si. Padrè, J.B. I mean it, you sound like a holy man looking to get his religion back. But, how you gonna find it in the desert? Or between the legs of a woman? I've never seen you like this. No, I won't try and talk you out of it. I see, no I can *feel* the difference. A loss. A hole. Look at me, here, in my eyes, don't blink. You, be careful. Be careful you don't lose the man who brought you out here. He's a good man. Best I ever met."

J.B. hugged Miguel, then held him at arm's length and said, "You're not so bad yourself. Padrè? I like that. But no, at least, I don't think I've got any religion left in me, now."

"Are you sure? Big, awful chance you're taking going out into the desert without something or someone larger or stronger to stand you up or some purpose. No, without a spirit to talk to, I don't know. I've heard it called: sand crazy, sorry, I know, I'm sticking my nose where it doesn't belong. Still, it's like this old Navajo Medicine Man told me: 'The man who hates God takes three lives to find the blessed hunting grounds, the man who loves him seven. The reason? The man who hates him is constantly thinking of God, while the man who loves him takes God for granted.'"

"I like that," J.B. said, "a lot. My trouble? Connections. Maybe that'll change out there, or I'll fool myself and find it while I'm in Vegas. I've just got to go. But religion? No, just one big collective sigh. Each generation just keeps building on the one before it, they just keep dreaming it up to a more difficult place, impossible to touch. What's the use in something that you can only use or realize it's full beauty after your dead? Sounds like one of Don's real estate pitches."

Miguel started to speak, but was stopped by J.B.

"Miguel, buddy, please, with you, shit only with you, this is the hardest thing I've ever done. Shit, you and I were gonna play with each other's kids, cry at their graduations. You're, the family I never had, man, I mean it. So, no . . . I'm not recommending this to anyone. No sir. Just the or rather a place I, suddenly, happen to find myself being drawn to, called to, I'm not sure which. Strange confluence of events. Still, I've got to find out if it really is just one man, one life, one answer winnowed out of the detours, switch backs, drops and rises; find out if that is how you have to go to find something that you can end up calling your life."

Miguel, still looked concerned, and slightly more than confused. He held up his hands and said, "OK, no more lecturing. Just be careful. Call me when you get a chance. Let me know which works the best, the desert or Sin City."

"You'll be the first, well, may be the second," J.B. responded.

"Who's first?" Miguel asked.

J.B. shook his head, obviously embarrassed and then pointed over to the corner, saying, "That son of a bitch."

"No one's there, I, are you OK? Nothing's there, just the afternoon sun and your shadow."

"Bingo! Exactly."

HIS HOUR UPON THE STAGE

(A STILLED POINT)

J.B stirred his black coffee three times clockwise then twice counterclockwise before putting his spoon down to watch the shimmering liquid settle back into a still, black reflecting pool.

"Mister . . . ah, sir!"

Metal, concrete, burning rubber, the mezzo-soprano squeal of the PETERBILT'S brakes pushed far past their limitations. Again, there it is, again. Won't go away, won't go. Me, that's me in a spinning car afloat, flying, the world suddenly slowed to complete, perfect silence, stillness and then boom! Down! The squealing and squalling of the metal and concrete, the grill of the truck, there! Barely a foot away as the car is pushed down, compressing into the road, everything, now leaning squashing, the smell and sound, how? How is it, I can hear the soft, normally imperceptible sound of birds, then and now here? Why is the sound of yes, birds looming up and over, covering the squalling and the metal and the smoke . . . yes, birds.

A flock of them, there in a single scrub bush that is so clear, yet I know it is a least a quarter mile away. And the distant mountains . . .

J.B looked at the shimmering black pool staring up from his white porcelain mug and thought, 'It all⁻everything⁻stopped. Was I collapsing star? Touched the speed of light? Is there, is that the way a man can actually glimpse into such a place? If so, where do we go after that?'

Still staring into his coffee, J.B remembered climbing out of his car and running over to the median. He looked back at the compressed and crumpled Prius . . . *and Mozart; his "Jupiter" symphony, the same piece of music he and Therese would listen to while making love, the same piece of music Cindy hated, the same music he always played driving to and from the factory was still in the CD player continuing to play on.*

Then asking himself, 'That voice, that persistent goading whisper haunting me. It sounds like me, but a hybrid or major chord, like young, middle and elderly speaking in unison. I have to find out who you are, or do I? Doesn't really matter, now, does it? Just move along, slick. Go on, not that it really every mattered or ever will not, right? Dead or alive the music will still play, those birds will sing and this road and the truck and the people stopping? You're just a story for supper, slick. A wow moment for the witnesses to recount to everyone at the table while finishing their coffee or second cigarette.'

"Dead! You most certainly should be dead! Understand me? I saw it all. Dead! Why and how you are here is anybody's guess. Dead! You hear me? Seen it with my own eyes. That man should be dead!"

"Pissed myself good, soaked clean through to the upholstery just watching you spin around and then boom, thought that rig done eat you for dinner, then squirt you out the other end. Shit! Yeah, boy, sure was something!"

"Dead! I tell, you!"

And then, there it is again, clearer now, no, I've heard his voice before, since I was a child, but it, he's so clear and loud and insistent.

J.B. took a long sip of coffee, closed his eyes and mused,

'That voice? Is that another one? No, it was never just a part of this particular incident or time or place or moment, it was always mine, but now is that a second one? Soft, and it's started coming to me late in the day, if a dry martini could speak it would sound like her. One of her vocal chords must be frayed, so smoky. Yes, it is arousing, I can only imagine what a woman who has a voice with so much oil and smoke could possibly look like. And-'

"Mister! It's Martin," she whispered, leaning over to top off J.B.'s coffee, motioning with her eyes to the large framed and leathered face man rolling a tooth pick in his mouth. Martin was standing at the cash register, shaking his head as he counted out the morning's receipts.

"He owns the place, it's the counter space. Small diner like this, me? Wouldn't give a howdy-do if you sat here all day and just drank coffee. Martin? He's like a badger with hemorrhoids when business's been bad at breakfast, then picks up, you know, the lunch crowd? If it don't move, then customers go somewheres else. It's all about turn-over.

"Sir, mister, we got a line out the door. Most uv 'um are construction workers, real hungry sorts, they are. And, shit! I mean, shoot, here he-

"Pie?" the waitress shouted out to J.B., "why yes sir, best peach pie in this part of the desert, how 'bout a scoop of vanilla ice cream? Wonderful!"

J.B. smiled, touched her hand and mouthed, "Thank you," before nodding his head to the passing Martin.

As, "Natalie, sir, or if you like Natty," leaned over to place the pie in front of J.B., he breathed in the soft and intoxicating mixture of her sandalwood perfume wrestling with the perspiration of the breakfast shift, being reignited. Add to that, the restless slide and brush of her stocking covered legs, the twist and turn of her hips and the flush of, yes, another scent, her own particular moisture wafting up and around him, J.B. smiled as his nostrils flaring, 'Not a wink of sleep tonight, nope, not a wink!'

Over his pie and coffee, J.B. continued to survey Natty and her beige, polyester dress as it desperately attempted to trace and hold in toe her ample, hour-glass form. One eye was cobalt, the other a faded dappled gray. Her smile? The spark that fired his imagination with a desperate, hopeful image of *her,* being held by *him*. 'Easy, she's half, no, well maybe not *half* my age, Jesus!'

Peering down at his plate and then back up at Natalie, J.B. smiled, and before he could speak, she touched his nose and said, "You're kinda cute in a quiet way."

Again, he thought, 'Not a wink, tonight, as he slid the fork down through the crust into the orange fruit, making sure to balance a small dollop of ice cream on top. 'Up all night, howling with the coyotes, not a blessed wink.'

Everything, from Natty's form and gait, to the morning sunlight, to an armadillo scurrying for cover, seemingly, had a twist and turn, or a push away from, or a pull towards the long, tedious translation that he was working on in the old line-shack ten miles away, alone in the desert. Staring into the words of a man who had perched over a steaming caldron twelve hundred years ago, trying to snatch the correct word from the French by way of the Arabic into English, the colors, the scents and the smoke and light and fire, all seemed to be swirling, dancing and sliding into and out of 'That wonderful little mixture of velvet smoke, mercury, cobalt and aromatic sandalwood vixen in the brown polyester dress, my, my, my so *that's the philosophers' stone: la femme cherché, found!'*

So? Same time, same place, the following day:

"Yes, another cup, Natty, please!"

DOUBLE, DOUBLE, TOIL AND
TROUBLE,

FIRE BURN AND CALDRON
BUBBLE.

(SUBLIMATION)

Miguel? J.B.! Just in town for the day. Seein' my shrink. Anyway, big favor to ask. A couple of dresses, slacks, blouses, all of your finest. Size two, have Maria make them, leave extra room in the bust and the hips. I'll pick them up next week. You're a prince."

J.B. put his cell phone away and looked around the room. A poster of Klimt's "The Scream" hung on the wall in front of him. To his left was another poster, in French, it apparently had been torn and repaired, then mounted and framed. It was an advertisement for a play, "En Attendant Godot." He walked over and looked at it closer, thinking, 'Waiting for Godot and "The Scream," Doctor Lowenstein's got a pretty dry sense humor to put these in his office, wait a second.'

He noticed a faint outline around both. 'Yeah, I can just make it out. There were two slightly larger pictures here. There, that's where the sun's bleached out the wallpaper. He purposely switched these out just for the day, for, shit! That asshole put these up for me! There's no one else in here and I bet that son of a bitch didn't schedule another appointment today.'

Continuing to walk around room J.B. took in the rest of Dr. Lowenstein's "joke."

"Psycho" Janet Leigh's terrified face hovering over him. A framed playbill from "Long Day's Journey into Night," Two Jack Nicholson posters: "One Flew Over the Cuckoo's Nest and The Shining."

J.B. felt the familiar cold flush of isolation run through his arms, legs and hands. 'Ten years old, again,' he thought. Ten years old and standing at the front door of a house he knew was empty. Home? He would search his front pocket for the house key, knowing full well as soon as he crossed the threshold the cold, isolating feeling he felt now, would only worsen.

Closing the door behind him, the house smelled of his father's aftershave, his mother's perfume, his brother's sweater lay on the couch, his sister's magazines were strewn out on the floor. Putting his backpack away in his room, J.B. walked through his parent's bedroom, lingerie, socks, a linen skirt, a wadded-up t-shirt covered the bed. The scents of Old Spice and Chanel Number Five were even stronger, here. Passing through his sister's room, the walls were a mosaic of nature and movie posters, James Dean smiled over the Grand Canyon. His brother's room? Locked.

Returning to the den, J.B. sat down in his father's chair and listened to the house, silent, save for the occasional cricket or cicada or blue jay, outside. It would be another three hours before they, one-by-one, the "real family" would begin to arrive. Each in his or her own turn would waltz in on the red carpet for their daily premiere to an adoring audience of one who anxiously awaited any form of acknowledgement. Three more hours that could be used to try and find a familiar, warm place here. Home?

Easing out of massive the red leather recliner, J.B. stood in the center of the den and turned, his mother's needlepoint hung over the fire place, his sister's certificate of academic achievement, three of them, were arranged in a line just below. Trophies, baseball and golf, his brother's, lined the mantel. His father's distinguished service awards from both the company and The Kiwanis Club, hung just above the television. And of course, the world travelers!

The photographs. Rome and Paris, Berlin and London, the first of many big trips. He could still hear his mother from his room, "After our "Irish" twins came along," she explained to yet another member of The Junior League, "we just had to reconnect with the finer, European approach to life."

Smelling the coffee and hot chocolate, the caramel and cinnamon was too much for J.B., but dare he? His stomach convulsed, no not from hunger, but from the fear of the passage, crossing the threshold of his room out into the house. Walking out, crossing the desert to reach the pastries and chocolate, always reserved for the visitors and the others, but never him because? "Dear, when you're older and have earned it and well, just you never mind, hear me? Go!"

Yes, Jonas knew that whatever was left would be saved for the harder working older brother and sister. His only chance was to venture out, now. Yes, ignore the icy reproaches, be willing to take a "blistering" later, use the cover of this elder Junior Leaguer to finally taste, yes there it was: a bear claw.

"Jonas? Jonas! What did we talk about earlier? You know the company rules? In here, now! Lean over the chair. You do know how I hate to do this."

One, then two, finally ending five, yes mother, *hated this, really, hated it.* Quick hard lashes with his father's belt.

"Go on, go! Back to your room. Now!"

It would be ten years later in art class, the art work of Fuseli, his painting of Banquo steadying a frightened and nervous Macbeth as they approached the witches on the moors. Yes, the same painting that hung over the fireplace, there, but now was too much. Yes, comical, that was him, there projected on the screen. Nervous, hysterical laughter, Him, my god, Me! Or rather I was there, really there as the belt came down. Staring long and hard, up into that very painting wishing for a friend to hold me back, steer me away, protect me, hold me.

"Mr. Ayer, I fail to see the humor in this painting. Please take the levity outside of my classroom! When you've composed yourself, you may return.

"I, but you don't understand that painting, oh never mind."

"Honestly what were we thinking? Another one, and at my age. Dear God, why?"

Through his door, the hushed, but insistent wave of conversation would filter under and through the closed door of J.B.'s room, "Oh, he's a little dear, right? No, no, of course, he is. Three? Well, I'm not sure that was in the plans. It's just such a bother. You have the two well on their way, so self-sufficient, so bright and independent, and then here it all comes again: the crying, the whining, the incessant questions. The oldest, my Dee has been a big help, took him to school the first day, makes supper. Stephen, our young man? Oh, when pressed he'll allow him to follow along, but you know how young men are. Got a lot of his father in him.

"Jonas? Well, I'll give him this, he never really pushes for anything, leaves us all alone most of the time, thank God for that! Maybe he's just mature for his age. That would explain his odd behavior, I mean, he does seem to enjoy being alone. Not really sure what he does back there. More coffee, dear?

"See? Up there that's when the four of us were at The Louvre, and there in front of Tower Bridge, Berlin was-"

"J.B.?"

Dr. Lowenstein had been standing in the doorway for several minutes watching as J.B. paused and studied each poster, playbill or painting. He noticed J.B.'s shoulders droop, his hands remained frozen to each side of his body, his eyes open, rarely blinking. A large, tanned, healthy, full-grown man with a ten-year old child screaming, as he beat his head against bars of the cage that held him hostage, inside.

'I might be sanctioned, even lose my license for this stunt, but he's stuck there; always returning there, the afternoons, alone, the latchkey kid, still, even now, going deeper and deeper into his isolation and separation.

'Or is he? Sometimes I think the tables are turned. Listening to him, I'm beginning to wonder if we all aren't locked up in our particular shrink-wrapped prison. Reaching out, talking, touching, but are we really, honestly stepping out of our own sphere? Does there exist any sort of meaningful, idea, truth or objective reality when the long and the short of experience starts and stops at entry point of our eyes, ears and touch?'

"Come on back, let's talk."

J.B. looked down at the floor and smiled, "Nice set of posters, Doctor Freud." Both men laughed, nervously. Then Doctor Lowenstein said,

"You have every right to punch me out. I know that I was invading a confidential space, using a difficult confession about your childhood to try and form a stronger, ah bond's not the right word, I guess release.

"Honestly, J.B., I'm just trying to help you get out of there. But first you've got to let me in, *there,* all the way in. J.B. we've all got some baggage, not unlike yours. It's just, you were forced into being way too accommodating as a child. Now it seems, you can't find a place for yourself, even though you have and you did, all along.

"It's always been, 'I've got to help the other guy,' be it your family or a stranger asking directions, you always slip back and pause and ask, 'How can I make them feel better in their own skin, place or help them secure an identity?' Now it's your turn. I mean, I want *you* to believe it. You've done it all along. It's like a parallel "J.B." who's been watching Jonas, and now this accident has brought in a third player. It's all fine and good to look to the past, identify with an ancient mystic, alchemist, whatever, just as long as you don't lose a concrete sense of what it is to be Jonas Ayre."

J.B. shook his head, "Actually they, the family, gave me a head start, then add into the mix, the accident and this dual path you just described-"

J.B. rose up out of his chair and walked to window. A teenaged couple waiting to pull their car into bay for an oil change were kissing. First just a quick kiss, then suddenly, long and passionate. His hand dropped from stroking her face, then disappeared into a gap in her blouse while she, it appeared from J.B.'s vantage point was stroking his crotch, her right shoulder gently dropping down before rhythmically moving up and then repeated. 'Without the prelude and the dance and . . . The actual sex? Take the first two steps away, even for a moment, and it's like the wreck. So much of it we have to manufacture. Or am I just a cat chasing its tail? And now, what? Fuck it! When, where is this all gonna stop?'

J.B. turned and said, "Seems it's all a haze until it's not. Spend all our time looking to get inside another body, make love, pick somebody's brain, write a good poem, paint a picture—whatever! It's all about trying to scratch the itch, figure out why and what the fuck are we doing here? No, I follow what you're saying Doc, but what the hell!

"Maybe there's a third option, now. Maybe I've got more to draw on. I actually "hear him" now, I mean, Jabir. No, no, that's not exactly right. I hear what I imagine he would have sounded like, hear his voice when I'm translating. Once the hole's been opened, why plug it up? Maybe I won't have the fear and reservations most everyone else has when the lights finally go out, I mean when I die. Rest of my life? Well, there's Natty, for starts.

"Natty, the condo in the tower, and the line shack, all of it is working pretty damn well right now. Those posters you put up. Spot on. Rather than punch a hole in the wall or curse you out, I can step back and into, remember what I was talking about a few weeks ago? The book I found in Paris when I was a student there? A French translation of an Arabic alchemist, name's Jabir. I'm translating it into English. Natty? I guess it all fits. Going deeper into the shadows of my own isolated experiments, I'm seeing now how I might possibly fit into any of, this or any other world. Still, the most important part of all of this right now is . . . Natty.

"Yep. As much as I would love to make it sound, interesting or profound, how I'm dealing with the rage, it still all comes down to just another hot-wired monkey, scratching . . . *men*!

"Don't get me wrong. It won't, can't last for very long. Nothing that good or intense or revelatory, can. When we're making love, we're still separate, but at least we're suspended—together—for a while, close, real close, but will we ever cross over together? Find each other *in there*? Not gonna happen, doc. Not on my watch. How 'bout yours?"

Lowenstein felt a momentary sting in his stomach, thinking, 'Son-of-a-bitch! Again, the touch of the èpèe. Focus.'

"OK, J.B. Fine. So, the posters? Not too much, too soon?" Lowenstein asked.

J.B. smiled and shook his head, no, saying, "Way past that now. Funny actually. You're good, kid! But remember, I'm still on top!"

Lowenstein, looked confused.

"The Cincinnati Kid, remember?'

"OK, yeah, yeah, but why are you bringing that up, now?"

"I want you to put me under again, you know hypnosis. I want you to hear him."

"Who?"

"The alchemist, Jabir. I swear I can actually hear him when I 'm translating. Figure if I can hear him, maybe you can through me while I'm under. OK?"

Again, Lowenstein felt challenged, disoriented, but fascinated, and little envious.

'He's pushing me, testing me, but why? So much there, and right when I think he's lost, boom, he turns the table *on me.* OK, I'm sure I won't hear anything but his own voice, but if he wants this, what can be the harm, and maybe another break through,' "OK, J.B. let's do it. I'll turn the lights off, you remember the breathing, there, CD's in place, fine."

J.B. closes his eyes.

FADE OUT

FADE IN — 8th Century Khorasan Desert J.B. IS IN A SMALL WOOD-FRAMED ADOBE WORKSHOP OUT IN THE DESERT IN PERSIA   JABIR, ANTIQUITY'S MOST FAMOUS ALCHEMIST IS SITTING NEXT TO HIM

"See my son, the flint to the fire, the disquieting song and chant and ruse is that we believe, no, cling to the notion that in each of us we have the capacity to inspire the elements: fire and water, air and earth, that we can make them speak. We foolishly believe ourselves to be ascendant, god like, bearers of some eternal truth. Truth? If there is any truth it is only found in the particular and deeper, more isolated stillness. The stillness we each bear alone. So, in your own particular stillness the experience created by the interplay of the four elements with your own stillness becomes the single expression that is seated, becomes the root and the source from which all others flow out from."

"So, did you get that first part doc? Amazing voice, he's got there isn't it. Sorry, he's starting back, listen."

"Look down at the desert, then up into the night sky: a mirror. Yes, a mirror. So many brilliant, crystalline worlds there, just there. Where? Which way, up or down? Both, the same. At your feet each particular grain is but an iridescent construction that when held aloft, up to the light breaks into flame of color. The reverse? A sea of endless black, dotted with these same explosions of crystalline marvels.

"So, the sense of *we-us-all* is the unattainable philosophers' stone, the transmutation of lead to gold, the elixir of eternal life; they sit on our chests like a liberating dream. As your heart pumps, so the dream branches out and flowers. A transitory, golden and yes, eternal moment for it touches all of time as it pulls you, draws you into the light-the singular fire that is in you-alone.

"You alone, why? Look up into the sun. Explain to me how and why and where it, first, made an impression on you. Fine. Would I that I could feel it as you. Do I know it as you? No. Impossible. I long ago resigned myself to the isolation of one. Then and only then did I begin to unravel the mystery of the stone, the philosophers' stone. I learned that it followed me as would an echo chanted out in a canyon, as the light chasing me in the desert, as a foil to my fear. Yes, my son, this conception and practice of my art is my shadow.

"It is why I leave the city to work, alone, here in the desert. From this singular position of I—me—alone, I can look back into the desert and see a reflection of my longing. I hear voices carried on the wind long before I see the creature appear. I look back from where I traveled and though I understand there are others there, I always ask the same question, 'For what purpose or reason should any of them matter?'

"*We,* yes the illusion of the collective *us* is a diversion, a step away from the base metals that make up our troubled souls. So, how to sublimate the particular, the singular? How to transform the raw and unflatteringly dull body and voice and eyes and heart of the one so that it can at least imagine and embrace this illusion of *us,* and, so thus, ring out of a nugget of gold? Survive in this impenetrable loneliness? Small paces that ascend and descend all in the same motion: golden steps of a sunset walking up and down, back and forward on the river's face. Over my bain-marie, the forge blasting heat, in the center of my head I am neither here nor there but suspended in a third, singular place of my own design.

"Perhaps if she were sitting with me, along the river, or out in the desert, and we were to study the same golden steps or flower, perhaps without a word, reaching out to touch or silently, in coitus, we would for a moment dissolve into the other, still, there is always the source. One can only step out of that particular place for a moment and never past the limits of the body. Understand?

"To become a vapor, a rising stalk of your own essence, perhaps as one breath of wind swirls to rub against another, the two of you hear it before it arrives, feel it as a memory and sigh as it disappears before it has a moment to take root. And even these bits of deflected light can only be gleaned, held and then understood through your own set of particulars.

"So, any lasting truth can only, tragically, apply to the solitary conception of a single life like the lone flower, I spoke of earlier, in the desert. Its very existence is miraculous, fragile, transient and profoundly true for its brief and particular time there, alone. Come over here, and I will help you with the first experiment, side by side, no not together. We will demonstrate that each one of the components that make up this world constitute a world unto itself. See?

"Here, watch this. Mercury, copper and iron shavings, cinnabar, camel hair, olive oil, goat dung, and blood from a fetal pig mixed quickly at first, then slowly as the heat and colors rise before us. As I suspend my head above the bain-marie, the fire beneath rages, the air above scented and colored and inside, as I close my eyes, the center of my head, the matter and make and fortune of perspective unfurls. It is the leap of a stag in the forest, the wind hoisting up an eagle, and all that I pray you or any other man will do is to read what I have written down, perform the same experiment and in that intertwining world of dream and shadow and suspension between the world without and my own particular within—we touch—as one breath pauses to insure that the next will follow.

A WALKING SHADOW

"My inquisitive visitor, it is only a matter of unlocking the elements within your own being, drawing up what exists outside of you so that it may rub its furry back against the soft underbelly of your own singular, isolated and lonely spirit–within. I never claimed there was gold or eternal life or a purpose to this and all my other endeavors. Only the experience, for a few short hours to take me into the bosom of a world that abhors my presence. Deeper and deeper still, and eventually I find the black, timeless hole that will accept my ill-shaped elements, knead, mix and light them with the four basic elements and release me back into the ill-directed energy that we, reflective and dream riddled animals have come to call ourselves–man.

"This man, there, in front of you who is mouthing words at *you*, yes, who concentrates on you. When he stops and studies *you*. Stand down, relax! *He* is actually a flight from the pain you were *lucky* to find. Why lucky? It launched you into abandoned shack in the desert, and into the cool comforts of your towered room in the city. But even these are only distractions from the shattered vessel that is . . . you. You bleed out what the world bleeds into your particular sphere, and in that flood is lost any purpose or identity that was once called you. Even as a child you had an impression of it.

"Again, you are fortunate. When that metal monster raged in your face, it was the same as the fire burning under this cauldron. A stilled point emerged, you as its center. The pay-off is in the floating, yes just above the cauldron. For a few hours, the stasis exists. Man has a place in the violence and the fire, can hang on the wind, burrow deeply into the earth, or wash the inner rage, cool and invigorating, away."

"J.B.? J.B.! Start back, ease on up, OK?" Doctor Lowenstein, put down his note pad, leaned over and taped J.B. on the knee, "Easy now, come on back."

J.B. opened his eyes, he felt unusually refreshed, his mind calm, and yes, his shadow was there in corner, smiling and nodding.

"J.B.? I-"

"So, you heard him, right? I know you did 'cause my man in the corner over there is nodding, "yes."

Lowenstein looked over his shoulder into the corner, then back at J.B, started to speak, then stopped, thinking, 'Yes, I did hear a voice unlike anything I've heard out of him before. Now, what? Am I to believe . . . ask him,' "So he's here, now?"

"Yes, and no."

"I'm not following."

"You will, if you just allow it."

"What?"

"I can't do it *for you,* you just heard why. I know I'm right 'cause he, Sparky there, my shadow, followed me here to watch. Followed me out of the desert to sit down with the both of us, here. That's how I know. Don't worry, doc, it's fine. No, I know it sounds loony, but it's just another door, I have now. It's a gift from him and the desert and a little of . . . being sand crazy. It's a chance you take out there."

"J.B., maybe we should bring someone else in on this. I'm worried. Seems you're crossing a line that, well, a little disconcerting. I-"

J.B. shook his head, "I'll make a deal with you. I'll write down directions to the line-shack, if in six weeks, I'm not back here, send in the cavalry. That is if I don't call or come back sooner. No, it's too good, now, something clicked. You'd be amazed, if you just let go, and tried it."

"What? What's that, J.B?"

"Walking straight out into the desert, walking straight out and through the heart of yourself, and not stopping."

"Huh, what? I mean, explain."

"I can't, but you'll get an idea of it, if you start walking. Anyway, six weeks, OK?"

"Fine, be careful."

. . . DOES MURDER SLEEP

Lowenstein watched J.B. close the door. After waiting a few seconds, he walked to the window and watched him climb into his car and drive away. Whether he ever saw him again was quickly becoming a hard question to answer. The last few minutes of the session had shaken, no frightened him. The other voice, the one heard along with J.B.'s was different, different enough to force Lowenstein to consider that perhaps a split personality was at work. Still, what was even more puzzling was the manner in which J.B. seemed to monitor it, handle it like a comfortable tool. Too convincing, weirdly, so.

'If I had been listening to that on the radio, rather than sitting in front of him, I would have sworn that he wasn't speaking as another, but actually interviewing Jabir. Yes, Jabir. He had read some of his work, though, third hand, paraphrased in journals describing Jung's work, but nothing even close to this sort of intimacy. Yes, it *was intimate.* I could almost smell smoke, my eyes seemed to burn. Whoa, now. Easy.'

Yes, the sound of his voice was disconcerting, but it was his words, they had the feel of a distant warning like an echo or, 'Shit, say it! Like a voice welling up from inside me,' Lowenstein thought.

'A challenge, yes it had sounded like a direct challenge to me,' he continued thinking, 'too personal, but there was no way, J.B. could have knowingly touched on that part of my past.'

"Walking straight out into the desert, walking straight out and through the heart of yourself, and not stopping." It had the ring and tone, a timbre of something he had read or studied, yes it was similar to a passage from one Jung's works. It was describing a patient who perfectly described an image from an ancient text that had yet to have been translated into English, the only language that the patient spoke.

"Walking out of the face of the sun, aroused and laughing, my essence, the manna of my loins was brought up and out, my life sprang forth and I made love to the stars." It was from Hesiod, the author of The Theogony, dating from 500 B.C. Jung was using as an example of the collective unconscious, that certain themes, images ideas are a part of every man's unconscious; a long, extended river in which all humans bathe.

'J.B. did that to . . . me, just now. Touched a nerve, a place I thought *only I was privy to*, shit!'

Sitting down at his desk, he opened the bottom drawer and pulled out a bottle of Michter's Kentucky Straight Bourbon, and poured a small amount into a glass and quickly downed it. The hard, sweet burn, the momentary jolt was pleasing. Kentucky bourbon, horse country. He thought of his native Maryland and the stables on his parent's farm just outside of Frederick. His grandfather had raised thoroughbreds, Talented Dancer, his pride and joy finished fourth, eight lengths behind the winner Vigil, in the 1923 Preakness. Malcom still had a photo of his grandfather atop Talented Dancer, the inscription reading: "To my favorite grandson, stable boy, and best friend Malcom. If only we could have trained my horses together, maybe we could have run with the mighty Vigil. Love, Grandpa Devan."

Lowenstein, swore he could smell a hint of manure and straw; hear the big Palomino: Gus, his favorite whinnying. Every weekend, either Saturday or Sunday, until the day he left for Johns Hopkins, he road to Frederick to work the stables, then hike in the woods of the Blue Ridge. The hardest decision he had ever made was to leave his native Maryland for Las Vegas, but it was Adele who had forced his hand.

They met when he was in graduate school. Married as soon as he had his Ph.D. No children, but they had the farm and the stables and the lush green grass in spring and summer and the flaming, twisting fires of maple, poplar and oak trees in the fall. "Two coats of paint, sweet,' she said to him twenty years into the marriage, "even now, this late, I still see you as that brash, wire-haired graduate-assistant who gave me D on my first paper."

'How else was I going to get to see her, again?' he chuckled, 'I knew she'd come screaming into my office. 'Sweet Del, two coats of paint, yes, as close as two people could be, right? Were we? And why am I asking myself that, now?'

"Very aggressive," was the diagnosis. Del decided against radiation or chemo, "Just let me sit on the back stoop on the farm, hold my hand, we'll watch the birds, hopefully be here long enough to catch one last blazing autumn."

'I never wanted to see another autumn, again. Ever!'

Lowenstein sold everything, and headed to Las Vegas to be, 'As far away from green grass, orange, red and yellow leaves, the smell of honeysuckle, straw, horses and sight of . . . Del, so . . . now?' Lowenstein mouthed J.B.s words: "Walking straight out into the desert, walking straight out and through the heart of yourself, and not stopping."

He took another short drink then picked up the phone, calling his answering service, clearing his schedule for the remainder of the day. One more call? Yes, he thought that Matt would be good to talk to, that . . . no. Lowenstein stopped dialing, put the bottle back in the drawer and locked up his office. Just before climbing into his car, he checked the marquis: Penn and Teller and laughed. 'Why would it be any different? Is it or *anything ever going to be* . . . go. Just go.'

So, Lowenstein drove. Looking up and around him, he drove. Looking straight ahead, ignoring all the sun-drenched plexiglass, marble, brick, stucco, bungalows, glimmering towers, extinguished neon, tattoo parlors, casinos racing past him. He drove and then, drove some more.

Out past the city limits, Lowenstein, looked around and, still not satisfied, drove even farther. An hour out of Las Vegas, he took the first road that would lead straight out into the desert, and drove some more. After another hour, he stopped his car, scrounged around his CD case until he found Mozart. Sliding it into the player, he turned the volume up to ten. Leaving the door open, he walked around to the trunk and pulled out a lounge chair and then walked. Out into the desert, with just a wisp of Mozart in the background, he looked at the city on one side, and then turned to look at the distant mountains on the other, and then a third place: up into the sky where several buzzards were circling. After taking a long, cleansing breath, he unfolded his chair, and sat down.

BRING FORTH MEN–CHILDREN ONLY

ONLY

(DISTILLATION)

A WALKING SHADOW

atty Helms kept her '93 Ford Ranger parked on the
crest of Gila Drive, the highest point overlooking
Valley View Apartments, only a quarter mile away
from her second story studio: 7-B. Parking on the hill was the only
way to ensure that she would not be late for work. The starter in
her truck had developed a "hick-up". If it refused to turn over, she
could simply release the brake, ease in the clutch, roll, take her
foot off the clutch, feel the jolt, hear the engine pop and then, "On
my way!"

Today, though, there was no need to rush. Perfumed and
manicured, her hair bouncing easily on her bare shoulders, her teal
colored sun-dress, seemingly infused with neon, glowing in the
late afternoon, she made the short journey to her truck, heels
clicking and rasping on the sidewalk, wondering what Jonas would
surprise her with, this time.

Easing the parking brake off as she pushed in the clutch, the
powder blue, baby pick-up truck quickly gathered speed. Three-
quarters of the way down the hill, Natty pulled her foot up off the
clutch, the Ranger, with a slight jolt and jerk to the right roared
into ignition, 'Houston, we have lift off,' she thought as she felt a
slight flush and tingle run through her body. 'What's the rush in
getting it fixed? S'kinda nice, that felt *real nice*.'

From Ada, Oklahoma to the desert, running from flat and green to barren and desolate, Natty had arrived just outside of Las Vegas three years ago, still looking for a place, with even more open space, in hopes of untangling the jangle and the static that had, forever, cluttered up her ever-whirling brain. Diagnosed, at age five, with dyslexia, the world had always seemed a room constantly being re-arranged. When the guidance counselor told her parents that a tutor and special classes would help Natalie cope, they shook their heads, smiled and said that it was nothing a little intestinal fortitude, and a lot of hard work, "C'ain't fix!"

For Natty, words on the page, even listening to a lecture, moved like bees pollinating a field of summer wheat. The newspaper was a tablet of hieroglyphics, text books a wash of ill-fitting symbols. Desperate and exasperated, she found Wallace Stevens, Robert Frost and, most remarkable of all: e.e. cummings, all a refuge.

Yes, Cummings more than all the others, the letters: tumbling towers, the riffs and nervous tics of symbols and switchbacks acted as foils to her scrambled processing, oddly freeing and calming it to down to a sweet, purring, easy idle. Her sophomore English teacher remarked openly to the class, that, "Miss Helms' oral presentation, her *explication de texte*, yes I know, the rest of you are probably unfamiliar with that term or approach; look it up! Miss Helms' insightful dissection of some the finest twentieth century American poetry ever written sounded like the synopsis of a doctoral dissertation. Bravo, Miss Helms. Bravo!"

Unfortunately, as she began to find an inward calm, the outside world roared its approval of her hypnotic mismatched eyes, her ivory skin and the ebb and flow of her flowering figure. Accustomed to being ignored and parodied, scorned and forgotten, now, she could not enter a room without the herd of aspiring bulls snorting, "Stacked accomplishments, rack of ages" and much worse.

None of the other girls would befriend such overwhelming competition. There was not one of the anxious, horny herd that was the least bit interesting. So, with the hum and chatter inside her head finally finding a place to sleep, Natty retreated, decided to remain inside and watch the storm around her, rage.

Mother wanted nothing of that, wanted nothing of a bookworm, schoolmarm: nerd!

"But you finally *got somthin' good* to show off! Honey, fruit of my loins, it'd be like shootin' fish in a barrel. With that bodacious body, that sweet face of yours, girl, you'd have yourself a good time with all the hunks, the good-lookin' ones. Hook yourself one with some real foldin' money, let him knock you up. You'd be set, sweetie, set," was the sage counsel her mother offered Natty in between puffs of smoke and sips of coffee at the breakfast table.

"Beach house, nice car, country club membership. Don't forget about your mamma, now. Don't forget who *gave you* all that equipment. I want my slice, you hear?"

Natty, smiled, nodded her head, saying she would certainly think about it and then locked herself in her room. Annoyed, but undeterred, she opened up another book of poetry and returned inside where she could continue with her latest discovery: words. Next morning at breakfast she shared her new-found excitement with her mother, "Count them, sixteen variations on something as simple as "place" she said to her mother while they both ate breakfast. The Eskimos have a hundred different words for snow. Now look at how this poet used that in this poem about a young Inuit girl walking out into an arriving snow storm. Just with this single word walking through the falling snow, see? I counted all the variations: seventeen. Each ties-in and then reflects a different, emotional feeling she is experiencing."

Her mother never looked up, she just turned the newspaper over, flicked the ashes off her cigarette, and then burped, muttering, "Too much sausage in last night's pintos."

Natty stared at the head of matted gray-white hair hunched over the newspaper; watched as the silver-blue smoke curled up and away from her mother's hand resting on the table. Looking around at the bubbling wall paper, the yellowing kitchen cabinets, the worn vinyl floor, and then back to her mother. Natty felt her newfound hope and excitement slowly seeping out, watched as her new and exciting world seeped slowly out and down to puddle and then spread out across the floor, thinking:

'There. Right, there! See it, momma? See that puddle of piss and vinegar? Is that what you want me to be? Want me to stay right here, be just like you? Really? Everything . . . *here* is just one long, slow leak. No one here dies, they just wake up one day and there's no air left in them. Their lives just slowly flatten out, and then the wind blows them away.'

Looking up, her mother released a long, thunderous belch, "Whew! Finally! Last time I use Pittman Sausage. Lordy! You say somethin' Natty? Run put on that tank-top, I bought you. C'mon, girl. Reel one in for us. Use the bait, God and your momma give you!"

"I need some air. Later, mom."

Isolated and alone, Natty turned to the one place, outside, where she could count on a fresh start and new light each day: the sunrise. It became a new and liberating routine. Rising early, she would walk over freshly plowed fields, smell the fecund odor of turned soil mixing with the dew, and watch as the light would move over the land, as though it were being transported by "little cat feet." Yes, she knew that Sandberg was describing the fog but it was more her own, this way.

Rejuvenated, almost optimistic, she would slip back into the house where she would find her mother, again, hunched over the newspaper, smoking one Camel after another between gulps of coffee, and bile.

'It had to be something she found outside,' Natalie thought, 'something a stranger introduced her to as a child. Poisoned apple or bile, it can't be something she manufactures inside of herself, on her own, can it?'

That was the only way Natty could explain, and still feel any connection to this person sitting across from her. Yes, she, that angry, cantankerous old, 'Stop, look at her, study her for a second. *Mother?* Yes, I passed through her, but . . . are we *really of the same flesh? Are any of us really . . . connected? And if so, how?*

The next morning, fresh off another hour-long walk, Natty experienced a new revelation. No, not so much a new revelation as it was a new twist to an ancient myth that involved her. It was one of her favorite stories: the birth of Athena. The first time Natalie read it she felt a twinge of excitement. It had never occurred to her that a girl, a woman could spring to life, full grown and in battle gear. She knew that it was a myth but loved the idea of this creature, this *woman* born out of the mind of the greatest of the ancient gods. Zeus' most inspired creation coming to life directly from his thoughts; and not just any woman, a goddess in her own right. Perhaps even surpassing Zeus, since she was a fully formed ideal come to life.

Looking at her mother, again, the two seated at the breakfast table, the story seemed particularly *pertinent* today. Yes, yet another nice, new word to use in more ways than she had originally imagined.

"Momma, it was just so fresh and wet, cool and soothing today. Over at the Sumners' farm, Charlie waved from the top of his big green John Deere tractor. The plowed fields were like a long, sweet sigh. And then the new light laying its soft hands down, kneading, turning it with shadow, vapor rising up, all of it was just so quiet and calm, so fragrant. Made me want to sing, and before I knew it, I heard Charlie singing too. No, not my song, he just felt like singing too. There was a time I always felt so awkward and alone, but now, mom?" Silence.

It was in the Lady's eyes. Not unlike the ramrod who drove Macbeth to ignore his best judgement and proceed, "Damn the costs!" First it seems she had stolen joy and purpose, then dreams, but most of all sleep. So now it was on to Natty, and the worse of all crimes: young and pretty and free to leave. This Lady watched, but missed the signal etched out in this time. A marker, here with Natty, that was scorched—branded—into this moment as it must and will and does burn and define a place and that person in every life.

Overstepping, too sure she could win, she was, now, unaware that it was her *daughter's water* now breaking. In this protracted silence a strange new calving occurred. Still, it was *mother, the Lady's* one last attempt.

Still, once more reaching out, speaking in a tone an octave shy of a moan, Natty said,

"Like I was saying, growing up and even now sometimes I feel so awkward inside."

The Lady was grinning, almost laughing, replying, "So what? If the shoe fits. Like I said, God and me suited you up just fine. With that body and face, who gives a damn what's goin' on 'tween them ears of yours, shit! Just stay on the pill or make sure the fun ones use rubbers, until you land yourself some money. And then I'll finally get somethin' for not havin' you hosed out of me when I had the chance."

The silence screamed out into the morning light, daring either to make the next move. The small travel alarm clock that the Lady kept on the breakfast nook table ticked off forty-seven seconds before Natty jumped free and clear of her life, there.

"No one, and I'm sorry to say, the hell I am, no! I am not sorry to say it. Most especially to you! Just at the moment it all seems to calm down, as I start to feel as though I can function and think straight and maybe find a foothold, happy, I'm happy, you! You, you just, no! Damn it! Damn you! Damn you, and damn that spot you can't seem to get off your heart or off your eyes or off whatever it is that's in the center of your head, the place, ah I mean, shit I don't know! So, you, you tell me where does that hateful rotting ooze come from? Where is the spot, the place, the center of you that makes that bile? Where does it comes from? You don't know? Fine. But not me, not now, or anymore! I'm not going to take it or let it poison me, anymore, woman, you hear me?

"Don't you understand? I still see that awkward, lonely little girl inside me, even now, when I look at the mirror. Even when I walk into a room and every last one of those horn-dogs, whistles and paws, I'm still not sure who or what I'm supposed to do. So today, right now, when I came back in, happy and confident you'd think my own God damned mother, that she-"

Natalie stopped and looked down at the smirking, chain smoking Lady. Her mother. No way to change it. After taking a long, deep breath, Natalie thought, 'Useless. What will it accomplish?'

"I love, no! That is not it. I *owe* you a debt of gratitude for pushing me out of your body, for making sure I survived. Thank you for that, Debbie Helms, thank you. I'm beginning to think that it's all just a big joke on *all of us*. There really is no connection, God knows, I don't feel connected to you in the slightest. Maybe we're just light or energy or frustration or anger channeled through each other. Maybe that's why I felt so good this morning. Charlie and I shared a common light, some of the same energy in the same spot at the same time, and then sang. No not together, just in the same place."

Natty paused and looked long and hard at the woman sitting there, still smirking and shaking her head. She realized that it would be the last time she would ever be standing over this woman, connected to her as *daughter*. She raised her hand, reached out to touch her face and stopped short. Pulling her hand back, she tightened it up into a balled-up fist.

The Lady continued to smirk as she rubbed out her Camel, reached over, pulled another out, lighted it, burped and muttered, "Always with the drama, you little . . . bitch! Like I said, it was a shame the old man didn't have the money to have you hosed out of me, would have saved us both a lot of grief."

Natty, yes it would be Natty from now on, not Natalie, lowered her hand and thought, 'Sure, I could beat her into a pulp. But where do "I" start if I jump back in there?'

"Good-by, Debbie. I'm gone."

Even after three trips out to visit J.B., Natty still had to look for the marker: the twisted and mangled post from an old road sign. From a distance it looked like a small dead animal that refused to decompose. Three-tenths of a mile past that point the side of the road feathered off into the desert. If a person looked closely, he could see the remnants of tire tracks that seemed to head off straight into the desert and disappear. Five miles down the phantom road were the railroad tracks, part of the Salt Lake Line. To the left was a hunched-over building, a dilapidated water tower and another small tool shed: Jonas' home, six months out of the year; his winter palace, "The Tsars have nothing on me, sweetheart, nothing, especially looking at you here, now."

Pulling up, she found J.B. closing the lid on his oil-barrel smoker. Tonight, they would be feasting on steak and lobster tails. A bottle of Moët Chandon '93 was packed in ice along with strawberries, grapes and kiwi fruit. "A little of my city life out here just for you, but first come look," J.B. whispered to her after kissing her.

Taking Natty by the hand, he told her to close her eyes just as he opened the front door.

Suspended from the ceiling, each corner and spread out across the palette that served as his bed was an array of dresses, blouses, slacks and lingerie, all original designs, custom made for Natalie by the head designer at Ayre Apparel, J.B.'s dream, now flowering, under its new owner Miguel Sanchez.

"I was in town last week, I phoned my old foreman, Miguel, he was the one I sold the business to. Told him I had someone, ah, remarkable I wanted to surprise. Asked him to talk to Maria, pull out all the stops. Wow me. So, what do you think?"

The steak was shoe leather, the lobster tails briquettes by the time they finished making love. J.B. and Natty sipped champagne and fed each other strawberries as the afternoon undressed and the evening light bathed the desert in aquamarine, yellow and black.

Looking at Natty's profile in the waning light, J.B. thought of his session with Dr. Lowenstein, what he said when the doctor asked him about Natalie.

"She's the fire, I'm the distillate. We talked about it, she agrees. She threw off, shed her old skin, fled Oklahoma, but realized that the desert, the desolation could only go so far in calming the riot raging in her head. Me? Used up, cynical and unloosed from time, the fucking accident did that, no. I guess what it really did was act like a catalyst, pushed me farther and faster along a path laid down, shit, who knows, before I was born. It's not just me, I'm beginning to think it's the species, whatever.

"I've always been looking out from the back wall my own skull, my own built-in movie theatre, wondering how I'll ever fit in, and then boom, now I know for certain it'll never happen. So, I look up and there's this apparition with two different colored eyes and a body that, you remember that great old cartoon with the wolf? Yeah, when he sees the woman up on stage, his eyes pop out about three feet? So, yeah, you get the picture.

"Natty tells me that she enjoys crawling up inside of my arms and being held with no expectations. Feeling safe and warm. After that if she feels really comfortable and connected to the moment, she wants me to enter her and thrust as hard as I can. She says it quiets the noise in her head. I'm more than happy to oblige, either way. Fine if we just hold, though, I do have to admit, better, if she gives me the green light.

"We're a hot burning fire. Jabir, the alchemist I'm translating, would use an incredibly hot fire in his forge when using metals, would even throw shavings into the fire to watch the colors swirl and rise up around him, said it was a dry rainbow, one to free the spirit and mind of purpose, to allow the voices from the four elements wrestling inside to hover on the outside: put the most secret side of yourself in full view.

"Natty will be gone in a few weeks, I'm sure of it. I want her to go. Even promised I'd help her go back to school. What else is the money for? Besides, I really don't feel as though I'm trying to rearrange her, or whittle her down to fit the image I want of myself, what you and I talked about in an earlier session. I just want to crawl up inside of her and sleep, then come out, make love to her and then crawl back up inside and sleep some more. After all that is the only time we're ever truly connected to another, isn't it, I mean in utero.

"Nine months is all we're given and then it's, well, shit. Well, there are ways to fend it off, transform it: the isolation, the indifference, being human. Again, with Jabir. All those experiments, the endlessly long recipes, the search and, ultimately, he says that it's all for just a few moments, at best hours, where you can trick yourself, transport yourself back to where it all felt connected, but you're outside of the womb, so you keep trying, maybe there is a chance to leap, fly. Even thought of using peyote buttons. After all it is the desert.

"But even he, Jabir, I think, was frightened. Even he wondered, back in the eighth century if this isn't some wonderfully sadistic, cosmic joke. Hot wire a group of monkeys, make them believe they are supreme, God-like, let them dream and imagine, let them believe that they have control of all this, only to then . . . wake up."

Wake up Jonas, time for school!

He always heard their voices before he saw them; smelled *their* breakfast before he ate his own. "It's your place, son." Your place: last in line. Last one in the house allowed to shower, pick from the dinner plate of chicken or choose what was next to watch on T.V, ah, well, that one? Never.

So, knowing he would be last, Jonas remained in bed and watched the light of the new day form. The square outline of his window sharpened, the dresser, the lamp, the doorframe, and the ever-constant backdrop of voices and aromas: coffee, bacon, toast, Old Spice; and laughter, completed the experiment. Yes, like hovering over the cauldron, the fire licking its sides, there just there rising up, the transforming tableau.

"Wake up Jonas, hurry up! Don't make your brother and sister late for school. It's important they arrive on time. Hurry, now, get a move on, now!"

Appearing in the doorway, still in pajamas the rest of the elders, groomed, dressed and waiting, shaking their heads, smiling and smirking, tapping a wrist watch, sighing, "Children!"

Turning, J.B. strokes Natty's hair, careful not to wake her. Easing off the palette, he sits in the middle of the line shack floor and waits; watches as the desert night begins to gather itself up to leave.

FADE OUT

FADE IN — Screening room. Three small movie screens, shaped and framed to look like perfect replicas of the three glass panes on the den door off the porch where J.B. played dominoes; exiled. In front of each panel/screen is a café table. Seated at the center table is an Arab male, dressed in a white linen suit. Seated to his right is a figure obscured by the light. The third is J.B. As the film rolls the same image is projected on the three screens. When each person comments on the images on his particular screen, the images change. It is up to J. B. to explain the changes projected out from his head.

J.B.: "Most interesting lesson of the desert? Confronted with the absence of water, my mind always wanders over to the glistening, wet memory of perspiration which leads to steam, steam that wraps around her soft flowing torso, much like the rivulets of champagne I poured between her breasts. Pausing for a moment, there, it then flows effortlessly down to puddle and pool on her stomach before fleeing, downward; yes always follow the trail of water, right? Perspiration-steam-water-streams.

"Yes, only in the desert, where this sound wells up without prompting, 'Without-water-anywhere-the-dew hisses, then begins to suckle on the new light. Cat-like and pleasing as it rubs its shoulders across my face turning the last, best dream into rapids, the slippery stones, glistening, imitating the sheen of her long, radiant form awash in whitewater. Blinking. Eye-lids clearing, welding-into-one-seamlessly-the two worlds becoming a turnstile: water-torso-steam-showers-and-more-streams. Yes, the desert creates a new form and definition of the most precious of the four elements; releases the taste and touch of its liberating, lubrication touch—between—us.

"This desert and my phantom water nymph, smile. Watch as she brushes out her wet hair . . . just there . . . outside my reach, mirage or mine? Air and earth, sky and floor, one blink more, window and door from which I drink the animated blue, white, rust, shadow, breast, hip and eyes, there poised among the brown, taupe and scrub-acned broken, paint-flecked discarded UNOCAL and UNION PACIFIC signboards that rise to house me, my dream, and guard my place alongside her smile. Gentlemen, my desert cabin.

FADE OUT OF SCREENING ROOM

FADE IN TO LINE SHACK

J.B.:

"So, awake, once more and striking out hard and fast, finding that the indifferent desert has returned to its honest form. Again, with opened eyes it is now simply a mirror of the real and the imaginary; the perfect looking-glass: for me. Yes, with opened eyes. What is *that?* Light, shadow, desert—stasis."

Looking back over at Natty sleeping, J.B. smiles.

FADE OUT OF LINE SHACK

FADE IN SCREENING ROOM

(J.B. turns to talk to the other two characters seated on either side of him. Both have been watching the three screens along with him. On his left is Shadow, his right, Jabir)

J.B.:

"It was the way I stirred my coffee. That's what caught her eye. Three times, clockwise, then two counterclockwise. It was from the passage I had just finished translating earlier in the day. It was about incorporating the four elements into thought. The master, Jabir, was ruminating on the idea that shimmering black liquid is a physical representation of the absence of perception. It is there that the groundwork is laid for the mind to produce a clean, vacant vessel. In such a vessel a new order already exists, or at least gives one the opportunity to create a new order. It was all there, that day. I saw it in my coffee. I guess Natty saw my eyes and knew that I wasn't really seeing just a cup of Joe, but a black, reflecting pool.

Shadow: "Black. So, why do you think *I'm black,* then, chief? Ever consider that one?"

J.B.: "Funny, you sound, different, I thought you would have *my voice.* At least closer to what I heard as a young boy on the porch, or similar to what I hear or think I hear standing in the rear of my own head."

Jabir: "Black, Tabula rasa, the vacuum, the vacant space behind the fire, ebony of the moment just there, see?"

J.B. scanned the three panels/ screens and saw himself rubbing his eyes, just before staring straight into his shadow.

J.B.: So that's what the inside of a shadow looks like, is made of, what it sounds like, what is driving me to stay here in the desert.

All three smiled.

Jabir: "Don't fight this, let the lightless part of you, speak. Your projections up here, on the three screens, wonderfully. . . releasing. Bringing your shadow here, giving voice to the black, the stillness, the absence of fire, the perfect blank slate is as close as one can come to finding the stone without an experiment. Contained in the firing, all the elements touch, knead, combine and then destroy everything, save for the moment of the transient revelation. Yes, a good firing is beginning, here."

Jabir closes his eyes for a moment, smiles and continues.

Jabir: "Drop shavings of copper and iron into the fire. Beneath the fire a pool rich with oil, ebony and charcoal. There, just below the fire, one stage holds up and informs the other, the universe being recreated there. Watch the rainbow colors lick the air and slither up and around and down into the black, then back up here and there, swirling inside of you."

J.B.: "Yes 'um, black, please, I said. Then the nylon of her hose strained, rubbing, creating even more heat in my imagination, then she smiled, and yes, there was what you, the master said, right there looming up from the blackness, suddenly a torrent of colored perception as she smiled, licked her front teeth, her smell and face and body seizing me, saying, "You're kinda cute, in a quiet way."

Shadow: "Hot damn, finally, finally admitting it! So, that's what you're after chief! Now, I'm starting to follow, horn dog. Why not? When every day is stripped down to the four basic parts: earth, air, fire and water, or as we like to say, here, deep inside the warehouse ("Blue light special, aisle three! Renewed perception of self and place!): your unconscious. No, no, that's good boss. Owning up to the four horses of, man's place here, in the universe, or anywhere you choose. It's a head-shot, remember what was stenciled under your desk? It's always been there, just that little waltz you took in the Prius exposed them all to the sunlight. The four horsemen? Sorry: desperation, disillusion, fear and isolation. So, it's the sweet, smell of the Bermuda Triangle, of course I remember, is what you're after to salve the wound, but not just any old approach, using the witch doctor over there, using his smoke, fire and mirrors to . . . dress it up. Clever! A new one, even for me."

J.B. feels a hand gently squeeze his shoulder. His stomach convulses. Looking up over his shoulder it is the figure from the third table, the one obscured by the darkness, his shadow, suddenly standing behind him, Again, he squeezes his shoulder, gently.

Shadow: "Easy now, chief. It's only me, well, you-and-me-making that voice in your head sing. The feeling you can never put your finger on when you feel as though you're standing behind the last row of seats: Shadow, Jiminy Cricket, wit of the staircase, again, that's good, I'll save that for another day. Damn, I wished I'd said that before you did. That guy, the witch doctor sitting at the other table, oh, and by the way, I like the cafè tables, Paris,

Therese, you've got a nice touch, the desert in a lot of ways is bringing the best out of both of us.

"Hey, Jonas, just remember this though, this ain't any walk in the park for me, either. I was doing just fine! Tucked away in a nice cozy corner, watching you score, laugh, cry . . . whatever. So, make a choice, numb nuts, pick a spot. The hole you've opened—in both of us—yeah, didn't think of that, did you, Einstein. You go to fucking me up, cutting me loose, after a while the desert's gonna feel like Grand Central station. Chew on *that* Ozzie!

"I mean, shit! Going and letting that fucking witch doctor . . . alchemist, whatever he is, take on voice, stature and form; it's like pouring cement into a pool of quicksand and then expecting it all to miraculously firm up. OK, OK, yeah, there you go again, good, firm it all up and forget for a while. Great, but you listen to me, boy, listen up good!

"I mean, I'm startin' to feel like two miles of bad road, out here, you hear me? Draw a line, now! It's just you, chief, and well, of course me, but I'm more Teller than Penn, you know the quiet one, the one nods and smiles and occasionally pulls the rug out from under you.

"So, do us both a favor, find your way back, soon. That's why I'm bustin' your chops. These early morning mirages, alchemical creations trying to patch up, fill in a hole, watch out! You're falling straight through a crack, down past the center of a place, like I was saying, so deep, even I couldn't hear the stone hit the water.

"That's right, this is your co-pilot, pull the nose up, cowboy. She, I mean the defining *she* will be found. If not in the flesh at least a look, a touch, a smile that reflects back to both of us . . . something that cobbles together a foil to this spot-on, open-ended-isolation. Virus maybe, yes, humans are like viruses, but even a virus finds a way to survive and thrive. Right, Sparky?"

Jabir: "Looking up at your projections, seeing the inside of your fear, I understand, now, why you have summoned me here.

Look, there, up on the screen, from the inside of my head, your translations of my work forming an instantaneous leap, a bridge, a perfect projection of you, J.B. making love as if were an alchemical creation. Wow, even I never thought of doing that, damn it! The booty I missed out on, go on, show me more."

(Jabir turns to J.B's shadow and nods in agreement)

Jabir: "I was after a defining theory, a cause and effect that would reinstate man into the cosmos. As I would float my head over the fire to extract the abstract from the concrete, the cold hard truth of desert revealing a moment's respite, and there it was for a moment, maybe an hour. Ah, but you, J.B. you build the perfect fire through and in the woman. Wonderful, but will it liberate, restore you? Of that, I'm not sure."

(Jabir looks at J.B., then at J.B's shadow, then down at the floor, back up at the screen and laughs.)

Jabir: "So, cowboy, Ozzie, is that what you called him earlier?

Shadow: "You'll see why in a moment."

Jabir: "So can you put any of this, of your dream of her using my black art, up there? On the screen? No internet, no soft porn in the eighth century. Can you do an old man a favor, just this once? Please."

J.B looks from Jabir back over to his shadow now seated again looking up at the screen, anxiously waiting, and sighs. Sensing the split is growing wider, he looks at all three screens and back into the dark, murky form of his shadow and then into the wistful, smiling eyes of Jabir.

J.B.: "So! It's come to this. As I separate into more and more disparate parts, and each part acts independently, I can at least pull it-me-them into a cohesive whole by plunging straight through her and into a quiet spot, at least, for the moment. Black holes, birth canals, the simple act of holding her for a while. Is there a place where I leap over it? The separation is real, I just, am looking for a moment that acknowledges the indifference, but leads me to a separated, calm and perfectly serene place here in me. In the center of the only universe I'll ever know, inside and out."

Shadow: "You will. Sorry, sometimes I get angry, short with you. But you will. Maybe it's the random pebble kicked up by a passing car that, like a gunshot, forces you to swerve and crash. Maybe the answer will take the form of another person, maybe a woman, the face of a destitute man, a child. I don't know. It will, though, have to be someone who is more wanting, more unmade, broken beyond repair who will force, you to take the most difficult step of all. You know how destitute and lonely, mean and cold it is, so go. Keep moving through and then past the indifference into a place where, even I'm not sure what you'll find. The worst is over. No, you'll never know that second heart beating just to the south of your own, but you can move. Go one step more, one step more and well, we'll see. We'll run it, her, whatever *she is*, down. We will, promise. But God damn, let me get some sleep!

J.B.: "That word, again, sleep. Put it all to bed, wait, it'll all be better the next day. Sleep, really, now? Sleep? Is that the only way we get by? Sleep? By putting all of this, the painful part to sleep?

(Shadow shrugs, waves, gets up and leaves. J.B. turns to Jabir. His face has changed. His clothes, now resemble a white-linen suit. Looking away and then back, Jabir has the look and the smile and the eyes of the book-seller J.B. met in the Latin Quarter.)

Jabir/Book Seller: "*Here in the desert, our particular, isolated worlds are mirrored best.*

Did I just say that? Why?

Each animal has his own kingdom, own place within nature. Useless for us, though. We are foreign to all forms of nature, save for other men.

Are you doing this to me? You were such a shy and reflective man in my shop.

I found the desert perfect. Isolated and indifferent place; useless for anything fertile and growing, stunting all it touches, yes, of course, like us, like one man talking to another."

LIGHTS GO TO BRIGHT IN THE SCREENING ROOM

ONLY J.B. IS LEFT, STILL SITTING AT THE CENTER TABLE

FADE OUT

FADE IN – KITCHEN TABLE

Mother: Jonas!

Five years old and four feet tall, Jonas Bellingham Ayre's eyes paralleled the expansive savannah that was the Formica-top of the kitchen table, perfectly; a posted sentry observing the work of his older sister and brother, Dee and Stephen lining up dominoes.

"A dragon curling up to sleep," he shouted. Silence, and stares, and then the alarm.

"Mother, he's doing it, again!" screamed Dee. "Spiral Jetty, you newt! Mother, please!"

"Make one move," Stephen said, "and you're a *squashed newt.* Compris?"

Even now, he can see the direct and easy path of his index finger as it evaded his brother's grasp. 'Like God extending his finger out to empower Man; it was the first and last time Jonas was to ever assert his place and power and purpose while still a child in that room and family. And as clearly as his own finger appeared, so was the convulsing stomach when he felt her fingernails drive deeper and deeper into his shoulder, as his mother jerked him up and out of the room. Dragged him out and into the living room, away from the other children so she could be free to use the belt in anonymity. First a cigarette to calm her nerves, steady her hand. It was, after all a man's job to discipline.

Still, if she had to do it, she would do it where no one could accuse of her not being a loving and concerned, mother. Grinding out the second Winston, she snapped the belt and muttered, "When are you ever going to learn? Bend over the chair, now!"

Away, isolated in the living room, staring up at the strange, frightened man in the painting. Out in the distance, three withes rose up and over the moor, the man who was, and was still desperate to hold onto the title of king with his trusted friend, there facing the horror of what this new truth would reveal: "Be bold, bloody and resolute! Laugh to scorn the pow'r of man, for none of woman born shall harm . . . who?"

And now, as the belt found its mark, repeatedly. Who will win? Who will rule? And what is the truth, now? Well, for now, whatever the belt holder chose. Here it was simply what was called for, "True? Of course, it was, you deserved every last one of them . . . dear."

So, J.B. flinches, and always flinched when-anyone-walks up from behind and grabs his shoulder. The shoulder, yes the nails digging deeper, the fear and angst. 'I'd do it again, I was king, ruler, one flick of my finger and the dominoes, jumped! So, what? Always the rules for him were different, not the same for the older, ones.

Yes, as a man, even, standing outside his office, looking down, surveying the production floor of AYRE APPARREL, the seventy-five stooped over, but grateful Mexican and Central American women, sewing, occasionally glancing up to wave and smile, blow him a kiss, or mouth, "Gracias," content that the actual living wage he was paying them made the long hours justifiable, and for the moment connected and happy and comfortable there was the issue of the hand, grabbing . . . resurrecting the sharp, frightened feeling in his stomach.

Anxious to show him the numbers, share the good news of their profits, J. B.'s foreman, Miguel, the beehive hum of the Singer sewing machines cloaking the sound of his steps reached up and grabbed his boss's shoulder. The emptiness and fear, first, and then the startled face, "Sorry boss, didn't mean to . . . are you OK?"

"OK, Jonas, come with me!" His mother's hand grabbing his shoulder, turning him around to face her. "Jonas what did I say? I told you, you could *watch* your brother and sister as long as you don't bother them. You know what's next. Run get your father's belt, yes the broad black one, let's go."

The perp-walk, again, and for what? he thought as she lectured him about his elder siblings,

"They are both so . . . high strung and sensitive, but that just comes from being gifted. We've talked about that. Maybe if you'd apply yourself. Bend over. You do know why I have to do this, right?"

After the sting and the fear and the resignation abated, "It's such a pretty day, sit out on the porch. Maybe one of your little friends will come by to play. And-"

"Mother!"

"That's Stephen calling. Jonas be a dear, you know how . . . intense your older brother can be. Run along, go out on the porch. And don't bother you father. He's resting."

No kiss or hug, *she* actually felt better after the blistering. Less distracted, more at ease to better deal with the "gifted ones." One more post-coital cigarette, then, gone. Jonas? Alone, again, and the isolation put even starker, more exaggerated relief. The porch, again? Yes, so red-eyed and quiet he would await the second barrage, become the object of yet another volley of gibes and taunts from his friends. Hovering like a hawk over a field, searching, there, a certain stasis to the moment was, yes, the punctuation of their voices from inside slithering out to crawl under the door and wrap themselves around his feet as he sat, again, alone on the porch.

Warm and muffled. Laughter. Mother and father, beaming, the light of their smiles a sun to the two prized offerings in the form of their eldest son and daughter transforming the kitchen table into a work of natural art.

Turning to face his foreman, J.B. tried to shake the waves of laughter and loss of connection, the porch, the belt and the living room free. Looking up he swore he was back in the middle of the desert, alone, under a one o'clock sun. 'No, it's the shack, the light's just now up. Natty's there, asleep . . . Miguel?'

"No, Miguel, s'OK. I've always been a little jumpy when my back's turned, it's me not you. Me."

Yes, it was J.B. on the porch, again watching the day wind down. No friends, they rarely passed by, again. From lemon yellow to rose then salmon, twilight to black, staring and sketching he saw himself move in and out and around the dying day. And always the odd comment and laughter nipping at his back, "Oh he'll catch fire, one day. No don't bother him, I'm sure he's fine. He'll come in if he wants to."

From the outside into his head and back through into the house, J. B. imagined the changing colors to be an expression of what it is, and was, and probably would always be. . .'*What it is to be: Me.*' To be . . . me.

So, when in the Latin Quarter, finally away from the porch and the whispers and the laughter scratching at his back, an accidental student in the heart of Paris . . .

"We're still not sure how he won that scholarship," he heard mother, and later father, too, on the phone.

A second-hand book store, peering up into the musty, sweet-sour smell of decaying and forgotten words. J.B. frozen, staring up and into what? Exiled to the porch, looking down on Cindy, as though in prayer, his moans, his hands pushing her head in closer, and the flight over, the droning engines, the carpet of black below, the stale air and suddenly—here. Empty, his motionless body and blank stare piqued the interest of the owner, watching, trying to imagine what the young man saw and felt and wanted.

Walking over, he put gently tapped the floor with his shoe so as not to frighten J.B. then put his hand, gently, on his shoulder. J.B. eased his head around, amazed that he was so relaxed and smiled, "Amazing place you have here, sir."

Over Turkish coffee and Iranian smoked fish, minutes morphed into hours of conversation that led to Jabir's "Sixty-Nine Alchemical Treatments", "Your French is very good. This has just been translated from the Arabic to the French. Now you can take it to English, right?"

J.B. smiled and thanked the thin, mustached man dressed in white linen suit.

'Just as he is here in the . . . Is that a dream? A reverie? Or is it really an alchemical thought experiment wherein I become the four basic elements?'

"I have heard that this is . . . well, best understood in the desert. Don't ask me why. Probably just another old-wives tale. Jabir had a wonderful laboratory. He was a nobleman, as well. Brilliant. Some say the Confucius of the Middle-East. You seem to have a wonderfully wandering mind, like him. No, there is no gold or eternal life to be found. Just transitory moments. Sparks of lucidity. Random . . . incongruous ideas and objects join up . . . for a moment or sometimes for an entire afternoon . . . the secret of life, *n'est pas?*"

It was full light now. The window, its frame, the squared view of the desert, all were one. J.B. rubbed his eyes and looked over a Natty, still asleep, then back at the window. His stomach convulsed. No hand on his shoulder, yet it convulsed.

'I've just finished the most intense, no, satisfying twelve hours of my life, yes I even forgot about Therese for a while. Natty and I made incredible love, drank champagne, watched the sun set, made love again and slept like the dead. I watched the light come up, disappeared into a place inside myself I never dreamt was there. Talked to my own shadow, Jabir and thought I could even hear it all mix and match into one: desert, dreams, her body and the light and still that fucking cold feeling, that, that sharp rebuke, screaming out, "Wrong Jonas! Try again, this time, do it right or, we all know where and how I'll have to deal with you, it a blistering, *n'est pas?*"

J.B. stood up and let his shorts drop to the floor. Walking out into the morning light, he continued to walk for the next hour. Out and back, each step traced and followed, a hundred feet to his rear, then suddenly, there—close—touching, his wandering shadow. Yes, one moment next to him, the next a hundred feet away. His nude body soon felt chilled then warmed as the sun burned hotter and higher in the sky.

When he returned to the line shack, Natty was sitting outside, sipping on her third cup of coffee, waiting for him. As his distant figure came into clear view, she saw that he was naked. Stepping out of her sun dress, she walked out and met him about a quarter mile from the shack.

As she approached, J.B., again, felt his stomach convulse when he realized she was nude.

'She has an answer for everything I've ever wanted and more,' he thought. 'My God, look at her! If I wasn't completely sure, I'd swear I was still sitting on the floor early this morning, dreaming, or no, in a coma, or doing mushrooms or peyote buttons.'

'She's called my bluff. No way I can complain about isolation, the wreck, the alien family, my god look at her!'

When the two finally came together alone out in the desert morning, J.B. took her into his arms as she pulled him into her. After kissing for a long moment, they continued to hold onto one another, she looking out to the mountains in the distance, and he at the shack. Natty, felt calm and free and connected to this moment in a way that surprised her. Nothing here could remind her of why she left home to come here. J.B.'s body was comforting; the sun warming. She even entertained the idea of having a child with him. All of this in a matter of seconds. As she started to speak, J.B. put his finger to her lips, signaling for her to stay quiet.

"Don't let me ruin this. I feel like doing or saying something really, selfish and stupid, like I'm in love with you and want to take care of you for the rest of your life. If it were really true then I wouldn't feel this isolation, this . . . shit! My God, if I can't feel connected to you here and now. Run girl!"

GARY BOLICK

A GIFT FROM THE DESERT

Again, he heard it before he saw the physical object appear before him, but that was not unusual since it was two 'o clock in the morning. Sitting out in front of the line shack, admiring the full moon as it brought a shadow box, cameo definition to the scrub bushes, cacti and the jagged outline of the faraway mountains. The constant breeze blowing was dry, but much cooler than usual, J.B. found sleep difficult, again. It had been three months since he had driven Natty into Las Vegas, put her on a flight to Phoenix and wished her the best.

She was enrolled at Arizona State; Natty was firmly decided, she wanted to be an engineer. Who was he to argue. Now that her dyslexia had been identified she was learning how to stop fighting and work around it. In refining the diagnosis, Natty was given a battery of tests. Just as J.B. has suspected her IQ was extremely high. So, with a nominal amount of tutoring and remedial courses, she would be able to start classes in three months; right about now, J.B. mused. He smiled when thought of her going in to the registrar's office to apply for student aid. Contrary to her wishes, J.B. had established a trust fund to pay for tuition as well as room and board.

"OK, Natty, have it your way. I'm more than happy to set it all up, if you'd just let me. That way you can just concentrate on the work. OK. I won't. Promise."

'Not!' he thought. 'She'll get over it, accept it. Coulda, woulda, shoulda. No, still, I'm not that much older, she was incredible, but shit, if I couldn't shake the feeling after what we had all that together, *out here,* then I-'

Again, the long, nasal drone of the engine's horn filled the night. J.B. walked over to the rail, put his head down and felt the vibration, 'Three miles, six minutes away.'

The wind kicked up throwing a shower of sand into J.B.'s face, then: nothing, the air was completely still, save for the long guttural drone of the train's horn. A second, harder kick followed catching him low, his stomach, seizing up with surprise. Again, complete calm followed. Another lone drone rode in on the wind, and suddenly the smell of water. A vulture hung on the updraft, the full moon catching its silhouette. A second later, J.B. thought he heard the sound of a baby crying. Looking up the rails he waited. 'Three more minutes, she'll be here.'

NEWBORN

A five-minute bus ride from town. The town, an hour from the border, still, time never moved, here, in the migrant camp except on Friday night when the week's wages were spent on beer and wine and occasionally, if they pooled their resources three bottles of tequila, and a "bleeder," a "working woman" on her period. Five dollars, US for five minutes and you did not have to worry about getting her pregnant. This was the camp where Tela came into the world.

Stumbling into the one room, tarpaper shack, Tela's father cursed the blood on his drawers as he finished the last of his bottle, washed himself in the basin and stood, swaying over his newborn daughter suckling at her mother's breast. Barely two feet away, he felt a universe apart from his wife and daughter, saw a hard, perfect circle form around mother and child. Felt the throbbing in his temples, felt the vise tightened inside of his head and then reached down to fondle himself, and yes, decided, 'Why not?'

Moving Tela to one side, he pulled the covers off his wife, smiled and whispered, "Me now." She turned her head and bit her lower lip and kept her hand on her infant daughter's face while her husband probed and sucked, wrestled and pinched, laughed and then fell asleep. Easing out of bed the young mother gathered Tela up, washed herself, wrapped her daughter up and left.

Rosa, her grandmother lived, outside of Los Cabos, near the coast. It would be hard, but she would make it, somehow, she thought. Boarding the last bus, heading for the train station, she was gone. She would sleep, all night on the train, and then in the morning there would be the ocean and the sun. She would hold out her little girl for grandma Rosa to first smile at, then cradle and hold. Yes, she would bestow upon her grand-Rosa a new, great-granddaughter, then take off her clothes, burn them and walk straight into the healing waters of the Pacific. Take her little Tela, wash and baptize her along with herself, and she and her child and the world would be new and whole, but most of all, good, again. This is the dream she kept turning over in her head as she held her young daughter, who in turn held her Raggedy-Ann doll, the three of them waiting for the train to arrive.

A hand covered her mouth as though part of lucid dream. Their eyes, all of them were glassy and dark, and each smelled of recycled beer and sweat and, no, it was not a dream, that she was having in the quiet corner of the train station, the perfect place, she thought, to sleep with her little girl.

The last memory of that moment before the blindfold went on was Tela, asleep still clutching her doll, wrapped up tight and warm in the blanket her great-grandmother had sent from the coast. Tela, did eventually, find her way to the water. But only after the angry woman who woke her, and then made sure that the conductor placed her up against the window, used an extra blanket and warned that if her granddaughter did not make it to this address, stuffing a paper in his pocket, then there would be un-shirted hell to pay. She would not see or know who this angry woman was until much later in Los Cabos. First from a picture on the mantel and then an angry exchange with great-grand Rosa. And mother, Eva, yes mother? Gone, these ten long years. Mother.

Tela's mother? Tonight, three minutes away, on a train moving through the desert, a full moon above, though she could not see it through burlap sack that now encased her. Nor could she scream, no they had seen to that with a knife, first to the throat and then her tongue.

Just twenty-nine, now, and *they* were finished, done with *her*. She—Eva? No, there was no Eva, now. Whomever she was in that train station, ten years earlier, no longer existed. There was no one left, there, now. *She* breathed, but now existed on a plain, in a place wholly created by the hands of man. A place so odd and alien, the natural world refused to acknowledge it. A place so particularly awkward no animal, save man, could or *would* dream of creating it.

Her particular place? The center of her own elastic cylinder where all the intangibles, the light and spark, spirit and center of her *self* had long ago been dissected and removed. From the outside working deftly inward, the scalpel they used systematically stripped her of all that Eva once saw as—*me*—staring back from the mirror. All gone, now. No Eva—or me—or I. Only the distant echo that she heard now as *she, only, she.*

Into her center they probed and, once there, sliced free all that *nameable.* Any and all emotions and sense, any and all things that could be reminiscent of *me* had been cut away. Carved-up, *cleaned* of all identity, Eva had been systematically deconstructed as they worked their way toward her center; and once there? No one stopped. All but *she* was gone.

Eva, incapable of even pronouncing her own name, was dismantled; her very existence erased from the ledger of humanity; ten years, now and counting. No voice, no memory of it to hold on, all that she could recall of her place, name and time were the faces, hands, sweat and stench of each one taking his place to have and use her, then go.

And still, it all become even colder, lonelier and terrifying as she found that this faceless, nameless transitory place was becoming even more alien and awkward, taking her to a newer, stranger and even more isolating place. Moving from camp to camp, then tent to tent; passed from one man to another and then discarded until the need arose again, she slept out her days in boxcars.

At nightfall, the ritual would begin, again. No days or nights. Only the troubled sleep and dreaming in manure and urine-soaked straw. Nights? More straw, even worst smells, accompanied by such pain and degradation, even her captors were amazed she endured. "This *one* . . . so used and scarred, mute and passive, yet she persists. Lives on! What she brings in barely pays for her food. Few, only, the worst off, will pay too have her, now. Why bother? What's that you say? Even a dollar is better than nothing at all, sure, OK, if she's there, why not? Right, amigo! No. No, not now. See it? She's gone, nothing alive is still in there, no use to us now. See? Dead eyes, worst face and her body? Sure, she's alive, how? And who cares?"

How? How did she endure? She could still remember the face of her daughter sitting on the station bench, her Raggedy-Ann tucked up in her arms, both smiling. Nothing else remained except for her daughter's face. Each day melted into the next until there was nothing left of time or space, air or water, earth or air. Nothing mattered, save the face of her little girl. She, Eva, now with no name or place or time or purpose¬now¬except to see, make sure, hold her little girl's face in her hands, one more time, one more time, yes, please . . . is how *she* endured.

The burlap smelled of rotting onions. There was a small patch of light, a wisp of shaded, ragged illumination coming through a worn spot in the burlap. A single, persistent blank stare, a Polyphemus-like eye, a hard, ivory moon following the train through the desert. She felt her stomach convulse. 'Tela, my sweet, my child it's over . . . this time.'

Eva was convinced that she would never see her little girl, ever, again. It was in their voices, the voices of these men were different; cold and indifferent. They had not stopped at camp, they had just riding on. To be bound and stuffed into a burlap sack, meant that they were through, finished with her. 'Tela, just to see her, touch her one last time, Tela.'

No? Just the sound of the wheels gliding farther and farther out into the desert. Looking through the ragged, pin-hole, catching a glimpse of the moon, occasionally one of their faces, riding and riding some. That is where *she* found herself, and then— him—one night in the desert.

HER FIRST NIGHT IN THE DESERT

He saw it now. Swaying side to side as it moved through the long curve, flecks and glints of moonlight exploding off the diesel engine as it pulled the seemingly endless line of fruit, freight and boxcars up from the south. A short blast followed by an accelerated triplet of pulls on the horn signaled the approach. 'Engineer must be an old timer, remembers when this was an actual way station.'

Bertrand Sparks waved from his slow moving, seemingly, floating perch high in engineer's seat, the deep guttural rumble and growl of the engine preventing any meaningful exchange of words. J.B. waved back, smiled and realized that he had begun to look forward to these momentary touches with another person, rising every morning at two, knowing that there was a possibility, an hour later, at three, of watching an impossibly long steel-like snake slither up and then out of sight.

Since Natty had left, J.B. thought back to the morning when he knew that he must send her away. Then he thought of where that morning had sent *him*.

FADE OUT.

FADE IN – Las Vegas. High-rise condominium. Late afternoon.

Twenty stories high, a large wrap-around picture window looking directly out onto the desert, mahogany paneling, red leather furniture, a wet bar, sunken bedroom and a seventy-inch wide-screen television. "As far away from the desert but still there, the desert, yes, right there sixty miles that way . . . see?" he whispered to Toni as he ran his hand over her bare buttocks, then began to kiss her neck.

J.B. and Toni, yes drop-dead gorgeous, Toni, his "favorite" from the stable of beautiful prostitutes at Shari's Nevada Ranch were admiring the view from his summer retreat. Toni was J.B.'s answer to Natty. After sending Natty away to school, J.B. realized that it was perhaps the best thing he had ever done for another human being. Standing there in the morning sun, naked and shivering, but ecstatic as they held each other, each had come to a very different conclusion. Natty mentioned the idea of having a child, while J.B. could only think of escape.

'If I can't find some resolution, some real connection or attachment with a beautiful, intelligent woman who has just said she wants to have my baby, I'm not fucked, but close to it,' he thought. And there to his left, his shadow polishing his fingernails, nodded in agreement, saying, "OK, chief. Pull up and out of this tail-spin. You bring this one along and you're more than fucked. Sure, go ahead, make a miniature *you*, drag him or her out onto the porch, into the desert, watch gorgeous, there, do a slow burn into a pile of ashes. As long as I'm here watching and listening . . . let me put it to you this way. We both know that all you really want to do is start walking until you can't stop. Once there, you'll have it. You'll have brought the entire universe—your own—to its knees. It'll all make sense, all be connected, you will be connected, but back to what? Me? No, I don't think, so. That's right, pal. Ditch her, now. Look some other place or just keep moving. Just keep moving until you can't see me here anymore. Maybe then you'll at least have a handle on what you don't know. First step, chief, once you realize that all you know for certain is what you are actually *unaware of,* what has escaped you up to this point . . . well, then it starts. It's the *actual first step.* I know, I know. Drives you nuts when I say things like that. Later."

Looking into her eyes, he gently kissed her and then shook his head, "no."

"Got to get you out of here! Here, this desert's *my* purgatory, not yours. Go! We'll get you through school. After you graduate, build a career, find a good man, then have yourself a bunch of toe-heads. Name one of them Jonas. Deal?"

After he put her on the plane for Phoenix, he returned to his line shack out in the desert and wept. 'Called my own bluff,' he thought. And so, for the next three weeks, he rose and watched the light return, allowed the dry, lifeless wind swirl and circulate in and through him and watched as his own shadow, a hundred feet away shake its head, turn and walk away.

'I am now', he thought, 'an absolutely perfect match for the desert. No give or take between us, just an open door. Not even a door, just clear, clean pathways, funnels in and out, through my eyes, nose, heart. Why does it hurt so much?"

"It has to, schmuck!" his shadow answered laughing.

'Funny, I've never seen him out, in the dark. Black on gray, more wolf than man, but a lot pissier.'

"So, it has to . . . hurt?" he asked his shadow.

"Birth, no, you'll never experience the real thing, but yeah, anything worth remembering, holding, keeping is gonna hurt like a son-of-a-bitch and bring you within a wisp of death. The accident was a good start. Remember look at what you don't know, push on. Stack the dominoes, look at the window off of the back porch, the one leading back into the den. You knew for certain that to cross that line was risking the look, the belt, but most of all complete rejection. Now you're here, better. At least here, you know for certain, that the universe, even you own particular take on it, just doesn't care. You know that now. And me, here. You're staring down the barrel of every buried dream and fear and loss, that's me. So, what's it going to be, chief? How you gonna shut me up and tuck me back into you head? Hurts, just even thinking about. See what I mean?"

J.B. looked away from his shadow and out over the desert waking up in front of him. A buzzard hovered on an updraft just above him. The sky was spooling through its early morning wardrobe of azure to pink to blue. A puff swirled an eddy of sand just in front of him. Closing his eyes, he was deep in the recesses of his father's overstuffed Easy-Boy lounger. From three in the afternoon until six when the rest of the family arrived home, it was the only time he was allowed to sit there. 'Easy, don't fall asleep!' he thought.

Sleep. He still remembered, no, felt the bruise of being hoisted up and out of the chair onto the floor. Waking up in the middle of the den floor, brother, sister and mother laughing as father settled into his chair, paper and pipe in hand, not bothering to see if Jonas was hurt.

The only words, J.B. did hear, "He won't think twice about my chair again, will he now?"

Again, more laughter. Even his shadow was laughing at that one.

"What I tell you, chief?"

He closed his eyes again, and there, just a few inches away the grill loomed in front of him: PETERBILT and the screeching and moaning of rubber, steel, concrete and air and sunlight all compressing into the moment that he was sure that, yes, 'Flat as a proverbial pancake and then: air, light, sound, sky and the chirping of birds collapsed into the same sound and moment. He felt even more alone and isolated than in his father's chair and suddenly— stopped.

Out of the car, looking back, 'How?' The tiny car mashed, compressed into the interstate. One, maybe two more revolutions of the tractor-trailer's tires and nothing. Nothing would be all that was there of him. Yet, now, the "Jupiter" symphony played. It was a clear, blue sky above. The air was fresh and crisp and none of it, most of all—he—Jonas, J.B. was no longer here, nor there or anywhere that vaguely seemed connected to anything or any one of the people who began to populate the roadside, hoping to see the carnage.

"So? Chief? Busted. Seems the grand design, this plan of yours has only succeeded in driving you deeper into the morass, farther away from me," his shadow said. "Want my advice? Well I'm sure you don't' but here it is anyway. One more cycle. Go back into town, back to the high-rise, back to Toni, then back to the doctor and then back here one more time, before moving onto, well, what you don't know. Remember that, first step is to find a secure place in all you don't know. The only certainty is to start walking toward that, right chief?"

Looking back out over the desert, then back at his shadow, J.B. laughed, "Deal, if one more cycle doesn't do it there's always . . . Branson . . . Branson, Missouri . . . Right . . . Elvis?"

Laughing, his shadow said, "I like your style, kid, I like your style."

J.B. gently kissed the back of Toni's neck, let his hand trail the gentle slope of waist and hips, drew in the scent jasmine scent of her thick, black hair, before pointing out of the window, saying,

"See that rock formation, yes that one, there. Well you go another sixty miles and you're there. Old Salt Lake Line. Oh, it's still used, but there's no need for lineman anymore. And this particular line is just used once or twice a week. All freight, mostly produce coming up from Mexico. Enough of that, though, let's continue with . . . you."

Once a week, J.B. would drive out to Shari's Ranch, put ten thousand dollars on the bar, and nod. Within minutes, Toni was there with her overnight bag, smiling. In her early thirties, olive-skinned, petite, dark-brown eyes, perfect hour glass figure, she was the "ideal vessel" for J.B. to pour himself into.

Natty and the wreck and Principal Burden and the coach, Cindy, his family and now his own shadow were rebelling. What had any of them shown him? Nothing, of course. How could they? And now he was being told to ignore everything except what he was sure he did not know. To start, no to actually stay there.

"Be careful, chief," Shep warned over dinner one night. "Be cocksure of what you want and what it'll bring you when you latch onto it. Chances are it'll be all shiny and new and perfect like a little boy and his new dime. Burns like a son-of-a-bitch . . . just like the first and last time I picked up a hot poker resting in the fire. Never once had anything play out like I planned it. No, sir! Half the time it fucked me over in a way I never saw coming. Once in a while it fools you, moves you in a direction that even surprises . . .

'The random, Sparky,' his shadow interrupted, 'Gödel called it the perfect system predicting its own demise. What? Don't looked so surprised, *you* read it. I just pulled it back up. See? Got you again. OK, OK, get back to Shep.'

"My old man called it bein' schooled by nature. We're so unfamiliar and outside the natural flow of things, impossible for us to predict any outcome. Sometimes, no, all of the time your best shot blows up in your face like one of those cartoon cigars. Once in a blue moon, you get treated and schooled by something that seems like a greater power. It ain't a god or spirit, it's just ignorance. You and I are the strangers walking around here. We just got lucky and fell into a situation where we see the natural order played out through us. Don't shy away from it. Actually, you can't.

"S'why I always go to the monkey cage at the zoo, get a good look at myself. It's us jumpin' around those bars. Us 'fore we got hot-wired and full of ourselves. Fucked is more like it. Fucked and still don't know it. Probably never will find out 'fore it's too late. Then blame it on, sheeit, everything and everybody, 'cept the dumb-assed monkey lookin' back from the mirror. Or that shadow, over there. Yeah, I seen him, use to have one following me, too. Hell of thing until you quit pushin' up against him. Lose him, you lose yourself and then it all starts to make a whole lot more sense. Trouble is, no one will listen, 'cause they can't, no sir they just plain can't hear you. Just like they couldn't see him, your shadow. Me, sure, but I'll never know—him or you—not like you, out here in the desert. School of one and a degree fit for a genius, that's right, chief. And you're the only one who'll understand what it's for."

'At least I didn't take Natty down with me. And Toni? She makes a fortune off of me. Perfect solution. What and who I can't find in the desert, I can just get lost in, here, for a while. Lose myself in and with Toni, yes Toni, not Therese. Sure, I'm sure her name was the first thing that drew me to her, maybe the second thing, God look at her!'

Natty was gone. Therese was finally laid to rest. The desert was no answer, simply because it was exactly as he had imagined, no it was harsher, more unforgiving than he had bargained for. Not, not the heat, nor lack of water, the sand, nothing about the natural side of the desert was what was so unforgiving. It was the unrelenting perfect reflection of what lay inside of him. Four aces to his full house.

'Can anyone really ever stay in that, yes, it is a place: past hope, nothing above it, nothing but the idea of despair. Having punched through, where now?'

Nothing was becoming clearer or closer to being solved. Even his sessions with Dr. Lowenstein were becoming bothersome for both of them.

'There's always Toni,' he thought.

The great experiment, it seemed, was becoming even too much for him to endure. Walking out into the desert each day had been proven to be more than a match for J.B. Since Natty's departure he felt increasingly over-matched. Still, he felt a fleeting sense of satisfaction in that he had been correct: nothing.

'It's true,' he mused, 'when confronted with a landscape that perfectly reflects your own sense of purpose, the desert wins in a walk-over, so what's next?'

He thought of Jabir hovering over his bain-marie, the few hours the great alchemist could steal and create a connection. His own attempts, out here in the desert, were equally as fruitful, or so he would like to believe.

'Really? All of this and us, everything and everyone are separated, alone. So, coming here to let the sun and heat and wind and sand roll over me, twist and turn me like a small twig in a little boy's anxious hands, the only answer I get is: Go deeper.

'But where and how? The desert, indifference, always wins.'

He turned Toni to face him, "Anyway, that's where I've been these last eighteen months, the cooler months, out there. I'm beginning to think though, why bother, especially, now. You are a *vision* . . . champagne?"

Walking out to watch the long, snake-like train slither up and past him, J.B. could not help but think of Toni. 'Might be the last time to wave at the engineer, count the cars, watch the moonlight jump off the rails, wrestle with the swaying cars.'

Looking up at the full moon, the mountains in the distance, the sand at his feet, the shack behind him, J.B. felt his stomach convulse, 'You win! All of you. So, it's Toni or Branson or, shit, pick out my spot in the monkey cage, I-'

Shattering glass and laughter interrupted his reverie. Looking up, the door of a boxcar slid open, three men, one with silver-capped teeth, the moonlight catching his smile screamed, "Now!" as two others heaved a large burlap sack out of the opening. Seeing J.B., the man with the silver grin smiled at him, showed him his middle finger and then threw an empty whiskey bottle. It shattered at J.B.'s feet. More laughter. The train lumbered on.

BRANSON . . . ANYONE?
(IT IS CLOSER TO MAN THAN HIS JUGULAR VEIN)

KORAN

J.B. walked over to the burlap sack. Both ends had been tied off with heavy rope. It lay there in the moonlight, motionless. 'Why wouldn't it,' he thought. "It's probably full of garbage, or no, with my luck it's toxic or . . . God knows what.'

Looking around, J.B.'s stomach seized up as he realized, understood that this isolated spot had now been cast into a different light.

'Perfect place for a drug drop. Not too close to the border, the abandoned line shack as a point of reference.'

J.B. braced himself, he was sure that in less than an hour one maybe, two or three large, black SUVs would appear. From these rolling fortresses, heavily armed men would exit, smile, shoot him and take the sack of drugs. Within days, his body would resemble the dog he found almost two years ago. He smiled, thinking, 'Too many bad movies, there's no way in hell that, shit, who knows? . . . still.'

J.B. turned to walk back to the shack. 'Throw everything in the Bronco and just go.'

Again, he heard it before he actually could see *it*.

A low, long, emotionless growl emanated out from the sack, then movement, and then, nothing. J.B stared at the sack. The full moon revealed small tears, stains and yes, there was an odor to it, now. More movement, and a second, less emphatic moan and growl. Nothing.

His silver teeth would catch an occasional bit of errant light and seemingly jump. His breath smelled of days of drinking and regurgitated food. He would take what was left of her one more time before throwing her out into the desert. He tied her to the door of the boxcar and with his fileting knife began to trace the outline of her breasts and vagina, buttocks and neck, gently, ever so gently, easing down just enough to draw blood a thin stream of blood, just enough to help himself become aroused. Yes, that always did the trick, that and her moaning? Whatever, it had worked, he was there, now, licking the sweat and blood mixture off her skin, watching her cry, listening to her attempt to speak, looking at her nude, scarred body. Yes, fully aroused, now. He was never sure which he liked better, using his knife or his penis. Maybe he would use them together, next time. Use them as one so that he would not become frustrated or feel let down after he finished.

Quandary, solved. We'll find another, another, but younger, just like her ten years ago and I'll use my tool and the knife together. Now a drink. The moon is full and I am my own man, see?

He cut her loose, motioned to the others that he was finished, and slept. Once the others had finished, she was deposited into a burlap sack that was secured with heavy rope on both ends. They had been instructed to throw her out as soon as they were finished. Throw her out in the heart of the desert, the perfect place for a crime to go unnoticed. No buildings or borders or points of reference insight. Yes, perfect. Instead, they slept.

When the man with the silver teeth was awakened by the blast of the horn, he rose up from his sleep and cursed the day he had ever met the other two. *She* was to have been jettisoned out in two hours ago; out into a place where no man would ever . . . shit! Fools!

Leaning close to the sack he listened: nothing, well, almost nothing. Through the coarse weave of the burlap, he could hear her desperate attempts to pull in whatever oxygen was available, to try and inflate her lungs. Each attempt grew more insistent as it failed. Smiling the man with the silver teeth thought, 'She is so good, listen to how she behaves, this one! Now she will save me the trouble of slicing her throat. Just throwing her out of the train will finish her. So, no matter, where or when, go ahead, now. If they ever find her? The bag will be in shreds, her body? Picked cleaned. All anyone will find is a bag of bones. They'll just assume it was a worthless, stupid tramp in the desert, some old, fool, crazy wife of an even crazier prospector or . . . who cares? Out with it! Damn my head hurts, I'm tired, hungry. Yes, it would be nice to have a young, fresh one about now. Very nice, but, yes, much younger, less used, a man like me deserves it . . . right? Of, course I do, of course! And next time together, yes, nice, easy slices as I firm up, oh my, yes, a real man's pleasure, for sure.'

It. Yes *it*. Yes, even they would not actually describe what they would do to her because *it* was too revealing and awkward and revelatory. It burned deeply inside of each of them and helped assuage, well, everything that they hated about the world, but mostly themselves. So, into her they inserted⁻*it*⁻and then extracted all that was violent to make it seem pleasurable for them. Through her they could watch the pain rise up and scream and listen to the sound and the fury of each innocent out their caught and trapped and punished simply because,

"She was there . . . available, right man?" So, her sound and their fury formed the perfect release for their own buried suffering roiling about within themselves, releasing still another more chilling reaction, "Yeah man, nothing like it . . . it's great!"

So, the virus, mutates, forcing her to succumb and endure. An unspeakable act? No, simply something *creatively human,* that frees the deliverer from his boredom and frustration. Yes, and afterwards, comfortable and clean, seated in rows of hardwood pews, under stained glass refracting the new light of this and every other Sunday morning these same men would nod and praise the absolute idea that each of them was, in fact, created in the image of *their* creator.

Their creator? Each man in his own way, of course. Isn't that the beauty of it all?

And so somehow. No, not somehow. It was simply her toddler. One perfect place still within herself: Tela with her Raggedy-Ann on the train station bench, ten years and counting. That single bond and image *she* clasped to her own heart and mind as she remembered her daughter holding her doll. Yes, Tela forced her to sublimate the pain, humiliation and degradation into something golden and eternal and enduring. Tela became her philosophers' stone allowing her to weather the forge and fire of an experiment that was never of her own choice or making. It was the one idea, the effects of it presented in such perfect detail that drew J.B. to her as no, not a disciple, but a willing heretic.

"Doc, she proved to me that a particular heart will create its own sense of reason. Yes, see? Collective, accepted rules of human reason, what we all deem proper, doesn't have a fucking clue. *Reason itself* has no clue as to what or where or how to react to this place, its people and our purpose, it's just as alien as we are. No, it is that one particular type of singular reason that only a *particular* type of love can create: perfect, indomitable will and reason. I saw it in, finally found its name: Eva. Eva and Tela. What that woman endured just to touch and hold that child one more time? I literally started shivering in the middle of the desert when I thought of it.

"Eva? For me? She just widened the hole that already existed in my center. Made me understand that about all a creature, a man, a human can honestly hope to do is reach out past his extended hand. I know it sounds funny, but no one is really comfortable once you get past the length of his extended arm. Past that, and it's all vinegar and piss, you know, like Sartre said, "Hell? Other people." Eva un-made me in the best sort of way; allowed me to reach past my own hand and actually touch the reasoning of another person's heart."

Eva's heart, speaking.

It would remind her, cajole her, to always remember Tela, sitting on the platform clutching Raggedy-Ann. And if and when the memory of Tela would momentarily stop working, she thought of when she had a tooth pulled at the public clinic, watching the bright, yes silver like his teeth, pliers disappear into her mouth, and the pull and tug, the taste of blood and salt, but no pain. Inside of her head, at the core of her body, any and every part of her that was meant to feel pleasure was soaked with Novocain. "Yes, it will be over and someday I will never feel any more pain, I, like that tooth, will no longer exist, but at least I won't feel, anything. That would be fine, no, wonderful!"

It no longer was rape, it was a cold, lonely, debilitating punch. Each day brought a new series of punches. Very little, no, nothing, now surprised her; so that when the cuts to her throat and the slices into her tongue, healed and scarred and made it impossible for her to speak, she simply slipped down farther into her protective cocoon. Using the nine hundred and ten days that she had been allowed to love and care for Tela, Eva thought of her little girl in her arms. Yes, Eva used each one of those days as a perfect, self-contained, permanent tableau.

Dominoes? Photos? All were lined up on the mantel encircling her brain. There, over and over again, she took each one and placed it, studied it, let her heart hover it, over and over again, all to keep Tela close and safe inside the ever-expanding buffer that allowed, she hoped her little girl as herself to survive.

Soon, then the touch of each and every man who paid to use her, yes, each touch, voice, putrid smell all were buffered, grew progressively distant. Each assault added a new layer, ever-thickening, new skin and an ever-lessening sense of all that the world, but most of all these men, insisted on inflicting upon her. With no voice to scream out, Eva soon felt as though she was watching—everything—from a distance.

As long as Tela is safe, as long as she is left out of this strange, distant dream . . . I'll continue to breathe, and look and . . . yes, go ahead, do it! Fine, there she is laughing at the clown, the day of the traveling circus, he shot me in the face with a stream of water from his flower. Tela laughed until she wet her diaper . . . OK, go ahead, finish.

And from the cocoon, Eva would take with her to the odd, occasional dream when she was left alone to sleep, her tiny, glowing face, hanging above like a sunrise, expanding out to light—everything.

Tela, my sweet, were you . . . how were you ever a part of me?

And then waking, Eva wept, longing to sleep again, to pass through the land and the place where her favorite dream, lived. Eva was convinced that it was an actual place where she was transported for a brief moment. It had to be real, yes it was, so please, put me back under, do whatever you wish, just let go back to the place where the sun is the face of my little girl.

No? Not again, tonight? No. No, you are right, I see it now. There is no such thing as me, now, or happiness. She, my Tela, is a trick that God plays on me. She is like the tooth pulled from me, leaving me unfeeling.

Even the notion of pain soon became awkward and strange.

Pain is for the living, those who hope to love and touch and be alive with their loved ones. No, I have seen my death. I will hold my little girl once more, and then she may strike me down for having allowed them to take her. I will always be alone and damned, but I will see her, hold her and make her understand that it was . . . impossible. Hold on, she may be here, breathe!

J.B. gently untied the sack and pulled it away. She was not dead, but barely breathing. Covered with blood, smelling of excrement, her clothes caked with grime, her face and neck bearing several knife scars, J.B. felt his stomach seize up, and then relax. He gathered her up and carried her over and placed her on his bed inside of the shack.

After heating up some water on his small camping stove, he gently removed her clothes and put them in a barrel to be burned later in the day. From head to toe he bathed, and then dried her, lifted her head up and let her sip water and then juice and then fed her broth. He dressed her and then pulled a sheet up over her, leaned down, kissed her forehead, and then walked out into the desert.

As she slept, he walked. As the sun began to appear, he felt his heart, racing at first, then settling into a strong, slow rhythm. He put his hand up to his neck and felt his pulse, and thought of a line he had just translated, a line Jabir had used from the Koran, a line asking and answering the question of man's alienation and identity, what pushed man forward like no other animal, what ruminated even under his heartbeat and breathing: "It is closer to man than his jugular vein." 'Yes, it's an ornery, angry push to shoehorn himself into life. Presented with overwhelming evidence that he should, will not, cannot find a place, the desire, like a fever, a virus that will not cool or die, drives him, flows just underneath his blood, haunting it and him to push and survive.

Looking up, he swore that he could hear the wings of a vulture beating, heard his own heart massaging the inside of his chest, and there, swirling, a short blast of the wind made   rose-shaped eddies of sand at his feet. J.B could actually see what he was feeling play out in the wind, the push and sweep, all moving, everything around him, forward.

"Alone with the morning in the middle of the desert," he whispered as he wondered out loud, "How is it, where is *it,* the thing . . . the notion, the essence of the dream that lines the inner most part of each of us that allows the 'unimaginable Zero summer?' Eliot's paradox that only a man could dream up an indescribable impression. "Here, now, I see it."

'I can see and feel the space between my heart and breathing, two things so close that I can actually envision the seed cracking, opening and spawning. Why now?'

Turning to look at the line shack, thinking of her, hopefully still alive, "What does she draw into herself from all of this that allows her to continue? To feed the desire to endure and thrive and simply stay *here*? There is nothing left of her; nothing to connect her to the outside, or doubt anything inside of her, as well. I'm sure that whomever she loved, or from wherever she traveled has been destroyed. From what wellspring does she drink, how does she survive?

He thought of the seemingly endless row of wheels of the tractor-trailer that came so close to killing him. There, they were, again, at eye level. And again, he heard the steel and aluminum of his car as the truck pushed it all deeper and deeper into the pavement. That single moment, the one that refused to find a partner or place or stretch of time to melt into and return to its rightful place in the natural world. Yes, that collapsed me onto myself, pushed past any limitations I thought possible to endure, and then . . . this woman.

J.B. looked up at the sky, down at the sand, and then tried to imagine how the woman could have survived all that humiliation and pain and torture. And then of the translations, the words of Jabir, almost a chant. Hovering over the fire, feeding the cauldron, J.B. saw it, now.

'Pouring everything that is particular to you and all that is impossible to share into a world that has absolutely no interest in it, you, and for a moment, it blazes up, a Phoenix, recreating itself, all for the purposeless push forward to see if the next moment is actually there. Perfect. It is what the three of us discussed, what my shadow was screaming about. Not the last, nor the next. Insist on this one. Pour everything, including yourself into the cauldron and well, yes . . . neither a line of dominoes or a story to be told; just the action and reaction that led life to be created. And it is, there in front of you, but for a moment. But yes. There. Anything else   is . . . a long shot, failed. Dropped at my feet, left for dead. And I, walking the desert, a dead man walking chasing his shadow. There has to be a bridge, an experiment, a cauldron the two of us can, if not share, pour ourselves into and see what flames up.'

J.B. laughed and started to walk quickly back to check on his new guest. Arriving, he slowly opened the door and peaked in to see if she was still alive. A quiet rasp filled the air. He stepped closer to look at her in the daylight. Her profile on the pillow, the gentle sweep of her jaw, the long angular nose, her long, thick mane of hair reminded him of an ancient Roman statue: Aphrodite, he had seen in the Louvre with Therese on his arm. Yes! So, what? Therese or Cindy, Natty, no matter, now. She, this woman, surpassed any sense or idea of beautiful, she was heroic, she was a gut-punch back at the desert, into the solar plexus of indifference. Now, if she only had a name.

Stepping quietly away, he eased the door closed and looked out at the desert under the early afternoon sun. Stepping out of his clothes, J.B reached down, gathered them up and walked over and looked down at the woman's soiled dress and underwear in the barrel and then threw his shirt, pants and underwear on top of hers. After soaking them with lighter fluid, he dropped a lighted match on them and watched the small explosion and subsequent dance of blue-yellow flames feather up and over the lip of the barrel, thinking, 'OK, first step, first our clothes, together, burning.'

After a few more seconds J.B walked over to the water barrel and washed himself. Rather than towel dry he walked, again. At first cool, the afternoon air soon warmed and dried his body. Continuing to walk, he looked up and around and for the first time thought of nothing but, yes. . . nothing. Complete calm. The desert? Agreed.

After another five minutes and a quarter mile's distance from the shack, he paused to estimate how long it would take to walk to the mountains.

'At least ten hours to make the mountain line,' he thought. 'And once there it be would over. Without water, the exposure of the sun and wind, I'd be exhausted and ready for sleep. Die in my sleep. Just put my head down on the sand and never wake up. She could have the shack, all the food, no one would bother her until she wanted to leave.'

J.B. looked at his naked body, 'A virus without a body to inhabit. We really are completely out of place here.'

Looking at the shack, he thought of her sleeping, of waking up alone, probably imaging that she had died and that she had in fact made it to some sort of afterlife. 'Space and time and at least one person who had not tried to take something from her, who knows, maybe I'll learn something. Try it, it's this or, shit, that'll be it! If this doesn't work, then?

J.B. began to chuckle and then laugh until his lungs screamed for help.

'Yes, sir! Perfect. If I end up failing here in the desert. Lose myself and shadow and place and time and purpose, there's always, perfect, got it! No, not Paris! Branson. Branson, Mizzou! "Danke Schoen . . . darlin' Danke Schoen."

Decided. New skin for the oldest trick of all. He would love and care for this woman, accept this gift given to him in the desert as his last, best chance to seal the huge gaping hole the wreck had not really exposed, but simply widen. If the desert did not have the answer he would, well there was always Toni. No. Hold the line, just now. Push it. The desert or Branson. Hold your hand to fire and see if it will last.

Walking back towards the shack, J.B. began to hum Mozart's "Jupiter Symphony." As he drew closer to the shack he veered off to the left where his Bronco was parked. Opening the back, he pulled out a pair of shorts and a t-shirt and put them on. Leaving the back gate open he climbed in and took the back seat out and put it to the right of the SUV. After about an hour he had arranged a small, very comfortable sleeping area. There was a copy of Kafka's "The Castle" on the front seat, a book he had not opened up since high school.

Easing onto the top of his sleeping bag, J.B. opened up the book and read the first lines out loud, 'It was late in the evening when K arrived. The village was in deep snow. The Castle hill was hidden, veiled in mist and darkness, nor was there even a glimmer of light to show that a castle was there."

Putting the book down, he looked over at the shack and thought of her sleeping, then turned to look out at the desert, now, fully heated up and baking, and then back at the first page, thinking, 'deep in snow . . . and the unimaginable, Zero summer.'

Both Jonas and J.B smiled. Looking over to his left he saw his shadow tipping his hat. Yes, there is nothing to feel except, no, absolutely nothing. Again, perfect calm; the desert nodding in total agreement. When he looked up from his book there was no separation, no feeling of standing at the back of a movie theater, no *other,* no one seemingly on the inside or outside of himself surveying the action. The air smelled of wildflowers, dust. A jet, passing overhead, left a white vapor trail and a light grumbling in its wake, leaving the impression that the air surrounding him was idling. Wildflowers mixing with the dry wind and the purr of a Rolls-Royce engine thirty thousand feet above him.

Closing his eyes, J.B. was ten and Jonas was thirty-three and together they were standing in the Buick dealership with his father and brother. An over-eager salesman, a cigarette in one hand and a small, spray breath freshener in the other, was trading off long puffs of smoke with short bursts of wintergreen, all the while desperately trying to close the deal with the elder Ayer.

"Skylark, Le Sabre, oh man, ah, I mean sir any Buick you choose, why, you'll be the envy of the road. Nothing says sophistication, assuredness and savior-faire like a new Buick! And besides, ah, hey there! What's you name little man? Jonas! Here, take a whiff of that son! Can't beat that new car smell!

"So, you'll take it? Mr. Ayer? Outstanding! Follow me, yes sir, right there. Won't take a sec to write her up and you and your fine young boys will be on your way in a Buick! Nothing drives or smells quite like a Buick! Nothing says, "You have arrived!" like a Buick and that new car smell!"

A WALKING SHADOW

OZZIE AND HARRIET
UNCHAINED

(HARRIET DREAMS)

FADE IN – *She* is having a dream. Still asleep on J.B.'s bed in the line shack, the woman thrown off the train in the burlap sack is in the middle of her last dream before waking. Camera slowly pans out of the window, focuses on a buzzard circling the shack. In the distance is a lone man walking across the desert towards the shack. Voice over, a song begins to play. Gene Kelly singing: SINGIN' IN THE RAIN. Camera pans back in through window, holds steady on the woman, still sleeping.

Gasping for breath, she raises up in bed, frightened, panting, sweating and completely confused. She does not smell feces or the ammonia stench of old urine or feel a sticky patina of grime covering her body. Taking another breath, she is stunned. 'No stench whatsoever.'

Reaching up she discovers that her hair is clean and combed. A soft cotton shirt, a man's shirt, covers her. It is clean. It smells of cologne. A soft pillow is under her head, a clean white sheet. 'Who's bed?'

Looking around she discovers a sparsely furnished shack. The bed in which she finds herself is wedged into the corner, away from the only window and ever-growing, brightening light, directly in front of her. Looking out, all she can see is the desert, the distant mountains, a lone stand of wild flowers, cactus and a scrub mesquite tree.

'Grand-Mama, Rosa taught me of Purgatory, a place of limbo, a waystation for those who had not committed a mortal sin. A place to cleanse before going before the Almighty, and then acceptance into heaven. But I know I have sinned, I left my little girl alone on the platform. Still, Tela, yes, she must be alive or I would be in hell, not here, now.'

She smiled. For the first time in years she did not feel panic or fear, only, nothing, thinking, 'And nothing is fine. I am dead. Free. No more of them. I could stay here for however long it takes or even forever. And, yes! If it means that Tela is alive, then here is fine, good. Yes, in Hell, I would be in Hell if she were not alive. And so, she must be . . . yes, alive!'

She hummed. Unable to fashion words, she would hum to let herself know that it was good and safe and, for the moment, another day she could count as alive. She wrapped her arms around herself, and hummed louder. Nothing. None of them to bang on the door, yelling for her to be silent. No more of them pulling her out of a dead sleep to use her. Dead. It was the best feeling she had experienced since being taken that night at the train station.

Pulling the sheet up to her chin, she looked around the room, felt a warm flush of contentment spread out through her body, closed her eyes, and slept.

GARY BOLICK

OZZIE WALKS THE DESERT

J.B. woke up, THE CASTLE, resting comfortably on his chest. His skin was flushed and bore a light patina of sweat. Reaching over to his right he opened the cooler and retrieved a bottle of water. The sun was low, six o' clock, a light breeze slid under his opened shirt, cooling him. Even during November there were days that it reached ninety or better. Still it was his favorite time, here, in the desert.

Crawling out of the Bronco he stretched his stiff back, downed the water and looked over at the shack. 'Still asleep, still, maybe I should check in on her, easy, now, don't wake her.'

Stepping lightly, J.B. eased up to the front window, being careful not to surprise or frighten the woman asleep in his bed. 'Still asleep, and peaceful. God only knows what happened to her. Her face, throat, scars and burn marks all over her body.'

Her hand rested comfortably alongside her face, the other hand was under the sheet wrapped around her body, her legs drawn up in the fetal position; her breathing was long and deep with a gentle rasp as she exhaled. Turning away, Jonas thought, 'More time. I know she is going to be frightened when she sees me, just. . . back off. Just walk. Maybe she'll wake up and come out for some light and air and see me in the distance and realize that it was a friendly stranger who helped her. Walk.'

As J.B. began to walk, he felt 'Yes, *comfortably* . . . unconnected, now' content that he was thinking of 'nothing!' He laughed, when he saw his shadow bowing to him from a short distance away. He, then nodded his head in agreement when his shadow called out to him and stated the obvious, "A sex slave tied up in a burlap sack, dropped at your feet in the middle of the desert. How's that for a movie pitch?"

Again, J.B. thought, never quite free of it, him . . . yet, so what gives? What am I missing?. Still, hanging on, still standing behind the last row of seats, even here, in the middle of the desert.

Then as he watched his shadow, coax a buzzard down to play hopscotch, he thought, No, it all made perfect sense, it all fit together, perfectly. I'm the odd one out here. Never really thought about using another person until I'd had my fill and then just tossing her away.

No, when I think about it, the woman in the burlap sack seems almost normal. Normal. When I think of those silver teeth, the raised middle finger, the empty whiskey bottle smashing at my feet. I guess I was the one who looked like the fool. I can just hear them now, "What a fucked-up gringo. I mean who the hell lives out in the desert in deserted line shack? Wouldn't go near a fool like that. No, sir, not me!"

J.B. laughed again. 'Jonas, J.B., fool out in the desert, all of them; I'd gladly give all of them back just to wipe the slate clean for her. But what is she to me? Really . . . is that what the shadow was signaling . . . saying. Look at who *she really is . . . to me?*'

OZZIE, HARRIET, RICKY . . . BUT WHAT ABOUT DAVID?

A WALKING SHADOW

To his right, the sun was just beginning to disappear over the mountains as the city lights on his left, jumped. Mozart continued to play as Lowenstein's eyes panned out and over the landscape. He had been sitting out here for four hours, watching as buzzards circled, a lone coyote in the distance stopped to study him and then move on. Pulling himself up and out of his lounge chair, he walked over to a scrub bush and urinated.

Walking back to his chair, he sat down and stared straight out, focusing on a mesquite tree a hundred-feet away. 'Barren and dry, sand, rocks scrub bushes and dry-powdery air. It's what I came here to find. Done. So, it's the why, now. That son-of-a-bitch! Why did he have to involve me . . . her!

'Eighteen months ago, about the time Ayre crashed, Del squeezed my hand, pointed to a pair of Baltimore orioles, male and female, smiled, took a drink of sherry and then asked me to help her to bed. Gone. Now, suddenly, here, in the desert, alone, looking for a sign. Bastard! I was fine. Just about there, just about to move on. I-'

Lowenstein closed his eyes and tried to remember Adele when they were younger, when she was healthy, vibrant forking straw up to feed the horses, hoeing out the vegetable garden, smiling as she winked, asking him to join her for a sherry and a shower. Watching her as she drifted off to sleep, stroking her hair, kissing her cheek and then wondering how it was that in such a warm and perfect setting, he grew restless, and oddly, enough, felt isolated.

'"Malcom, dear, don't fret, so. Sure, when we were younger, hormones and student debt, we didn't care a bit, just as long as we could end up in each other's arms at the end of the day.

It was nice, distracting, it's just, well, dear I think . . . we, women, view it all so differently. Oh, never mind, here help me stow these saddles. Lordy, I'm tired. Too tired for that, dear, just, supper and sleep, sweet."

'So, now I'm walking straight out into the desert, through the dry, rough, hard-scrapple place that is, has become *my center, my place,* now. I fled any and all memory of her to find some peace, here. Start fresh, to try and piece it, her, everything back together, here, yes, here. Why?'

"Malcom, dear, please, give us a kiss. I never told you, and now with so little time . . . it was never that I didn't want children . . . I."

Adele paused and coughed, took several deep breaths and then a sip of sherry.

"It was never your imagination, sweet. There really was, how do I say it? I guess, outright, so little time. Just before we eloped, you were so attentive, too much so. Smothering. Remember, I went north to Allentown for the weekend, to see Deb, my old roommate, my bachelorette party. It was then, no his name isn't important. Anyway, that's why we had to postpone. Why, oh dear, such a thing to say, and now. The doctor said it was staph, from the procedure, sterile dear. We were not married. An old crush, I . . . I'm sorry. No, it's never been your imagination. You *are such a dear.* I felt closer to you than anyone, two coats of paint, right dear?"

Lowenstein watched the last rays of sun disappear, and then marveled at the aura and the glow emanating up and out over the city.

"Why did that son-of-a-bitch have to pick *me* for his therapist? Me! Bastard! Me!"

David? You still there, dear?

FADE IN LOWENSTIEN'S OFFICE
(Twelve months ago. Fourth visit.)

"So, J.B. I know we've been over several points from your childhood, sore spots, the isolation you started to feel as early as eight or nine and how the accident acted as a catalyst, but I'm curious. I mean, you're not the only baby of the family to feel shunned, made a mascot, neglected. Sure, from what you described, it was particularly . . . nasty at times. Seems, especially, your mother, blamed you, or used you to justify her own failings and short-comings. An excuse to, well, exorcise her past.

"So, tell me, what about later, I mean as you aged? All I've heard up to this point is about your experiences as a young child and as an adult, what about the . . . middle years . . .?"

FADE OUT

FADE IN – J.B. is still in the desert, looking at the shack, smiling as he wonders how to best take care of the woman thrown from the train. Turning to his left, he is now standing in the living room of his childhood home watching as he, Jonas, gathers his older siblings, home from college, and his parents around the VCR and television to show them a recently finished project. It is his fair well to the family, an X-rated parody of OZZIE AND HARRIET.

'I'll be rid of all of them, most of all little Jonas,' he thought right as he slipped the cassette into the VCR.

"OK, everyone. This is from my film class, I got an A and a standing ovation, enjoy!"

Then looking back at the desert, J.B. smiled, thinking of her. *She, there in the shack, the one my shadow thinks, no is telling me is so necessary, important, I'll never know her real name, not until I find a way to coax it out of her, find a way for her to understand me, write it out.* So, Harriet sounds good to me, for now, laughing, 'Ozzie and Harriet in the desert.

J.B. picked up a handful of sand and let it run through his fingers, then stretched out on the floor of the living room, then looked back up at the desert sky and then over to his shadow, who was now applauding.

'Of, course I can do both, this is my movie!'

Looking up at the darkening sky, pale blue to salmon as twilight approached, he latched onto a vulture riding an updraft. Stasis. Frozen, poised, in and out of time, there, now circling, gone.

'From carcass to carcass, moment to moment, survival is a series of fits and starts. But what about . . . what would be that vulture's take on time? Shit, listen to me! Asshole. Nothing to do but indulge in this . . . experiment. Remember what the book seller said? Jabir was a nobleman, he had the luxury of researching and writing, exploring a wealthy man's ennui. J.B. suddenly felt embarrassed, and angry at himself.

He looked at the shack and wondered what the woman was feeling and thinking and how would she approach the rest of her life, thinking, 'She's probably in her late twenties but looks a hell of a lot older, the abuse. They tried to break her, completely. Grind her down so that she would just give up and die when they were finished. She's down to fumes and vapors, a living experiment, there in the shack. Yes, stretched out on my bed lies all the elemental parts. Pieces . . . fragments that will rise up Phoenix-like, but, no . . . there's more there. Something else has kept her alive.'

J.B. felt his stomach fold in on itself. 'Am I doing it, too? Am I just like them, the ones I'm about to gather around to shock and humiliate. Is everyone you come in contact with just an experiment? No, with her, *she,* I swear it'll be new. And I'm sure, awkward, I'll be trying it all out for the first time. Nervous, sure, just like the living room, but this will . . . yes, I want to do this, this time for all *the right reasons, no revenge.*

She and I will no, we will remain where *she chooses.* I just want to learn how and why she survived. Interesting dilemma, since she cannot speak.

Turning away from the desert J.B. looks at his family and himself, gathered around the television and begins to scroll through the re-runs of OZZIE AND HARRIET that his older sister and brother forced him to watch.

Mother: "Quiet, now. Jonas here, has a little school project to show us. I know, Dee, nothing like what they're throwing at you at Duke, dear. You *do know,* how so very proud we are of you. I was just telling Stella about you making the Dean's List, *again!*

"And Stephen, be a dear, pour me a stiff Drambuie, and one for yourself and your father. My, you are the image of Robert Redford, now, aren't you? Don? Dear, yes, I know you're reading the paper, but this won't take long. Yes, something about a project, film. Jonas insists we all see it. Just a couple of secs, then you can get back to your Wall Street, hon."

'Perfect, now roll it!'

KITCHEN TABLE – MONDAY MORNING – FAMILY EATING BREAKFAST

Ozzie is reading the newspaper as Harriet rushes about the kitchen serving breakfast. Ricky and David have still not come to the table. The clock on the wall shows 7:45.

Harriet (shouting)

Ricky . . . David you'll be late for school. Breakfast's ready and getting cold. Shake a leg, boys. You'll make your father late for work. Come on, you sleepy heads.

Ozzie (visibly distraught reaches under the table and pulls out a bottle of Old Crow, takes a long drink, leaves the bottle on the table and smiles)

Fuck 'um both! No better yet, you! Horny as hell, and ready to fuck you, now!

(Ozzie rolls up the newspaper and pops Harriet on the butt, goes up the stairs and locks Ricky and David in their room and then returns to kitchen)

Ozzie to Harriet (scolding)

Why are you dressed? Get that dress off! In the den, on the couch, now!

(filtering out from the den the audience can hear Harriet moaning and screaming "yes" as the camera fades out to commercial)

'Cut! That's a print!'

When the family, Ayre, in unison, screamed, "Stop!" Jonas was, once again, sent to his room. Jonas smiled and chuckled and sipped on a pint bottle of Jim Beam as he listened to them, all so very . . . "Shocked and dismayed!" as they discussed—*him*. Jonas listened for a few minutes, allowing the Kentucky bourbon to baste and mix and then wrap the whole bundle around his brain, and then looked down at the black lettering and remembered that it had reminded him of her, while riding back in the tow truck. Jonas, J.B. and now me, in the desert.

Then and now and forever and more, it still softened the edge so as to dull the sharp separation of flesh, spirit and finally touching—him—now as it did then, moving forward perhaps with her—she—there in the shack, soon. Just then as now, J.B. emerged from Jonas, and knew him and smiled and smashed the bottle against the door, looked at the camera past the wall into the desert and sighed.

Silence.

Camera shot is from overhead. Omnipotent observer.

(Mood in the other room, now, subdued. Older brother raises up from his chair, offers to talk to young malcontent. Father waves him off. Mother clutches handkerchief, sister begins reading magazine. Young protagonist slips out of the window.)

Before climbing out of the window Jonas looks back, scans his room searching for something to take with him, anything to justify returning: nothing.

All day Saturday and Sunday he watched old movies, listened through the paper-thin walls as one after another various prostitutes plied their trade at the Tarheel Motor Court on Highway 158 outside of Winston. He thought of trying out Lydia, of using her just like all the rest of the long line of truck drivers, laborers and the occasional salesman, until he heard her speak,

"That's right sailor, hundred up front and fifty after we're finished or Rondell there in that wheezin' Coup de Ville over there under that big ol' Live Oak tree will give you a free appendectomy 'fore he hands you your dick in a Dixie cup for free, Compris cheri?"

Yes, J.B. heard her before he saw the actual embodiment of a wet dream turned vicious and violent and real. Jonas cracked opened the door, saw Lydia standing with her back to him, adjusting her skirt and blouse, checking her rouge and make-up in a hand held compact mirror.

'I guess I was hoping for Jamie Lee Curtis or Julia Roberts or-'

"Rondell!" Lydia breathed out with a plume of fire, "Git your sorry ass over here. And you better have my corned beef on rye and coffee, now, or this lady's outta here. Right? You damned well know I'll walk if you don't start buckin' up! You sorry piece of motherfuckin' shit! It's me doin' all the work!"

Jonas eased the door shut, turned the T.V. back on and ordered a pizza. He did not return home until Monday morning, for breakfast. His father, leaving for work, smiled and patted him on the shoulder on his way out the door. His mother shook her head and simply said, "Someday you'll appreciate what you have, no *had* here when you're grown. You didn't even say good bye to either your brother or sister . . . at least *they* . . . never mind! You'll be late for school. Go on now, go!"

Peering back through the kitchen window, Jonas saw his mother throw her coffee mug across the room. After shattering against the wall, she walked across the room and stood over the scattered pieces, the mud brown liquid, and silently stared. It was five minutes before she, zombie-like, crossed over to the broom closet, pulled out the broom and dust pan and began to clean up the broken porcelain. After a few seconds, she looked over at the garbage can and then back at the floor and dropped it all: broom, dustpan and shards.

Reaching up behind the flour canister, she pulled down a pack of Winstons, walked over to the liquor cabinet and selected the sherry bottle and a milk glass and then settled down at the kitchen table. The last image J.B. had of his mother before climbing into his car and driving to school was of her staring blankly into the air as she raised one hand to pull a long drag from the Winston, the end flaring orange-red, and then the other hand, lifting the tall glass of sherry up through the silver-gray smoke to take a generous sip.

'Mother? No, a stranger who happened to smile every once in a while, even warmly at times. Yes, if the stars were aligned, her mood would soften. And if she did not need anything or anyone to distract her from, what? That was always the toughest question. What was she ruminating on? Why, always, the edge? Still? Yes! Yes, if there were no distractions from the children, and her husband was out of town, yes. Yes, and if she was thinking about the past, no, it had to be a certain, perfect time, in a past I'm not sure *really* existed, no matter, if she was *there* . . . "For God's sake leave her alone, there!" his father once warned.

'Yes, if she wasn't trying to work something out, then there was a semblance of kindness that worked its way through her personal INFERNO to exit unmarked, and miraculously arrive as, some might call it . . . love. Or close to it. With her, it was always like something learned from a book. Mother?

'Mother I discovered was a child first, and then a young woman recovering from, I really never knew, save for the bits and pieces she cobbled together to make a woman. So, as it filtered down to me last, the learned love and sweetness, the best attempts at deciphering the schematic of how and why and, most of important of all, "wanting" were lost. Yes, so the physical delivery out of her body of affection was always a . . . qualification.'

J.B., alone and drifting, in the desert stumbled onto a partially buried skull that invariably sparked the notion, the memory that would connect him back to her and release them both. Does it matter when that notion first arrives? Little boy, teenager, middle-aged man? It will always start and remain as a curse. Or it is the beginning of salvation? Yoke or freedom? "Can I get an amen from you, brothers and sisters? Yes, amen!

He learned later that she, no not her, but his mother was trapped in her own random desert. No, not thrown from a train, but locked into a cell. When offered the key, she refused.

'What was it she said just before the pills eased her suffering, "I, was, well, never much of a . . . I'm sorry. Everything seemed to always be hovering just outside my reach. Everybody seemed to always be walking up from behind or below me, never just up in front where I could see what they wanted. He, dad, no, I'll say it, that son-of-a-bitch did the dirty work, but it was mom who really wanted to break me. They didn't actually snap me in two, but I was . . . that's just it, 'Who am I when I look at the two people who made me and then think about what they conspired to do and then carefully and systematically carried it out? I was just a girl and then a young woman, so scared to say stop. But it was their betrayal just, and just because they could, they did it. I cried, they smirked and whispered, 'Now she's not so sure of high and mighty self, is she, now. '

'No one stopped them until, well it was your uncle. Once he was big enough to scare both of them; it stopped. When I met your father, so handsome. I could keep it under wraps, somewhat . . . somehow, then. He was strong. Dad hated him, mother loathed him. Perfect, I thought, perfect! You kids? Again, fun for a while. Never mind. Never mind. Just hate I left college and New York early for . . . no, that wouldn't have made a difference, either.

'Balzac was right, 'Men are hopelessly vain and women profoundly corrupt.' Nothing like the truth to set a girl free.

J.B.'s father found her in bed the next day, eyes glued to the ceiling. He leaned over and kissed her on the forehead, called the doctor, put on a pot of coffee and read the newspaper until the ambulance arrived. He and the doctor shook hands. Dad showed him the empty bottle. Doctor James shook his head, patted Dad on the shoulder and asked him if they were still on for eighteen on Saturday.

'What did she, Lydia say to . . . yes, the angry trucker, "Now easy now sugar. Easy! You understand? I ain't some disposable doll or . . . jungle gym. Hate when a man ain't never had no mother love. Always want to git it all back at once. Everything's sore for two days, my tits and coochie ain't enough, soldier boy, to get what you lookin' to get back. Easy, now!'"

The Monday after the Ozzie and Harriet "show" when Jonas arrived home from school his father was in his office, the door closed, his mother was upstairs, in bed, the door closed. A note was taped to the kitchen cabinet: "Not feeling well. Don't disturb me or your father. Money for dinner is on the counter."

Looking over at the kitchen table, Jonas saw a vase of roses and a note from his sister: "I had a wonderful time. Sorry it ended on such a sour note. You've done everything a mother can or should do."

Walking past his mother's room, she was on the phone, laughing, "You are such a dear to call. No, no I'm fine. Resting. I know, but you were always so attentive to me, almost like a second husband. Don't fret dear. Just keep working on that law degree. Shame you weren't twins. No, that's not it dear, really, all a mother can hope for is at least one son like you. Jonas? What do you think? Lord how he tries my patience, and so ungrateful . . . bye-bye dear, there's another call."

Jonas, up until now had been, "Well, just fine, a good sport, the family . . . mascot, if you will. Always knew his place, but now, yes, unfortunately with . . . no Dot, I'm not sure that it is his age or testosterone. Just so damned ungrateful, a real annoyance! Lord, please, strength, for one more year. College? Don't be silly. We're hoping for . . . anything. Miracles do happen don't they Dot? Please say they do!"

Jonas stared at his mother's bedroom door, out into the desert, back at the line shack and then looked down at the carpet. 'Here, standing here, nothing's changed in all these years.'

He walked down the hall eased open his bedroom door and then quietly closed it behind him, stopped, looked around his room and wondered, 'Where? Each of their faces, the sound of their voices the words; first soft pellets, then armor piercing bullets. The belt? Nothing . . . the words, the looks . . . the condescending head shaking . . . where is the place? Where is a place where it can all be purged . . . where? Is there a place where I'll be able to start over in silence, play by my own rules and hear only the sound of my own . . . words and heart beating . . . directing me to . . . where?'

From his back pack, Jonas fished out the copy of THE CASTLE, a book his English teacher had given him to read.

"Jonas, your papers remind me of graduate school. Your take on HUCKLEBERRY FINN and MOBY DICK sounded as though you've been reading Camus and Sartre. Here, try a little Kafka, no, not for credit. I'd love to hear your take on it, is all. You have a unique gift, son, you already see and trust only the parts of the world you know the best, that is you . . . your own . . ."

Mr. Johnson paused, waved his hands and continued, "That's not fair. My demons, not yours. Read it, and we'll talk about it at Starbuck's, coffee's on me. Deal?"

J.B. opened his eyes, THE CASTLE was lying next to him. He picked it back up and read the inscription on the inside of the cover: "To Jonas, The most frightening thing imaginable is for a man to see his specific place, his isolated, inner world, projected out in front of him. Suddenly, it looms as Everest, Mars, or as Kafka so brilliantly portrays here, a castle in full view, yet entry is impossible. My best. R. Johnson."

'We spent the entire afternoon and most of that evening going over this. Mr. Johnson was like a man possessed, he seemed twenty years younger, laughing . . . for a second, I thought we were going out for beers and chase tail. My English teacher.'

J.B. ran his fingers across the worn, dog-eared book and closed his eyes, remembering K the main character working, trudging, cajoling attempting everything, talking to anyone who would listen, and yet he never arrived, never passed through the castle gates. Looking over at the shack, he smiled, thinking, 'What . . . two hundred feet away, out in the middle of no-where, right there, and yet . . .'

He put the book away and stared at the shack. She has no name. I'm pretty sure she cannot, will never be able to speak. From the scars and burn marks that cover her body, she has been subjected to, God knows. No, that's not it, don't bring a fable into this. Only a human would ever dream up and then actually do something so hideous to another woman or man for pleasure.

He remembered the dog he found soon after he arrived here. Now her. Maybe the dog had been luckier. He died jumping after, following love. She? That's the trick, isn't it? Is it really possible to continue if there is only indifference followed by the certainty that only hopelessness will follow?

'Boy, you're gonna make some woman just a fine little companion, shit! He pulled himself up to the tailgate of his Bronco and looked out across the desert and saw his shadow playing with a vulture. Just as the large bird would light on a carcass, J.B.'s shadow would ease up behind it, block out the sun and then begin to fashion hand sculptures on the face of the sand.

J.B. took a deep breath and realized that he was past any sort of "normal" hallucination. He had succeeded in projecting his inner most fears and reservations out onto the desert. 'Sand crazy' is what Shep called it. "Say it happens anywhere you end up with only yourself and a naked environment. The artic and the desert, a deserted island or solitary confinement. Your brain ain't got no one around to distract it. Starts eating itself, same as those people trapped up on that mountain in the snow. Man becomes a cannibal to his own psyche. Me? Shit. Never happens to me 'cause I keep movin' and only go to bed with a woman who honestly wants to be loved . . . or I pay for it. Payin' for it is a whole lot easier. No strings. And we both know why we're settling into the business.

'No, sir, I'd love to find a woman who wants love as much as I do. Wants it without all the white noise. A man just wants to hold on for a while and feel a part of her. Will break his back and do most anything if he knows when he walks back in she'll just take him in and hold him, love him and for a while let him lose himself.

'Fore long, though, it, the love making has to be . . . different. New rules, new ideas, new meaning. Seems the only thing a woman truly loves day in and out is her own child if she has one, and if she don't? She'll find a way, use all she got to get a man to give her one.

'Shep cackled, then continued, And all *that* amounts to is pointing a finger at any one of a number of men standing at the bar and askin: "Want some of this, sailor?"

'Yes, sir! Get herself knocked up and then toss him aside. Oh, maybe not right away. But before long that dumb son-of-a- bitch will either have to settle for being her house boy just to get a look or taste every Christmas, or so. Or just leave.

'Woman got the one things she wants, so the dude is expendable. What else can he do but take off. All she wants from him now is comfort and protection. Men are the ones lookin' for the romance. Part of the job. Seduce and spread the seeds. It's what we do.

'Sounds harsh, but it's true. S'why I keep movin' and don't never get sand crazy.'

J.B. looked over at the line shack and thought of her. 'I'm going sand crazy and she's been left for dead. No, she's past dead, but still breathing. Amazing.'

'All this time, I've been trying to figure out how to get inside of the other side, taste and touch and feel whatever it is they have that makes . . . *her* . . . *the unimaginable   Zero summer . . . and me crazy!*   I have been tracking any and every woman that vibrates that wondrous tuning fork inside me. I always wanted to call it love or romance or a profound need to attach . . . shit! None of it works . . . not for very long.'

J.B. started to walk. One step in front of the other he moved briskly across the desert floor, striding straight towards the mountains a hundred miles away. He thought of Therese, in Kenya, probably bouncing a baby boy or girl off her knee. And Cindy? No problem, wherever she walked there was always an anxious trail of ready and anxious suitors. Natty? Again, no problem. If it wasn't one of her professors, it was a graduate student or a med student. Whomever it was, he's in way over his head. Perfect!

Jonas, yes, Jonas now, eight years old looking out from the back of his head, seeing the desert as he saw the house, alone, waiting for someone to return. Looking to his right, he saw his shadow dancing, jumping and then laughing as it pointed back at him. Shaking his head, his shadow, turned, dropped his pants and showed Jonas his ass. 'Touchè, better than what I did to coach Barnes,' he thought.

Eight to eighteen, times two make thirty-six, now add two and in the compilation, there was J.B. now ruminating on the perfect, stilled point of himself in the desert. It worked. Each person and every age, even his shadow of them all, were all present and accounted for. Sir, yes sir!

Sand crazy or not, the alchemical dream was playing from the inside out, pivoting to reverse—there—on the desert floor. Stasis. Lead to gold? Time twisting? There in the desert, alone, all possibilities exhausted, the only woman available was to go untouched, so the universe opened up and allowed him to see just a small bit of ankle as the continuum of space and time threaded through his shadow, there, yes, right there.

Yes, he saw it there, his shadow melt into a swirling black pool, a perfect vessel. Standing over it as it coursed one way and then another, each and every one standing behind the back row came forward. Yes, for an instant, there, at least it *felt that way* and for a moment that was . . . sure, probably sand crazy, but hey, who isn't when it all feels . . . just fine.

Sitting down, Jonas watched his shadow return to form and begin to play in the desert. Each and every stage of his life up until the last moment seemed be in his shadow's hands. His life a collection of brightly colored rubber balls: red, blue green, yellow and orange being juggled, and a moment suspended, yes there, right there in the desert.

'Profoundly and perfectly sand crazy, or not,' he thought.

Turning to his right, Jonas saw a line of dominoes. His shadow had placed several thousand in intricate patterns: spiral jetty, circles, squares, and a another: a long, direct line, an arrow pointing straight towards the line shack.

J.B. now, not Jonas, was sure that he was asleep or hallucinating or worst. He closed his eyes and opened them after several seconds: nothing. A light breeze stirred the sand, a buzzard circled, making two passes before moving on.

In the late afternoon light, the line shack appeared almost cartoonish, something out of a movie, as though it had been dropped down on the desert. 'A sequel to THE WIZARD OF OZ. Maybe it landed on my shadow. Dorothy inside? No, that's Harriet, remember. Oil can what?'

He laughed out loud, saying, "If it's not a bout of psychosis, then it's something someone slipped into the Scotch or no, no! Admit it! It's what I've really been asking for, isn't it? And why and to whom am I talking out loud here in the desert?"

J.B. smiled and began to pick up one handful of sand after another, letting the stream of pulverized rock thread through his fingers back onto the desert floor, thinking,

'Cause, it's always been over. Started as a little boy and just got stronger, more concentrated.'

Moment to moment, it's always been the same tune called. Dance to it. Dance to it 'til the day you die: "See that hill, son? Here's a big shiny quarter and a pretty medicine ball. Sure, it's heavy. The quarter? 'Case you git thirsty. Go on, now. Go and play. I know. I know. Simple. Just roll it up to the top and watch it roll back down. Sure, you'll have a swell time, I promise!"

J.B. and Jonas, his shadow, the man in linen suit: Jabir, and everyone else who had come forward from behind the last row of seats began to walk back to the line shack singing, in perfect harmony: "Danke Schoen . . . darling. Danke Schoen!"

Turning to each, smiling and then putting his arms around Jonas and Jabir, J.B. joined in the chorus, thinking, "I hope she, Harriet likes my cooking enough to want to stick around for a while."

EXPERIMENT IN THE DESERT

Mechanically, reflexively, she pulled the soft cotton comforter up over her face, then pushed it away. All night long, from warm to hot, to a pleasant slow cooling. She had never felt anything so soft and warm. Never had she had the luxury of lounging for as long as she cared to, alone in a bed without fear of yet another intruder. She had awakened only once during the night. Her eyes never completely focused or adjusting to the dark. Awakened by nothing. It was quiet and cool. Could any of this be anything other than, yes, it had to be a dream.

During the first weeks after she was kidnapped, she had long, angry, paralyzing nightmares that she was being attacked and could not move or scream or lock the door. Before long, she realized that they were not, in fact, nightmares, but only fitful periods of waking, of being there in the moment when yet another had come, paid the man by the door and was now on top of her.

After a while, each night after the last man had finished with her, she would close her eyes and hope that the darkness just behind her eyelids would become permanent, and the next long, painful breath would chase the others into a hole, and together there, she and this place and the men and the stench and the knives and everything would simply stop. Very soon, she began to sleep without dreams or nightmares or any soft, warm thought. That was what made the cover so special. It was as though she could cover up or deliver herself, whenever she wanted to, to a soft, warm or cooling dream, now.

The blackness behind her eyelids would be the last soft memory of nothing, and then there would be no sense of anything that was had ever been or would ever be. Even, now, she could no longer recall her own name. Nightmares? No, being awake, was much worse. Awake she would revisit, inhabit the body of the woman who allowed her child to be stolen. So, she had to remain nameless, dreamless and accept what these, no, they are not devils, nor some kind of demon. Devils and demons only wish to destroy the world of love and compassion. No, they were simply men. Only ordinary men would think and desire to this to . . . *she*.

Yes, She, that's what they call me, "She is ready for the next. She will not be any good after I take what's coming to me. She only likes it if you use the knife, make her scream, only way she gives back is to scratch and cut. She's dead inside, so I use whatever it takes to get my money's worth. She . . ."

She eased both feet onto the floor and was amazed that the floor was cool and the wind pushing the thin line of cotton covering the window, hot and dry. She could taste a faint sweetness, then salt on her tongue. Her hair was clean, and the large shirt she wore as a night dress was soft and smelled of cologne. 'Strange,' she thought, 'purgatory . . . limbo and yet I'm still feeling and smelling and tasting memories of living as if they were real and here and happening to me as if I were still alive.'

Pulling the drape to the side she felt another burst of hot, dry air sweep across her face. The sun was just above the mountains, in the extreme distance, a place that seemed unlike here or there, and . . . railroad tracks? 'So, God fashions a place from the last memory and holds you there until you have been cleansed or pay your penitence, until the atonement is over.'

Looking over to right she saw her reflection in a small mirror perched over the wash basin. She recoiled. Hanging over the wash bowl, a diagonal swath of mirror, even with its cracked and cloudy glass, could not hide her scars. It had been, no, she could not remember when she last looked at herself in the mirror.

Unbuttoning the top of her shirt, she gently traced the shining worms of smooth skin that ran from around each breast up to her neck, where, there, another larger, almost as thick as a garden snake formed a half moon from one ear to the other.

Her cheeks? As a young girl and woman, always compared to the petals of spring roses, were now like coarse sand paper speckled with flecks of black and scabbed-over red. Her hair? How was it so clean and brushed?

Speaking, a muted growl, followed by a scratchy, high-pitched shriek. 'How, OK,' she thought, 'if I am dead, even in limbo . . . purgatory, surely you get you back your voice and face and body back, right?'

She returned to the palette and sat down, looked around the room and thought of Tela, her daughter. Surely, they left her, and some nice couple found her, or I would not be here, I would be burning and screaming and listening to the other damned souls whispering through the smoke.

Her neck began to throb. Looking down at her hand, she noticed that her left wrist was swollen. 'Yes, OK, yes, when they threw me out of the train I landed on my left side, caught the ground and then my head hit, then I begged, I prayed that it was finally over.'

Outside a vulture screeched and . . . humming? She heard the sound of someone, no not someone, that is a man singing to himself. Her stomach was suddenly roiling with acid and bile. 'No! Not another one of them, here! It's over, please, yes, yes, I must be dead!'

She tried to scream, but all that she could produce was another growling, high-pitched screech. A man appeared at the door. He was holding a plastic bottle, no, two, one clear, one dark. She pulled the covers over herself and tried to scream, again. Silence. She was back, there.

'Slow down, breathe and leave. Go to the small room deep inside until he has finished. One more time. Just one more time and this time I will, no, no, it's too much. After he has finished I will go even deeper inside and never come back. It's true. My little girl is gone. That is why he is here. God has left me for this one, and probably others until, yes this is my sin and penance.'

J.B. had fallen asleep in the back of his Broncho, for a moment, upon waking, he thought he was back in Las Vegas, snuggled in his small, tenth floor condo. It was the middle of the summer, he had just returned from Shari's Ranch, with Toni, his favorite, looking forward to a long, steamy weekend. 'No, maybe, not the condo, so maybe I'm back in the burbs, back at home with . . . great, Cindy's in the shower waiting for him. No, that can't be right. Natty's in the shack, she told me to wait, a surprise. No. What then?'

The sun was slipping over the mountains. He looked over and saw his dog-eared copy of THE CASTLE, and remembered the full moon, the glinting silver teeth of, 'Yes, that man, those men and the burlap sack and the woman . . . she's in there, and that's why I'm here.'

Waking up fully, it all collapsed at once: those god-damned scars! Bathing her, the poor woman was a Rand/McNally road map of scars. Knife, teeth, fingernails, nail files, broken glass all used on her stomach, chest, neck and face. What could have possibly kept her alive? And her hair, soiled and knotted, putrid. She never really regained complete consciousness while he gently bathed, groomed and dressed her before easing her into bed.

Water and salve, he thought. She'll need plenty of water and lotion. He reached into his cooler and pulled out a large bottle of water, then opened his first-aid kit and pulled out a bottle of aloe gel, walked over to the shack and eased the door open.

The moment she saw him, she screeched and disappeared under the covers. 'Ozzie never had it better,' he thought.

Ozzie and Harriet in the Ninth Circle

Standing in the doorway, holding the water and aloe, J.B. studied the convulsing, screeching mound under the bed covers. Betrayal? He thought of Dante's INFERNO, the deepest circle, the ninth was reserved for those who betrayed a loved one. Yes, it seemed, he thought that there was something more than just a kidnapping and forced prostitution, here, though, that was certainly enough.

'No, there's something else, something eating at her center, at who she is, was and why and how the people she loves and who should care for her have created all of this . . . pain. Don't know why, but it's got to be more than abuse. The scars and abuse have become like a turtle's shell. When I washed her hair and bathed her, she never woke up, still she reacted to my touch as if to say, "It's you, please say it's . . . finally you. Yes, please. I remember."'

Yes, the nameless one. The center of hell would not be complete without her, yes Eva's mother. Ten years earlier, not the least bit frantic, oddly, coldly decided. (Yes, I know, usually they show a little remorse. This one? Watch your back after you pay her, watch your back.)

"Remember, you are not to touch the girl, Tela, my granddaughter. Leave her on the bench. I'll come by later. Her great-grandmother lives just outside of Los Cabos. I'll make sure she gets there. Now the other? You said five hundred, cash! Now. Good. She's pretty. Will give you all you want or make you a bundle if you want to farm her out. Five hundred, that's my price. Yes, the train station. She doesn't even know I'm back. Go on now before I change my mind! What? Fuck you! It's a mother's prerogative. Nothing but a boil on my ass, anyway. Five hundred, now!"

J.B. looked around and tried to imagine what the shack would look like to someone seeing it for the first time; someone who, like she, this woman, dropped here to die. He thought of the smile, the glinting silver teeth, the other men, standing next to him in the open boxcar, grabbing their crotches, flipping him a middle finger and now this, the screaming mound of fear and desperation, hopelessness and pain under the covers in front of him. J.B. whispered, "Shit!"

Then thought, 'She thinks I'm just another John, thinks I've just cleaned her up to have my way with her, again. My god, I.' J.B. stopped, started to try and consoled her, then screamed inside of his own head: 'Go! 'Just get the hell out! She's terrified. Leave the bottle of water and aloe, there by the bed and leave. Go. Let her calm herself, go. Wait, then talk to her through window. Go!'

Standing outside, looking in J.B. watched as she pulled the covers off of her head, looked around and discovered the water and aloe. When she thought it safe, she grabbed the bottle and drank it down in a matter of seconds. Out of breath, she smiled, then remembered that someone else might be there and scanned the room for him. Nothing.

Picking up the aloe, she opened it, sniffed and smiled again. After rubbing her arms, chest, face and neck with the salve, she pulled the covers up to her neck and waited. After a few minutes, she was asleep. J.B. remained silent, watching it all from the window.

It was almost nightfall before he decided it was time to go in and speak with her, reassure her that it was safe. 'Why is this so much like a watching an old sit-com,' he thought. 'Why am I thinking of Ozzie and Harriet? Easy, no really, just think about it. If you don't make a joke out of it then it would be impossible to process. If I really started to walk her through all the places she has been and look into the all the faces of the men that have raped and abused her; just as she probably does each waking moment of every day . . . fuck! I feel ridiculous even comparing it to INFERNO. Much worse. Shit. I've got nothing. Zero. What can I really do? Honestly?'

He remembered the video he made to shock and sever all ties with his family. It had succeeded better than he had ever hoped. Insanely offensive, blue and over the top, weirdly absurd and . . . perfect. That's it, that was the best I had up until now. She's got a royal straight-flush to my pair of jacks. I am over-matched. And I feel as embarrassed and as angry as a man can possible be at himself, all men.

'Shit! Insane! No, worse than sand crazy, nothing. I ain't got a motherfucking thing, here. I've got nothing. No point, no reference, not even a pimp standing over there with a knife, someone I could at least scream out, fight. Hell, I can't even find my shadow, right now. Suddenly, even that S.O.B. has gone AWOL! Damn it! After what she's been through, those scars, that pathetic screech of a voice. And she's still alive, still breathing. So, what do I do?'

J.B. closed his eyes. Back in his bedroom, seventeen, piecing together, splicing editing, overdubbing, 'I mean, look at me, then and now! Wanting for nothing, then and now and . . . Be careful, you, asshole. No game here. Seriously, I mean, who is she? What has she turned *me* into? Fuck who and what I was before and after the porch, the wreck, will I ever be able to see or feel anything—at all—without first seeing those . . . scars?'

What was it Leander said? "Pay it off, son!"'

J.B. thought of his great-uncle, Leander seething as he growled out, "Pay it off, son!" And Sal. Yes, Sal, his life slowed, no stopped, just a series of photos, frozen moments sitting side-by-side rather than any sort of easy flow or continuum.

'Is that it then? You get deeper into this weird experiment, each action speeds you up so that all life slows down. Enough happens to you and you approach the speed of light so it all basically stops. Is there a limit, a point we reach and then we just shut down? Afraid to move past it? Afraid to stay in that place for too long? It was all so slow and there right within my grasp as the car spun. Two maybe three seconds and even now, two years later it grows and lengthens, stretches everything to the breaking point and more. Each person and place and idea are tacked to a wall. Right there.'

What was it that Leander said?

"Sal shook his head, spat to one side and said to me that their faces, dead eyes, cut throats of his wife and little boy only grew more vivid with each passing, well I used to call them days, now it's every second. So? Go on, give it to me, right there on the chin, your best shot, Slick, go on, then, maybe, I'll feel something, again."

'So, you make it up as you go? No. No more Ozzie and Harriet or the riffing. Seems it's all about a whole lot of riffing. Moment to moment, play off what the other introduces, run with it, solo with it or simply lay down a soft, series of notes to allow her to catch her breath and-no, yes, I'm dyin' here. Dyin', where's the rope? The schematic, quick draw something, anything a map a circle, square, anything in the sand!'

He heard the gentle flap of wings before he looked up and saw it. A buzzard hovered directly over J.B. Hanging on the updraft for what seemed several minutes, it finally dropped down and swooped towards the desert floor. A snake was slithering towards a small group of rocks. With just a few feet to go, gone. Skyward, writhing in the vulture's talons, the snake's body was all . . . 'All motion and matter pushing back against the sun and sky, but most of all the unexpected intrusion of another. She and I are going to make quite the couple if she'll have me. She'll push back, I know, but if I don't try something. Worse than damned, 'cause I don't believe in the voodoo arts. No, it'll much worse than if I believed in voodoo, religion or any higher power. Worse than any of those kinds of damnations, 'cause, I'll know it was *me, and me alone, with absolutely no one else to blame, but me.'*

VIVA LAS VEGAS

J.B.? Sweet? Do you want to go again? You paid for it. I'm yours 'til the morning. J.B.?"

J.B. rolled over and looked up at Toni standing next to the bed. A sheer, silk bathrobe covered, but did little to hide her body. She smiled, stroked his hair and then sat on the edge of the bed.

"It's never easy with you, is it cowboy? You pay me for twenty-four hours and we end up talking for twenty-three and somehow, strangely, neither of us feels cheated. I usually don't get this involved with a client, but if you keep this up,   why . . . I-"

Toni turned and walked to the window, opened the curtain and looked out at the wash of neon that stretched out below J.B.'s tenth floor condo., Amazing woman, Toni, not only beautiful, but fiercely intelligent, she was only two semesters away from her Masters in Financial Engineering.

"I've started looking forward to you, ah, I mean *us here.* Sort of a fantasy couple up above the desert floor, away from the Ranch. So, will you ever show me the desert?"

J.B. shook his head "no" climbed out of bed, walked over and kissed Toni gently on the neck. For the next several minutes he held her tightly to him. After nuzzling her neck, J.B. gently kissed her, holding the embrace for several seconds. Then, for a few minutes they stood by the window letting the collage of casino lights spread out below them, wash over them as they looked into each either eyes for another extended moment then kissed even more tenderly than just a few minutes earlier.

Toni felt herself oddly aroused. It had always been a hard and fast rule to never become emotionally involved with any of her clients. And even though, she had a standing arrangement with J.B., she had been faithful to her own rule, up until now. It was the sweet, easy and earnest way he pulled her up and encircled her with his arms. 'Strong, but gentle and so easy to lean on and feel safe,' she thought.

So, when J.B. whispered, "Now," Toni felt like, no, not like high school or college, she was older and wiser, now. It was easy to drop her guard, completely, with J.B. in a manner, that though, reassuring, was also, a little frightening.

Picking her up, he carried Toni back to bed and made love to her. Afterwards, she slept while he made supper. An hour later, still in their robes, they shared a light supper of smoked salmon, fresh fruit and champagne.

"So, what's so special about the desert that you can't talk to me about? I mean give me a break. I see you here, pretty much on an exclusive basis for almost six months, then no word, no cards nothing. My phone rings, and then I'm yours. We've crossed so many lines, I . . . J.B. it's not the money, now. Lord knows you've been generous; it's just, something, now, I mean, this time . . . you've changed.

"*We've changed*. It's not business for me anymore. When you hold me and make love, the way you caress me, now, it's as though . . . don't misunderstand me, it's nice, but different. It feels as though you're reaching past me into something that I usually just keep to myself. I'm finding it easy, too easy to let you go there. I'm growing very attached to, I know this may sound silly, attached to, well, it's almost like there's a little boy in there behind all the love making.

"You always take care of me first. Then we make love. I don't know whether to mother you or show you the wildest tricks I know. It's confusing and exciting and it's . . . not so much in love, it's, it's . . . when you touch me I know you are there to reassure and please me. I know that you want to step out of yourself to make sure I'm fine, then once you know I'm OK, amazing. It's just the best feeling, I've never known . . . lovemaking like that, I mean, only with you. I-"

J.B. smiled and then held his finger, gently signaling to Toni to stop.

"Thanks Harriet."

Toni looked confused.

J.B. laughed and offered, "Coffee? Some Cognac?"

"Please . . . I-"

"Here's a nice tall glass of Martell. Well, you wanted to know about the desert. Sip it, this may, no *this will* take a while."

GARY BOLICK

Madonna

(batteries and Jesus not included)

The next morning, an hour out of Las Vegas, J.B. laughed, "Been this way so many times, I could probably take my hands off the wheel and the truck would probably just take over."

Easing his Broncho over the first large pothole on the left, then a smaller one on the right, he adjusted his pants as he thought of making love with Toni after they watched the sunrise.

Toni? She was smitten with J.B.'s story of the train and the burlap sack and the woman. Surprisingly, it had acted like an aphrodisiac. After J.B. had given her all the details of how "Harriet" had been dropped, literally in his lap, how he cared for her, had sworn to let her find her place, a secure place in her own manner and time, she pulled J.B. over and kissed him. Kissed him not as a duty or to fulfill any sort of debt, she held him and kissed him in a manner that J.B. had never experienced with a woman. It was as though she wanted to be part of what J.B. had just recounted. After the long deep kiss, she insisted that they make love one more time before he took her back to the ranch.

"You keep this up, cowboy, and I'm all in with you. Cottage with a picket fence. Feels awfully nice to be alone with you. It's like absolutely no one else exists for you but the woman you've set your sights on. I'm a girl who likes all that pressure and attention. Makes all the white noise and urgency just seem to run down the drain. We're going to have to get a few things straight if we're going to keep this arrangement going. I'm getting *way too attached* to you, sailor. OK, that's enough, take me back. So, next week, we talk. I mean *really have it out*! I need to know where we're going! Understand, sailor?"

"Sure. But it still all deepens on what Harriet wants. You and me? I would never want to stop any of this with you. I'm just afraid that you'll, no, I'm sure you'll want to change this arrangement."

Toni looked confused.

"As long as I know it's safe to leave Harriet, I want you. I want you in the best and worst ways a man could want a woman. And you're right. You deserve to have absolutely all of my attention and focus. When I make love to you, I'm trying to go as hard and fast and deep as the man in the back of my head tells me. It's like I'm trying to find a place, hear the sound of when all of this was, well, to get back to when or what I was before I was ever . . . this is going sound crazy . . . human."

Toni shook her head and held up her hand, "Slow down. I said I was falling in love with you. I just want to quit the ranch and follow through with what you and I seem to be sharing and I-"

"Of course, you do," J.B. interrupted. "I want you every single day just like this. I want to crawl into and through you, go back into a place where it all makes sense. That's what I'm talking about. Oh sure, I'm a great guy . . .wait! A great guy until you finally understand that it never stops with me. Seriously, think about it. A lifetime. Right now, you think you love all this intense focus and insatiable passion. Six months, a year, ten and every day the pace quickens, becomes more intense, and we're still not quite . . . there yet. So? Dive down deeper, work harder and faster. Baby, I still can't get enough of you! See? Sweetheart, you may, no . . . you *will* feel differently. I-"

"Stop! I'm not a child. I think I know what you're doing. As soon as someone gets close, you just keep upping the ante. Make it impossible for her to hang on. You don't want to slow down, if you do then you'll have to treat me as an equal and trust me. You're right. I'm more about numbers. Give me an algorithm and I'm off and running.

"This metaphysical, transcendentalism, I admit it, not really my thing, still, I do know that what you are talking about boils down to an empty space inside. Guess what, I've got one too!

"It's when you start talking about that poor woman, you change. I love *that man,* but this one? The one who seems like he's tucking tail at the first sign of, no, not commitment. Trust. Seems you got a lot of clever tricks all designed to make it work, just for you. See what I mean?"

Toni's kick in the teeth surprised him. Still, it served to completely clear it all up, now. J.B. smiled. He walked over and pulled Toni into his arms and held her. Brushing her hair clear of her eyes, he gently kissed each cheek, then softly touched her lips and whispered, "Yes, I do see it. We'll talk, yes. We do need to talk about this, don't we? Did not see that one coming, didn't even hear it."

"What?"

"I'll explain, next time. Maybe even show it to you. There's a place on the rails, you always hear the train, long before you see it. Like I said, I never heard or saw you, on that one. Surprised me. That was nice, very nice, sweet. Nice."

SOLILOQUY

J.B. parked his Broncho and before climbing out, he did a quick inventory in his head to make sure he did not need to return to Las Vegas until next week. Under a makeshift tent were several boxes of provisions for "Harriet" and himself: bottled water, canned goods, plenty of sweets for her and a case of scotch for him. It had been a week since she was thrown out of the train, and the two had still not seen or touched or talked to one another. Except for the first night and day when J.B. had bathed, dressed and put her in his bed, they were complete strangers.

Just before sunrise, J.B. would leave a box of provisions by the front door, then retreat to the cot in his truck, read THE CASTLE, sleep, drink his scotch, and sleep some more. He was content to let her acclimate herself on her own terms. He would play the contented, neutered, tomcat sleeping in the sun.

Occasionally, he was awake when she briefly exited to pick up her box of provisions and water. She would glance, quickly, about the immediate area to see if she was being watched, then just as quickly duck back into the shack. For a brief moment, when her eyes met his, there would be an awkward instant of staring. It reminded J.B. of a deer bending over to drink water, anxious and aware that there were predators about. He would not look away, but insisted on, made sure that she saw him smiling. After a week, she lifted her hand, once, and waved; that was the long and the short of their relationship, for now.

'Funny,' J.B. mused, 'in THE CASTLE, "K" the main character never makes it to the castle. It's there, up on the hill, seemingly just a matter of walking up, crossing through the gate, pound on the door and walk in. Never happens.'

J.B. put the book down and studied the outline of the shack against the lengthening shadows.

'"K", journeys through four hundred pages, tantalized, frustrated and then dies, but still never breeches the threshold. What about Harriet? And me?'

Jonas, *yes Jonas the small boy,* looked around at the desert, then turned and smiled at J.B. as he pointed out their shadow playing Frisbee with a coyote.

Jonas then said to J.B., "Toni really stung you, didn't she? Every step of the way seems we've been learning the ins and outs of isolation. Started right out of the shoot and never got better. You and I are overmatched with Harriet. Even calling her that is awkward. I know. Where else can you go? Funny, when the desert starts offering more stimulus than the indifference and isolation inside your head means it more than being sand crazy. I'm back because you're lost, again, chief, yes, again!"

J.B. began to walk as Jonas continued to talk to him.

"Sure, go ahead and walk away. Keep walking this time. Go straight, there, into the mountains, strip down, die in the sun, let the buzzards have at least one good meal. You know where this is going, don't you?"

J.B. shook his head. Looked deep into Jonas' eyes, the same that would look at the door knob out on the porch as he listened to the rest of the family talk.

"Walk, that's fine. But you will go back. Harriet needs something, you know it, so find out what it is, and do it. Me us? Shit, we both know that hand was played a long time ago. Toni just finished it, put down a royal straight-flush to your lousy pair. Do I have to say it?"

J.B. nodded, yes.

"It's pretty clear. No, it's always been too clear, right there on the table just like the dominoes. All the wreck did was to open the last door. It all really does slow down to a stop. Speed of light. All of them touched on it. Dante, Einstein, Jabir, and now you asked for it and it's been given to you. So, don't complain, you sap!

"Harriet will let you find her. Yes, for some reason you've attached the feminine gender to the collapse and reforming of you, the cosmos, life as we know it, or rather man's place here. No, it's not the actual woman, not Therese, or Natty, God knows not Cindy, or your mother, either. We really can't go there. Woman is a woman is a woman, no, not really. It's the search for what is a natural, connective bond that, yes, that is the greatest cosmological joke ever: That you as a man . . . human can touch it. Make a god, write a poem, cipher out the math or dissect the biology of it, but, hey Chief, you're slipping down the rabbit hole, again, and I'm with you, this time.

"Woman, yes both the conception of and the actual physical creature, is just the double-helix, the DNA for the itch inside of your loins. As much as you try, as hard as you woo and seduce, it'll always just be a fleeting moment. Right? So move onto the next idea and person, right so far? But that woman, there? Holding that creation, bouncing him/her on her knee as it suckles her breast? That my boy is an entire universe full-grown-kicking-and-screaming to get out.

"So why wouldn't you want to go back in and through and out again? Into the rabbit hole, Chief I'm all in, with you all the way this time. No more AWOL, you may not see me, but I'm there. I mean that's where you and I ultimately have to end up, right? So, Sparky, you've got to hold serve, wait, there are bigger fish to fry and this time, well, we"ll see, but for now? Get off your ass! Move."

J.B. stopped and looked around. The mountains were still there, but his shadow was gone, and Jonas had stopped talking.

Looking at the shack, he felt, only, calm. Sounds, seemingly, were filtering out from everywhere. His heart was a bass drum. He swore he heard the feathers of a vulture flying over him, the actual feathers rubbing together.

'Jonas is right. It's been with me all along. I wanted this complete break. No, not sand crazy. Life crazy. She is the Madonna. I see it now. The only creature who has ever forced me to stop and embrace something completely outside my own world. No religion. No sex. No desire for anything other than to make this person whole again. I do that, and I can move. Yes, finally move on to-"

J.B. paused and looked around.

'Here, I'm already here, I've always been here.'

J.B. sat down, just as he had the night of the wreck; sat down in the middle of the desert and wondered out loud,

"This time, though, I'll walk back and it'll be Harriet. Harriet, and no one else, not even me. Whatever it is *she* needs, we'll do it. Whether it takes another day, week, month or year, she is owed that. Me? I'm sure it'll be Toni for a good long while. She was right, almost. No one needs to stay here or see this place. Who and why in the fuck would anyone want to come out here unless it felt like home. And that's the kicker, isn't it? The wandering sailor finally found his home. Who knows maybe that's actually Calypso inside. Or, shit. The hole just keeps getting wider. Sand crazy? Maybe. More likely, I'm just learning to be more honest. So, when I wonder out loud like this, step up and into the screen, look down at the audience as I snake round through this soliloquy neck deep in time I-"

J.B. stopped, shook his head, and then screamed, "Of course! *She* must have a child somewhere. That's the only thing that would pull her through that hell."

Unfortunately, the revelation concerning Harriet only made the conclusion concerning Ozzie that much harder to swallow.

'Me?' he thought, 'Oh shit! So, what drags a man through the desert?'

Looking up in the sky J.B. smiled, wistfully.

'The vulture's always been on point, had me in his sights from the start. Moving from the desert to the city and back. Looking for Therese I found Natty, looking for a way to forget the wreck I found this place and now she has found me, but it will never resolve, only, spread out. S'why Toni's getting so attached to me. It opens up for a brief while, then closes as quickly as it started. Gives a man a chance to touch her for a moment. Don't know if they ever feel it like we do. Probably not, bigger fish to fry. Make a life. It's hers forever. A god. We're so much sand and debris. We never really connect not like them . . . women. Impossible.'

J.B. drew a map in the sand. It showed every place he had ever set foot. He scratched in the names of each person he had ever known in that particular place. In trying to find a connection, there was none. Spread out in front of him was an intricate mosaic, almost a mandala of places, people and him, Jonas, J.B. But now?

He asked himself, 'Who am I here and now? Yes, still an unconnected, unfettered wandering stranger looking, no staring down at all that has come before and what probably lies ahead, still trying to find a point and place where I, or any other man can claim inclusion. Nope. Still no place. See it? It's all spread out in front of me there, nothing. The map in the sand proves it.'

Looking up he saw his shadow squatting next to him, shaking its head. After a long moment, his shadow reached over and patted him on the back, "Sucks, don't it," his shadow said, "Just plain sucks."

GARY BOLICK

REQUIEM

(WITHOUT THE MASS)

A WALKING SHADOW

S he looked both ways before reaching down to pick up the box. She had seen the man twice now. Once as he walked away from the shack, another when she sneaked out just after dark to use the outhouse. He was asleep. His arm tangled over the edge of the open end of his truck. An empty liquor bottle was on the ground just below his outstretched hand. A thick, worn book lay just to the side. 'He seems almost too peaceful, almost dead,' she thought.

She had seen too many dead bodies these last ten years. Passed from camp to camp, abandoned boxcars, busses, anything that could be used as a temporary brothel. Bad liquor, knife and gun fights, she even saw one man strangle another while he was sleeping, then pull his boots off. Always the same peaceful look of sleep, no, he wasn't dead, this one, but he seems to hate being awake so his sleep is a liberation.

Freedom. She took a deep breath and looked at the desert stretching out in every direction, 'I supposed I really am not dead after all. All of this open space and air, if I only had Tela with me. She closed her eyes and tried to envision what her daughter would have looked like had she lived. Shaking her head, she fought back tears and started to walk towards the shack. Collapsing, she pawed at the cooling sand, and wept.

J.B. woke from his single-malt stupor and thought he had simply slipped into another more lucid dream as he watched the young woman writhing in the sand, growling and screeching. That screeching, the metal of his Prius being ground into the highway, the world around him slowed to a stop, he was back, but this time watching another about to be folded into the highway. He started to pick her up, to hold her but she shook her head violently, no. Scrambling up, she nodded, embarrassed, tried to smile, and then disappeared into the shack.

J.B. stared at the closed door and felt nothing but the thumbtacks that were beginning to work their way into the center of this head. 'Way too much scotch! Great little honeymoon we got going here.'

J.B. then walked over to side of the Broncho, urinated, drank a bottle of water and went back to sleep.

The ballet continued for a month. Box delivered, door opened, arms, shoulders, head—gone. J.B. could almost recite THE CASTLE from memory. Laughing, he mused that he was truly past sand crazy, and well into acceptance. Yes, he was becoming a welcomed and permanent fixture in the desert. He even had a pet vulture. Every evening at seven it would land twenty feet from his truck, walk over and eat whatever scrap J.B had put out for it. He had affectionately named it K. So, for a few minutes he and K would both look at the shack, both anxious for *she* to come out. When she refused, K would look back at J.B. shake its wings and then fly away. Absent until the next day.

She inside?

She could not lose the image of her baby girl, Tela, sleeping in the train station. If she were not dead then perhaps that is why I am still alive, she thought. Looking out of the front window, the sun was just descending over the distant mountains. J.B. was sitting on the ground leaning on the back wheel of the truck, a half-empty bottle of Scotch beside him.

She watched him as he turned his head skyward to admire the sunset. Flint-gray, salmon, rose, streaks of chiffon layered over an ever-diluted blue, filled the sky. Pleasantly drunk, J.B.'s eyes felt like they were hovering just out in front of his head so the colors of the sunset seemed to be both in front and behind his eyes.

Looking over at the shack, he saw her looking at him through the window. This time she did not avert her eyes. She held him hard and steady with her stare. Her eyes were soft, now. She smiled.

'Great,' he thought. 'The first real smile. Now, give it another, year or two and she might even come out and say hello. OK, easy. Remember. Give her all the time she needs. Besides, finish this bottle and I'll be out, sleep till four. Get cleaned up. Go into town, stock up and, hell, who knows.'

J.B. pulled the brim of his hat down over his eyes and eased into a blissful nap.

Her steps, at first, were silent as she crept out of the shack tip-toeing towards the man. J.B was almost asleep, but heard her before he saw her approaching. No, not a C-flat or an E-Major chord, no train approaching, this time. She was much bigger, more intrusive and more insistent than any diesel engine, now that she had finally exited and was approaching, standing before him.

At first, she attempted to speak, but stopped herself. Suddenly she was bashful. Yes, J.B. marveled, 'She is actually . . . blushing.'

She smiled, nodded and motioned that she would start over. Pointing to the ground, with her left foot she scratched out: LOS CABOS, pointed to J.B. and then to herself, folded her arms as though holding a baby, nodded her head and with her fingers fashioned a stick figure, walking.

The sun was now just a sliver resting on the top edge of the distant mountains, casting a halo up and over outlining her form. Silent, motioning again, the action of holding and rocking to sleep, an infant, she loomed up over J.B. like a dashboard Madonna. His hand blindly searched and finally located the bottle of scotch. After taking a long drink, he crawled over to her, wrapped his arms around her legs, and held her. She stroked his head, bent over and kissed him.

The next day they were on the road heading towards Los Cabos.

TO-MORROW, AND TO-MORROW, AND TO-MORROW . . .

EVENTUALLY ALL MEN WILL ENCOUNTER THE
WALL THAT DEFINES THE LIMITS OF HIS MIND.

ALFRED DE VIGNY

A WALKING SHADOW

D r. Lowenstein studied his sleeping patient. J.B. had nodded off shortly after recounting the story of the young Mexican woman thrown off the train. In his notes the doctor wrote that he believed Jonas was becoming more and more detached from reality. Rather than reconnect to the world around him, the sessions seemed to solidify his desire to flee all normal connections to any other human.

It is obvious he never connected to his mother or family. Almost from the start he has clung to the notion that each of us lives in a wholly separate and isolated world. That was his starting point and for the rest of his life he has sought out validation of that idea. Unfortunately, he has found it. Every, potentially, meaningful relationship: his mother, wife, his first and subsequent lovers, siblings all have not only contributed, but have actually reinforced this idea. So, what is the situation here? Is he really looking for it, or is it simply the reality of his own particular experience, or is it broader, more inclusive, than that? Has he pulled away a curtain? Did the accident simply destroy a barrier that, perhaps, we all have and are never forced to acknowledge? At the root of his experiences is he encoding them with some sort of unconscious projection. Is Jonas a reflecting pool? A living commentary on all of us?

And the abused woman? The poor creature who was literally dropped in his lap and survived, even after suffering through unspeakable atrocities. She was almost an affront to him at first, and then a challenge, and now, seemingly the perfect resolution for his own feelings of alienation and loss and isolation. In helping another, more isolated and alone than himself, he seems to have concluded that his lot was cast before he knew it was even minted. Still, he is more confident, now, much calmer. Resolved. But has anything actually changed?

Dr. Lowenstein looked up from his notepad. J.B. was snoring.

Never snored, before. Either he feels completely safe here with me or he's moved on. For him, for all of us, is there a door that, once opened can never be closed? Is there a particular trauma that unifies the person around what has always been there, and cannot ever be undone or changed? And once experienced, and having survived it, does it remain a trauma? Or is it just another snapshot? What J.B described as, "The stillness of each moment—now."

He said that in the heart of each moment was a motionless, indifferent signature culled from the original source, the Big Bang. That out in the desert he learned that all life stops for a brief moment, each moment, then continues on, but only by reflex, like the pause between breaths.

So, does a trauma like the one J.B. suffered, is it, does it become a portal of sorts; a look down and into something inside all of us that, perhaps, is just too much to process? I never considered the world or the universe as "indifferent" until I met J.B. Now I see it everywhere. It has even begun to alter my sleep.

He called the desert the perfect place for him because so little moved. Just one big photograph, so it provided the illusion that his life was back to normal. If everything is still and quiet and in a static state, you don't notice the difference.

Flipping back through his notes, the doctor found entries from a session almost a year old. 'Yes, here it is. The part about projection: If he could only project his isolation and alienation into or onto something that had a constructive or positive outcome, it might bridge the divide, allow the "child" closure, allow the adult to reassume control. Maybe he's finally done it. Or, perhaps he was forced into being an adult prematurely. A child trapped in the arena of adults forced to concoct an elaborate dance, as we all do, but as adults, this coping is exposed, shown to be simply the loneliness and isolation of being human. No, those are his words, not mine. Still?'

Dr. Lowenstein then flipped his notes back to the end of today's session.

J.B. is more than reverential, he strikes me as a man who has witnessed, yes, it oddly enough reminds me of what Oppenheimer supposedly observed when the first atomic bomb was tested, a mixture of awe, horror, relief and anxiety at what he was seeing play out before him. That's what J.B reminded me of when he said, She finally walked out from behind the Life Guard Stand and into the water. She was almost waste deep in the surf when her daughter turned around and saw her, recognized her. They collapsed together, almost disappearing under the water, their hands frantically touching, outlining the other's face. Two sighted people blinded by the absence of years away from one another, probing, discovering and filling their hearts with the love so long denied them.

The patient, J.B., has succeeded in one fashion. He witnessed the resolution of his own problem, was in fact responsible for making it happen, but unfortunately was unable to participate in it, personally. Or is this by choice?

Dr. Lowenstein stopped writing. He looked at the still sleeping J.B. then wrote, Job? Sisyphus? No, snake bit.

'Now there's a clinical description for you!' he mused.

Scanning back through his notes he found an entry from earlier in the session.

It is not a validation of any higher or spiritual existence, just the opposite. My Madonna? Just a name I gave her. She could not speak. I dare say she lost all hope and religion long before she found her way to my doorstep. If anything, she was her own, completed universe. Me? A simple satellite.

S'why I love to drink and screw and move. Like most, no, all men running from that cold, flat feeling of being, knowing that all you're good for is a seed spreader, the disposable part.

Don't believe me? Go into any Advance Auto Store, give 'um your name and they'll look you up on the computer, go back, search the aisles and before you know it, sitting up on the counter is a younger, prettier, stronger version of you!

The obsession with this alchemist, Jabir? Interesting and a little, unnerving. This notion that each of us is completely and wholly a world unto ourselves and at best all a man can do is step out for a brief few hours if—

Dr. Lowenstein stopped reading, took his glasses off, rubbed his eyes and stared long and hard at the sleeping J.B., thinking, 'So what if he is right?'

Lowenstein thought of his own, 'Day in the desert. Of all the gin joints in all the world, he has to pick mine! Here's looking at you, kid, asshole! It was almost closed, almost scabbed over enough to move on. No, no. I always knew Del was strangely distant at times, suspected something. But it's funny, not until J.B. showed up, did I go back to the early years of the marriage. Two coats of paint . . . yeah, funny isn't it, she was reassuring me to hide-'

J.B. coughed, woke up and smiled, "See you in, well I'm not sure . . . should I see you again? What ya think, doc, so what's your take on it? Seems to me, what did Einstein say? "Repeating the same mistake over and over again hoping for a different outcome . . . so is it sand crazy or spot on?"

Lowenstein laughed, "Hold on, we'll see, but there is one other thing, J.B., you never mentioned Toni. Last session you had talked about what she said, how she seemed to stop you in your tracks."

J.B. shook his head and paused, then said, "She did. Don't they all? Stacked deck, loaded dice. After she pinned me down, I got to thinking. Remember in THE ODYSSEY how Odysseus spent ten years with Calypso? Took care of his every need, everything, but that cowboy was convinced he had to leave, finish up, and then proceeded to land in the middle of history's greatest shit storm. Don't you think, I mean honestly, when all was said and done, he would have gone back to her, to Calypso? Beautiful enchantress, who adored him, took care of everything, sheltered him from the hateful, spiteful world all around them. That island, maybe that's what I'm really after.

I know there's a shit storm out there, and I know I'll never really connect with anyone, really, none of us ever do. It's a ruse. So, if you find someone who can divert you, who buys into the ruse by making up one of their own, well, making the same mistake over and over again, at least, well, you don't' realize it or you simply don't care. No, I know there's no one perfect place or woman, just the idea of co-existing with someone who wants to keep digging the same hole with you. Right?

"Toni? Yeah, sorry, Toni. After that talk, we had something really good for about two months. Digging a real deep hole together. Then bingo, she started talking about going off the pill, quitting her job out at the ranch. First night we were together, first time we made love with the idea it might end up with a baby, *she changed. No more Calypso.*

"It was incredible love making, don't get me wrong. It was the sense of it, though. Now it was all to create and finish off something she always thought she needed, something that would define her. I could actually feel her move off the spot, out of the hole, if you will. So, I knew, literally the night we decided to make a baby, that once the idea of a little missy or junior could be on the way, it was over. We retreated to our neutral, or rather, our natural corners. Once Toni just *thought* she might be pregnant, it was, 'Hey sailor, packing my bags and heading for the coast, I got what I need, see ya.' Me? Back to square one. No, I guess I never really left.

"Shep was right, move on. Move on, I guess, unless you find an island, and an enchantress, but yeah, the shit with that is it's probably going to be too late before you realize it. Just like Odysseus, poor S.O.B. didn't realize what he had until it was too late. Looked at his wife, his grown son, and then remembered the island, What the fuck, am I doing, *here?* Anyway, Toni.

"When she got her period, she was disappointed, but even more dedicated. Felt myself being moved even farther over, and she was becoming more centered. That was my signal: move. I guess I accept the loneliness and isolation a little better now. I see that most, if not everyone doesn't really want to jump in, go down too deep. After helping Harriet, I'm sorry, Eva out . . . no, you know, I'm not sure it can be repeated. It's a start, for me, though, the experiment worked. I was really outside of myself for a while, felt what Jabir hinted at, 'The mystical, magical sense of creation as one breaks down and then resurrects the self through the transformation of the four basic elements.'

"Yeah, I know, doc, cat chasing his tail, again. But for a guy, men? What else is there? The ultimate diversion is the creation of a universe, a life. Just like my shadow said before leaving, 'So, Sparky, what'll it be upper or lower deck. No way you're ever gonna blow your fast ball past this one. *They* actually do it! Fire, caldron, vapors a life created. No, not imagined or removed. There inside them. So, Sparky, sure, a few hours each day you lose yourself, then it all starts over, again. Like I was asking, upper or lower deck. Even you best heat can't even think about getting' past that notion. '

"But even a woman, even a woman who has borne a child is still just a sphere, a collection of experiences, however you want to describe a life. Still, she does have that astounding connection, but is it ever really shared? Or is the best we can hope for just to brush up against another's particular collection at your own peril. Look, but never touch. You can't actually touch.

"That's the message. Found it out with every woman and man, actually, I've ever taken the time to try and get to know. It's all in our particular wiring. Hot-wired monkeys skittering across the high-wire, all without a net below to catch us. Women are just better equipped for a diversion, for . . . no, they actually do create life. So yeah, hard for them to see the isolation, just as it's impossible for a man to imagine another heart beating inside of his own body.

"So? Well, the desert did teach me that well, I gotta try. Try and mimic the entire process, find a place where the universe and "I" intersect. Every time it seems like I'm getting close, opened one door, when I reach out for the next, it always seems the next door has a Do Not Disturb sign hanging on the doorknob.

"Yeah, the desert and . . . Eva, I see that at least there's the chance to crawl outside, move just past the reach of my extended hand for a moment before the next door closes, and that damned hand comes out and hangs another Do Not Disturb sign on the door.

"Sorry! Toni? Married and pregnant. Philips Petroleum VP. Perfect, wouldn't you say, doc? All the money and space she needs. Big business guy, probably keeps a stable of babes on the side. So yeah, I mean, we avoid it. We all know how cold and lonely it is there, alone, inside your own skin, so why not create as many distractions, indiscretions and pipe dreams as you can, so you never have to set foot inside of yourself. Right?

"Ever wonder why all the drunk poets, painters and philosophers are men? My shadow and Eva showed me why. All that lost, lonely time in between benders; in between a relationship, job, anything that serves as a distraction. Moving and a good bottle of single-malt scotch, same thing. Loses the self, distracts the monkey for a while.

"No more arguments, just move on. Put my head down on the rail, listen, do the math, figure out when the train will pass by, wait, start running, jump up, catch the handle, swing myself up, and move on. Good and cured, right doc?"

J.B. laughed and then began to pick at the same loose thread on the arm of his favorite chair.

"Thank you, Doctor Lowenstein. May I drop you a postcard? Yes, leaving. No, not sure how or where, but going, can't be sure that I'll ever be stopping again, unless by some odd turn of events Eva gets in touch and asks me to help out with Tela.

"Huh, maybe that's it after all. Eva and Calypso. Always something there, just around the corner. No, you might never really share anything other than, yeah that brief respite, looking down into a hot, burning cauldron and suddenly all the colors of the universe just seem to jump. For a moment you're out of yourself. Take care, doc."

The two men shook hands, then hugged. Pulling away from each other their eyes met and stayed there for a while. Silently, J.B. nodded and Lowenstein nodded back.

Dr. Lowenstein, walked J.B. to the door, shook his hand, again, and watched him climb into his Broncho and drive away. He looked at the strip mall, sterile, baking under the late summer heat and then looked back at his office and saw that it was—empty. No, not simply devoid of people, actually vacant, a vacuum.

Locking the door, Dr. Lowenstein, lowered and then closed the blinds on each window. Reaching down into the bottom drawer of his desk, he pulled out and uncorked a new bottle of bourbon. From another drawer, he pulled out a small CD player, and one of his favorite CDs: TIME OUT Dave Brubeck.

As Paul Desmond began to wind his way through TAKE FIVE, Dr. Lowenstein, sipped on a large glass of Michter's. The blinds seemed more like a movie screen, and he felt as though he had just walked into a matinee, similar to the B-movies he would go to, as a child, during the summer to avoid the heat: blank, meaningless diversions, "Chewing gum to pass the afternoons away," he said out loud as he admired the color of the bourbon, felt it's warm, stinging touch as it eased down his throat.

Searching the dark, both here—in his office—now and there—back in the movie theatre of his childhood—he found a place . . . *his place*, again.

'There,' Dr. Lowenstein thought as he smiled, 'The movie hasn't started, just the previews, maybe it'll be better . . . a really *good movie*, this time, make it easier to lose the rest of the day and the heat and . . .'

He took another, longer, deeper sip,

'Better' he thought, 'Kentucky's finest is much better than stale popcorn. Yes, there was, there always was that hope in all those summer afternoons that something *more* would be there. Hope's still there, now, always is. Lowenstein closed his eyes and thought of the Maryland farm, the fresh, cool mornings raking out the stalls, listening to day wake up, looking around, wondering if anyone else ever felt as connected and happy as he did to be up so early, working, alone, here? Yes, just once, it would have been nice to have been surprised and connected to Dad or Mom, Del . . . anyone on those wonderfully crisp, fragrant mornings.'

Looking at his half empty glass, he chuckled, 'Perfect picture of . . . damn him! Yes, what I'm feeling *right now*. This moment, and the trip back, the memories, the pictures, places, the time, all right there as clear as that mirror on the wall, yes so clear *to me, here and now.*'

After downing the rest of the glass, Lowenstein, sighed, closed his eyes and whispered, "Yes, J.B, you're right! It would be nice to share it all with someone . . . anyone, even if it was just for a little while."

About The Author

Born and raised in Winston-Salem/Clemmons, NC. Lived and studied in Paris for a year before graduating from Wake Forest. It was at Wake I had the honor of studying under and being mentored by Germaine Bree. Amazing woman and scholar. Writing A WALKING SHADOW was a true labor of love. When I was living in Paris, I was able to track down a copy of the first ten treatises of Jabir's "Book of Sixty-Nine Treatises". Finally, it seemed, studying French was paying off. No English translation existed of Jabir's work. I could read antiquity's greatest alchemist in his own words. When Jonas' shadow splits off and begins to both comfort and mock him it was, as Carl Jung speaks of in "Psychology and Alchemy," the conscious and unconscious attempting to find balance.

ABOUT THE PRESS

Unsolicited Press is a small publishing house founded in 2012. Based out of Portland, Oregon, the team strives to produce exemplary, sometimes unsung, poetry, fiction, and nonfiction. Learn more at www.unsolicitedpress.com